FICTIONAL TRUTH

A Stella Kirk Mystery #4

L. P. Suzanne Atkinson

lpsabooks
http://lpsabooks.wix.com/lpsabooks#

Cover Design by Majeau Designs
Editing by Tim Covell

ISBN
978-1-7776-0052-5 (Paperback)
978-1-7776-0053-2 (eBook)

1. Fiction, Mystery/Detective-Cozy/General
2. Fiction, Mystery/Detective-Amateur Sleuth
3. Fiction, Mystery/Detective-Female Sleuths

Distributed to the trade by the Ingram Book Company

Table of Contents

Facts do not cease to exist because they are ignored.
—Aldous Huxley, *Complete Essays, Vol. II, 1926-29*

Things come apart so easily when they've been held together with lies.
—Dorothy Allison, *Bastard Out of Carolina*

Other works by L. P. Suzanne Atkinson

~Creative Non-Fiction~
Emily's Will Be Done

~Fiction~
Ties That Bind
Station Secrets: Regarding Hayworth Book I
Hexagon Dilemma: Regarding Hayworth Book II
Segue House Connection: Regarding Hayworth Book III
Diner Revelations: Regarding Hayworth Book IV
No Visible Means: A Stella Kirk Mystery #1
Didn't Stand a Chance: A Stella Kirk Mystery #2
Sand In My Suitcase: A Stella Kirk Mystery #3

For David, always

Thank you to Barb, Marguerite, Harriet, and Beverley
for all your help, and a special thanks to my editor Tim Covell for his
patience and support.

Recurring Characters:

Stella Kirk	Owner of Shale Cliffs RV Park; amateur sleuth
Aiden North	RCMP Detective
Rosemary North	Aiden's wife (Mary Jo & Toni – her sisters)
Nick Cochran	Park Manager; Stella's love interest; 10% owner
Alice & Paul Morgan	Park Employees; (brother & sister)
Eve Trembly	Park Employee; (Del Trembly's granddaughter)
Duke (John) Powell	Park Security
Kiki	Duke's Pomeranian
Trixie Kirk	Stella's sister
Brigitte & Mia Kirk	Trixie's daughter (runs Yellow House) & granddaughter
Norbert Kirk	Stella & Trixie's father
RV Park residents	Mildred Fox, Buddy McGarvey, Curtis Walsh & Elroy Brown, Sally & Rob Black, Ted Metcalfe
Jewel & Ken Winslow	Former fish plant workers, now caretakers at Painter Farm
Hester, Cavelle, Jacob Painter	Siblings
Farley Tompkins	Owner of Grey Cottage Realty
Paulina McAdams	Murder victim May 1981
Lorraine Young	Murder victim May 1980
Lucy Painter	Murder victim November 1980

CHAPTER 1

ID Isn't Official

Sunday, September 27, 1981

"We have a body at the hall." Aiden pauses.

Stella processes his words.

"I.D. isn't official, but he's the son of the two writers in your rental cottage."

The bleat of the phone disturbed the promise of a warm and cozy Sunday morning. With one leg wrapped around Nick's thigh, she'd been floating in the soft spot between awake and asleep, soaking in the perpetual magic of his continued presence. She reached to answer, he stirred, and her moment ended.

"What? Owen?" Stella extends her hand and touches Nick's arm, as he rolls toward her and studies her face.

"Yeah, Owen Ellis-Thomas. Can you come into town?"

She squints at the clock radio on the bedside table nearer Nick. Barely seven. "And his parents, Aiden?"

"We'll visit them together, but first I must get a handle on the writers retreat. Despite having met many of the players on Friday night, I need your help."

Nick pats her leg in unspoken support. "Okay. Half an hour." She flies out of their cocoon and sprints to the bathroom. The coolness of the bright September morning slides across her bare skin.

"I'll make coffee, Stella. And toast."

"Thanks." She hears his belt rattle when he grabs shorts off the chair nearest the balcony door. Today is the fourth and final day of the inaugural Shale Harbour Writers Retreat. Despite a rocky start which involved the arrest of their event manager's wife for murder, and an unorganized registration day, the success of their venture has been undeniable. Sponsored by local businesses and managed by Farley Tompkins of Grey Cottage Realty, the sessions have been lauded.

Participants and presenters began arriving Wednesday. Stella's RV park has been busy. Alice, her assistant, assigned sites and booked trailers, campers, and motor homes into adjacent spots before she left the job to return to school earlier in the month.

Frances Ellis and Edward Thomas rented her Shale Cliffs RV Park cottage for the duration. Nick provided a camp cot for their adult son, Owen.

When the family arrived at the park, she found little opportunity to interact with them, although their son habitually wandered around campsites and throughout the grounds. Since her staff, except for Duke Powell, her security man, are gone for the season, she and Nick manage most of the office and site tasks this time of year. The retreat created a significant increase in park business for near the end of September.

Many of her seasonal residents will stay to attend the final potluck scheduled for Saturday, October 3. She and Nick are tired and anticipated the completion of the 1981 season with relief...and now this.

****

Three Days Earlier
Thursday, September 24, 1981
"I'm sorry, Aunt Stella, but I'm stuck. Can you work my shift on the registration table from two to four today?"

"Your mother continues to avoid the public, but won't she watch Yellow House and Mia for the afternoon?"

Brigitte muffles an uncharacteristic snort. "I count on her to mind Mia, but not the business. Can you cover registrations? Please?"

"Whining is unbecoming," Stella teases, to lighten her niece's mood. "Yes, I'll help. Did you say two o'clock?"

"Right. Thanks." She pauses. "Aunt Stella?"

"What else?"

"When you have time, after the retreat, will you find a few minutes to talk with Mom? Invite her for lunch or coffee. She needs to smarten up and I can't be the one to encourage her back to the land of the living."

"Oh, you believe I can 'encourage' your mother? Brigitte, you know her as well as I do." Nails drum in the background as her niece's anxiety palpates. "But I will try, my dear. I promise I will try."

Stella leaves the kitchen in search of Nick. When she answered the phone, he was on his way into reception. She finds him waving to a couple breezing past the front door, tent trailer in tow. He turns when he senses her presence. His whole face glows, like when the sun bursts out of the clouds. Warmth trickles through her.

"B 17 left." He wraps one arm around her shoulder. Nick Cochran, her business partner, friend, and lover, came to work at Shale Cliffs when she took over the operation from her father. Undeterred by their nine-year age gap—not in her favour—and the fact he could do whatever he pleases thanks to an inheritance, he's chosen to purchase the majority of Trixie's share of the park and stay for the long haul. Their deal closes December 31. Stella still needs to find ten thousand dollars to cover the remainder of Trixie's shares. At that point, she and Nick will be equal partners. Last summer, he told her he wanted to give her the money—no strings. She remains hopeful the books show enough profit by year-end for her to withdraw a shareholder's loan-payback. Her focus is on finding a path forward without accepting the final portion of Trixie's stake in the park as a gift.

"Brigitte asked me to help with retreat registration later. Her mother refuses to cover the children's library and book shop for two hours. Her support involves Mia only. Brigitte sounds frustrated."

He gently squeezes her shoulder. "I'll be okay here for the afternoon. The check-outs are finished, and if there's the odd check-in without a reservation, we have room—plus I have Duke to fall back on."

She elbows him. "Duke can lead people to their sites and report any issues to you, but for God's sake, don't let him into the pump house or on a lawn mower." They giggle at her joke. Duke Powell and machinery aren't a good match. He handles security for Shale Cliffs—responsible for the gate at the end of the access road, both morning and night. He whirs around the park on the golf cart, checks for unattended fires, and ensures campers follow the rules: dogs on leashes, vehicles parked in their registered spots—the normal day-to-day aggravations in the management of a seasonal campground.

Their summer staff, Alice, and Paul Morgan, along with Eve Trembly, left employment after Labour Day to return to university. Duke moves to his efficiency unit in town once the park closes. Stella provides him a free site with a view in exchange for his services. He may pretend to be John Wayne with tasteless flair, and act sleazy on occasion, but he's reliable and trustworthy with work. She manages both Duke and his Pomeranian, Kiki, despite the fact they appear regularly in coordinated outfits, and test her patience daily.

"Maybe you'll find a chance to meet the writers and presenters who chose to stay in town. Give them a personal invitation to our party tomorrow night." Nick darts into the kitchen and returns with a slip of paper. "I have a grocery list of snacks. We have lots to drink, but we're in desperate need of junk food."

"Okay, I'll go into town right after lunch and deal with your list."

****

Stella pushes a small cart along the quiet aisles of the Shale Harbour Groceteria. She grabs chips, crackers, fig newtons (Nick's favourite), a pound cake, and a box of macaroons. She purses her lips—too much junk for her pantry since the staff are no longer around. If people don't eat tomorrow night, she'll drop off the lot at Brigitte's for her to use when the children come to reading hour.

Places to park near the community hall are in short supply. Stella pulls into the side yard at Yellow House before she scurries along the sidewalk to take her post across the street. A bottleneck of shoulders confronts her at the front door. One of those who remain outside on the threshold tells her they've run out of room inside.

"I'm here to help with registration," she states, as a means of explanation to an older lady who has clutched her sleeve.

"Registration is beyond help," mutters a heavy-set gentleman, as he leans against the hall's siding and smokes a long and offensively smelly cigarette. "I've been out here since noon."

"Let me in, please. Coming through." Stella pushes her way past at least a dozen people wedged into the minuscule foyer, to access the six-foot table provided by the retreat committee to manage registrations. "Hope, what the hell happened?" Stella drops into an empty chair beside Hope Carlyle, the local weaver who lives near the hall on Main Street. As she notes the woman's flushed cheeks, Stella fears Hope may burst into tears any minute.

"Farley forgot to pick up the registration forms. He produced a few, but

Mr. Gorman's wife is sick again, so he didn't deliver the rest. Farley went to retrieve them." She pauses to catch her breath. "I expected him back over an hour ago."

Stella surveys the table—no gift bags. "Give me a moment, Hope. I'll call Grey Cottage Realty. Maybe Cavelle's around."

Hope's manner suggests perhaps Stella has lost her mind. She gallops to the little office behind the foyer, anyway.

"Grey Cottage Realty."

"Cavelle. Stella here. Is Farley nearby? He's supposed to be at the hall. The place is chaotic."

"Hi, Stella. Farley is at his desk with the door shut. I thought you were finished for the day. The worktable in the front is covered with gift bags. What's the problem?"

"I have no idea. I think Farley might have come unglued. Can you deliver the bags and the registration forms? We're up to our armpits in frustrated writers." She stops for a second. "Seriously, Cavelle, the place is packed. Farley left to retrieve the registration forms and the remainder of the gift bags he forgot for some unknown reason, and now he's with you. Tell him I'll wring his neck if he doesn't return to the hall."

"Okay." Silence follows.

"Please, Cavelle, will you deliver the bags and forms? I need your help and I can deal with Farley later."

"Have you seen Hester? I dropped her off, and she hasn't arrived for a ride home."

Stella glances up from the desk to discover Hester, a sentry positioned in the centre of the office doorway. "Yes, I've seen Hester. Once you arrive, I'll finish her paperwork, and she can drive back with you."

She addresses the statue when she replaces the receiver. "Hi, Hester."

"I hate to criticize. Not everyone is as intelligent as me, but this retreat is not well organized. I clearly understood registration would occupy twenty minutes of my time, I could mingle as I chose, and return for the author readings this evening. Without an intervention, Jewel will have my supper ready, and I will not be home to eat."

One of Hester's many characteristics involves her visualization of people and issues in black and white terms. She possesses no skills related to nuance, despite her advanced capacities in other areas. "Problems," Stella explains.

"Farley Tompkins seems anxious and distressed. Mr. Gorman has a sick wife. Both were supposed to be here to help. Farley ran over to the printer to retrieve the forms Mr. Gorman couldn't deliver. The extra gift bags are still at Grey Cottage Realty, and now your wonderful sister is our new helper."

"Where's Farley? I assume he wanted to make a good first impression with both the authors and the attendees. You have but one chance, as you are aware."

"Farley missed the mark, but we'll be organized any minute. Come with me."

The two women return to the foyer and Stella shouts to the crowd, both inside the building and wedged in the doorway. "Mr. Tompkins has been detained. The additional registration forms and extra gift bags are on their way. Please have patience for a few more minutes and we'll be ready." She waves before she returns to her seat beside Hope.

She pats an empty chair near her for Hester, who whispers, "I am an attendee, Stella, not an organizer. I am not entitled to occupy a position behind the table."

"Sit," Stella commands. "Once Cavelle arrives, I'll register you and you can go home."

"Thank you. I have been standing for a long time." She perches on the chair, knees together and feet flat on the floor. She places her crocheted, drawstring bag in her lap. "Certain attendees went into the theatre. I wasn't sure we were allowed. I stayed in the hall."

"You mean more registrants?"

"They wanted to sit."

"Supplies were depleted before lunch," Hope leans to whisper in her ear. "People are upset."

"Be right back." Stella wiggles through the assembled group, toward the theatre. For a second, her mind returns to Paulina McAdams' memorial held here on July 11.

"Could I have your attention, please? The registration desk ran out of supplies, but they are on the way. We should be ready to take care of each of you in fifteen minutes." She starts back to the foyer and stops. "Thanks for your patience."

"Great to see you decided to attend." Stella resumes her conversation with Hester. "I knew you debated the idea."

"Yes." Hester continues to stare straight at the opposite wall while she talks. "I want to learn how to construct an effective memoir. Mayko Doan was invited here to teach a workshop and I'm convinced I will benefit from her experience."

Hope leans across Stella to address Hester directly. "Mayko is billeted with me, Hester. She drove all the way from Fredericton, alone with her small white dog. If you're interested, I will ask her if we can invite you to tea."

Hester remains blank-faced. "I will meet her at her workshop, an important event, Mrs. Carlyle, but I also want to meet her dog."

Stella's eyes twinkle when she glances at Hope. "Hey! Here comes Cavelle."

Both women jump from their seats to manoeuvre and grab the bouquets of paper shopping bags, emblazoned with the Grey Cottage Realty logo, and clutched in Cavelle's hands.

"I have more in the car. The registration cards are on the front passenger seat." Hope races out to Cavelle's sedan while the other two women drop the gift bags on the table.

Stella peers around for Hester and finds her positioned at the start of what she must expect will be the line. "You are a lifesaver," she whispers to Cavelle. "Where's Farley?"

"Farley 'can't-get-his-act-together' Tompkins remains in his office blubbering about how the event was really Paulina's idea and he misses her desperately." She groans as Hope returns with more gift bags clutched in her fists and a wad of forms wedged in her arm pit.

"We should be able to organize folks now, Cavelle. Thanks for your emergency assistance." The weaver starts to place the offerings in parallel rows. She bustles around the table and stacks the cards in two piles. They will register attendees in pairs.

"Cavelle, I'll complete Hester's paperwork. She's impatient to go home for supper so she can return and listen to the authors read from their work." She leans closer. "I'm happy she gathered up the courage to attend."

"You may be, but Jacob and I have serious concerns. Hester wants to write a family memoir. We have an older sister in jail for the murders of our parents and Jacob's wife." She touches Stella's sleeve. "We're excited to relive the sordid Painter history, right?" Heavy sarcasm laces her words. "See you tomorrow night."

"Writing a memoir will be cathartic for her, Cavelle. Only a select few will ever read her manuscript."

Cavelle's eyes widen. "She's a good writer. My younger sister will find a publisher, I have no doubt."

Within moments, registrants create lines in front of both women. Stella registers Hester first. They are behind schedule but still able to end by four-thirty, after the last attendee has left the building.

"Time to go home and visit with Mayko. I promised her chowder and biscuits before the author reading later."

"Are you expected to babysit her dog while she comes over to the hall?"

"The pup has a crate where she stays when Mayko isn't around, but the little creature will be snuggled in an airline bag at Mayko's feet tonight. She's attentive—a Maltese. Her name is Tanchau." Hope pauses for a moment to consider. "She told me Tanchau was her village in Vietnam—and no, I won't be in attendance this evening, but will drive Mayko to your house tomorrow for the party."

"Great. Tell her Tanchau is welcome. Hester will be pleased. I'm off to give Farley Tompkins a serious kick in the pants. I'll return the extra gift bags and cards to his office."

"Thanks for your help, Stella. The large crowd made me nervous." Hope turns to walk down the street, past the café, toward her weaving shop, and home.

Exhausted, Stella loads the remainder of their paraphernalia into her Jeep. She drives across Main and along Birch to Grey Cottage Realty. Farley's car is parked out front. She pulls in behind him. The entrance door sits uncharacteristically open.

With the leftover bags and forms plunked on the table, she yells, "Farley Tompkins, where the hell are you?"

He appears in the doorway to his office, red-faced and snotty. "I'm a mess. I am unable to go on." His body shudders with dramatic flair. He blows his nose, and the noise reminds her of a ferry approaching port.

"Pull yourself together. We have three days of work, and I refuse to let you bail. What can I do to help?"

"I gather leaving me alone isn't an option?" His attempt at a smile is watery.

"No. If my memory serves me, you are the host for the reading event tonight."

"Yes. That was the plan. Honest to God, I did not anticipate bereavement beyond belief. I am worse now than when we attended Paulina's memorial."

"You did a fine job in July, and you can rally again. Everyone depends on you, Farley."

"Did the afternoon turn into a disaster?" He makes a vain attempt to straighten his sport jacket.

Stella relaxes. He may be coming around. "Not terrible. People were patient, but the committee needs you," she emphasizes.

"Therefore, I must channel my grief into another love story for my book."

"Good idea, Farley. Channel your grief. Call the story 'Bereavement Beyond Belief.' You'll be at the hall tonight, right? Don't make me come back," she threatens, in as light-hearted a tone as she can muster.

Stained fingers rub his red, swollen cheeks and then scrape through his uncombed hair. "I won't let you down again."

❦

CHAPTER 2

I Am but a Child of Death

As she returns home after registration, the ocean vistas and scenery between Shale Harbour and Shale Cliffs RV Park impress her as usual. Poised on a scrap of real estate connected to the mainland of Nova Scotia by a single strip of roadway, held together by sea-grassed dunes, sits the village of Shale Harbour. The isthmus supports the community, the RV park, and a collection of cottages, many now permanent residences. No matter where you drive, you're never far from the twinkle of Atlantic Ocean waters.

Winters are often brutal. If a storm arrives from the right direction, the isthmus can be cut off when crashing waves swallow the causeway. The isolation created, if you choose to make your home in the area, has both advantages and disadvantages. Stella didn't move back to the park out of choice, but her birthplace has proven to be perfect at this moment in her life.

To blame Farley for his dramatic behaviour today would be fruitless. His wife hired a professional killer to shoot his lover, Paulina McAdams. The hit man happened to be Trixie's boyfriend. The murder occurred May first and Stella found the body. Her work with Aiden North, the local RCMP detective, proved to be both gruelling and heartbreaking. Neither Farley nor Trixie have recovered from the trauma. She continues to minimize Nick's concerns for her welfare, but you don't find a friend dead in an armchair with a bullet hole in their skull every day. She wraps her fingers around the steering wheel and digs her nails into her palms.

After the writers retreat ends, and the park closes for the winter, she wants to determine a path to finalize the sale of Trixie's forty-five percent of the business shares—forty for Nick to give him fifty percent of the park, and five for her, which will balance their partnership. Stella wants to scan the books again next week in the hopes she can retrieve a portion of her shareholder's loan investment. She needs to unlock ten thousand dollars, after she pays five to her sister in monthly installments by the end of this year.

She expects the author reading party tomorrow night at her house to be educational. Frances Ellis and Edward Thomas, two writers and workshop leaders from Port Ephron, plan to host the amateurs. The other retreat authors, plus any attendees and park residents who are interested, have been invited.

Owen Ellis-Thomas, the twenty-year-old son of Frances and Edward, is scheduled to read. He's peculiar and resembles Hester in many ways. He doesn't work or attend university and was home-schooled, according to his mother. From what Stella has heard and observed, Owen is an introvert. He wanders alone, with a notepad and pencil for company. The young man is tall and walks with a rolling gait, as if he recently disembarked from a ship. He carries his hands knuckles forward, in a position resembling the crawl stroke of a swimmer. He nods but establishes no eye contact.

His mother has written several romance novels. She's a short and round woman. Her hair is long and dark, streaked with grey. She wears it in a fat braid halo. Frances is gregarious and pleasant. By contrast, Edward, his father, presents himself as professorial in corduroys and sweater jackets. He writes futuristic fiction and is shy and unassuming, often usurped by his more outgoing spouse, or by his popular books.

She manoeuvres the Jeep into the parking space at the back of her house, near the veranda, and climbs the stairs. "Anybody home?"

"In here."

The response does not come from Nick.

A pot of spaghetti sauce bubbles on the stove. Duke and Kiki are seated at the table. Nick turns to greet her, a wooden spoon in his hand. "I invited Duke for supper."

"You're the one who hollered when I came in," she addresses her security man. "I gather the place is quiet, unlike the afternoon I endured." She throws her purse on a chair, the bag of groceries on the counter, and plants a quick kiss on Nick's cheek. "Smells good. I'm starved."

Duke and Kiki disappear to make rounds after supper. Stella and Nick remain at the table.

"Who do you think will be here tomorrow?"

"Besides Frances, Edward, and Owen, I expect most of our retreat guests to come," Stella responds. "Other than them, we don't have many literary types out here."

"We could still fill the living room."

Nick's right. "I want to call Trixie to encourage her to attend since Cavelle will drive Hester. Hope Carlyle said she planned to accompany Mayko Doan, the Vietnamese memoir writer, billeted with her. Bryce Blanken, the western romance guy, in the trailer beside Naomi and Gregory Whittleton, will no doubt turn up, along with the Whittletons. They're travel writers if my memory serves me. Two other presenters are booked at the hotel. I don't know specifics, but one is Greta Walmsley. I've read her self-help books. I'll be disappointed if she doesn't show."

"Let's plan for thirty, at least," he says as he rises to clear dishes. "Are park residents invited?"

"To be sure. I'll take a run around on the cart tomorrow and remind people—as long as Duke permits me to borrow his ride for an hour," she adds sarcastically.

They retire to the living room for tea after clearing the kitchen. "I hope we're done for the night. I'm bushed. What a mess at the hall today."

"What happened?" Nick settles in beside her. He places his tea on an end table and covers her knee with his hand.

Comfort in his nearness warms her. She tells him the story she avoided with Duke in the vicinity. "Farley troubles me. I know Edward and Frances—Frances—will run the workshops and manage the authors, but Farley is the pivot person. He's the local they turn to if the hall isn't open or if a writer experiences a problem with a lecture room. He will manage any food issues and work with Mercedes and Matt to coordinate the volunteers."

"The retreat is a big endeavour, Stella. Matt might appreciate an alert. He should know Farley has proven unreliable, especially since Meredith is no longer in the picture."

"Yes, and Theo Gorman's wife has relapsed. We can't depend on him, either. Now there are three calls to make in the morning."

"Three?"

"Trixie—to persuade her to come to the party; Matt—so he's aware of Farley's behaviour; and Aiden—to invite him and Rosemary, if she's okay."

****

Friday, September 25, 1981

"Trixie," she appeals, "Cavelle and Hester will be here. And we expect Greta Walmsley, for God's sake. You've read both her books: *Creating a New Self* and *Improving on Self.* Other than we four, and maybe the Norths, no one else knows you—no curiosity seekers." She listens to Trixie breathe. "And stop grumbling. Mayko Doan will be here, too. She was in the news. Remember her? She escaped from Vietnam?"

"Okay. Okay. Now I'm curious. What time and do you need food?"

"Not necessary. You and Brigitte will take the leftover snacks home in the long run. See you at seven."

After she dispenses with Trixie, Stella decides to contact Aiden next. Although not living at the park this late in the fall, it might be fun for them to attend tonight. The investigation of Paulina McAdams' murder finished at the end of June, and Aiden wanted to spend more time with Rosemary. She's in decline again, to the point where she may require admission to the psychiatric ward once more. They managed a few summery weeks in their trailer, but she started to deteriorate in earnest earlier in the month.

Sergeant Moyer answers her call. "Good morning. Is Aiden around, Sergeant?"

"God, Stella! Did you find another body?"

"No, not today, but thanks for your concern." Has she developed a reputation after three murders?

"Hold on." The phone line crackles.

"Stella! Glad you called. Still no suggestion you'll be asked to testify at Meredith Tompkins' trial. Russ, or Harry, I guess, will do the talkin'."

"I didn't call for a prosecution update, but good to hear. I thought you might be interested in attending our little amateur writer reading tonight at the house. Anyone with a spot in the park is welcome. I know you've moved home for the most part, but I wanted to extend the invitation—and to ask about Rosemary."

"To answer your second question first, Rosemary is back in hospital. Although I've done my best and followed her sisters' advice—off work every night by five, strict avoidance of you and the park, and my spare time devoted to my wife—she's hit bottom again. I visit each day over lunch, but she won't even talk to me. Toni and Mary Jo report she has decided you're welcome to me, and she wants a divorce."

"Oh, Aiden. May I go see her or will an appearance by me make matters worse? I can tell her I'm not interested in you." She pauses for a second. "You know what I mean."

"You tried once before without success, Stella. The doctors want to attempt to regulate her medications again. Depression is an ugly beast." He curses under his breath. "I may sell the trailer—not sure our purchase of Lorraine Young's rig and the plan to spend the summers at Shale Cliffs was my wisest move."

"Understood. Do what's best for Rosemary. Come out to the park tonight for a drink and an hour or two with different people."

"Okay. What time?"

"Seven. See you."

After a quick conversation with Matt Savioli, where she advises him of a possible lack of support from Farley and why, she hollers toward the kitchen where Duke and Nick are drinking coffee, "I'm taking the golf cart."

She first stops at Bryce Blanken's spot and finds him hovered over a pad of paper while seated at the picnic table. He's dressed in standard western garb of blue jeans, a plaid shirt with snaps, and a Stetson.

"Sorry to interrupt." She alights from the cart. "I'm Stella, one of the owners, checking to get an estimate of numbers for tonight. Do you plan to come to the house for the readings?"

"Yup, little lady. Lookin' forward to chin-waggin' with the younger ones."

"You write western romances, correct?"

He nods and places a protective paw over the scrawls on the paper beside him.

"Are you from Alberta? We host lots of visitors from out west."

"No." He doesn't elaborate.

"Okay. Hope to see you tonight." She glances at his work. "Sorry I disturbed you."

"Okay. Gotta go soon. Teachin' a workshop in an hour."

Naomi and Gregory Whittleton aren't around. She expects they're in town at the retreat. Before her return to the house for lunch, she stops to sound out other seasonal residents, including Rob and Sally Black, Mildred Fox, Ted Metcalfe and his friend Lily, Buddy McGarvey, and the boys—Curtis Walsh and Elroy Brown.

Curtis takes a pause from deck duties when she approaches. "We are almost ready to abandon you for another season, Stella, but an evening at the house to listen to writers read from their works sounds like a perfect way to end our year."

"See you near seven. There will be lots of people."

She's not surprised Curtis and Elroy are the only takers. By the time she returns, Nick has prepared lunch and included Duke. As they enjoy their egg salad sandwiches and barbecued potato chips, Nick reveals his plan for party set-up. "We can move the kitchen chairs out to the living room. If we use the six of them plus the dining chairs, there should be enough spots, especially since there's also the furniture from the veranda for an emergency. Duke and I will push the dining table against the wall and load it with snacks. Good?"

"The party's organized, I see, so now I have the time to go upstairs and take a nap."

His eyes widen. "Are you okay?"

She giggles. "I'm fine—delighted you're here to help."

"And me, too, right?" Duke sprays egg salad when he talks. "Me and Kiki—we help, too."

****

Trixie's subdued attire matches her mood of late. She arrives at six-fifteen. Prior to her boyfriend's arrest and murder confessions, she craved to be the focus of attention with her short skirts, plunging necklines, and platform heels dominating her fashion statement. Tonight, she has chosen jeans and a cashmere sweater. Her wavy hair hangs to her shoulders. Her makeup can best be described as minimal. One familiar trait remains. She isn't empty-handed. A trip to visit her former employer, the local fish plant, netted her cooked shrimp. Paired with dipping sauce and an old platter which belonged to their mother, the dish is guaranteed to be a favourite.

"Pretty sweater, Sis." Trixie struts toward the kitchen while Stella adds, "I'm happy you decided to come."

"Don't call me sis. I hate the word. Makes me feel ancient."

"We're in our forties, not our seventies. What's the real issue?"

She turns. Her eyes narrow. "Stella, you can celebrate a victory. You and Aiden rooted out a murderer—two murderers. I'm the one left to suffer."

"Even if Russ-Harry had not been caught, he was the wrong guy for you. I think you're lucky we discovered the truth before you moved in with him." She brushes her sister's arm. "Come on. Help me with the food."

Cavelle and Hester Painter arrive ten minutes later. "Sorry, Stella, but Hester insisted we be here by six-thirty.

"I am scheduled to read a poem tonight. Frances is aware. I require time to choose a proper place to sit and prepare. I told Cavelle you are understanding."

"Welcome to you both." She takes their coats. "Hester, find your spot. Cavelle, Trixie's in the kitchen." She leans closer to the latter woman's ear and whispers, "Try to cheer her up. She needs to move on."

After Cavelle wanders toward the kitchen, and while Hester chooses the perfect location, Nick answers a loud knock on the veranda screen door. The reception bell jangles simultaneously. Edward, Frances, and Owen arrive from the cottage while Hope Carlyle appears with Mayko Doan and her Maltese in tow. It isn't long before Naomi and Greg Whittleton enter via the front. They are supporting Mildred Fox, dressed in a purple caftan and bedroom slippers. Bryce Blanken lumbers in shortly afterward and helps himself to a beer thanks to Nick's offer, and Curtis and Elroy make themselves comfortable on one of the leather couches.

Greta Walmsley and Elsbeth Strauss materialize on the veranda. After they're settled, Stella scans the room, disappointed the number of amateur writers isn't greater. Hester and Owen will be the only readers. Perhaps the professional authors will contribute. "Attention, everyone. Each person introduce yourself before we begin. I'm Stella Kirk. I am one of the owners of the park, and welcome to those of you who have chosen to stay with us over the next few days." She turns toward Nick.

"And I'm another partner, Nick Cochran. Tonight, my job is to make sure you partake of refreshments." He attempts mocking formality.

"We are Frances Ellis, Edward Thomas, and our son, Owen Ellis-Thomas, who will grace you with an excerpt from his work-in-progress." She points in the general direction of her son, who keeps his head down and doesn't acknowledge the introduction. "I write romances, as you may know." She peers around the room from under her eyelashes. "My husband writes futuristic fiction." She pats him on the knee. "I don't understand a word, do I dear? Nevertheless, many people are fond of his stories." Both Edward and Owen are silent. Owen has chosen a chair as far away from Mayko's dog as he can get without relegating himself to the kitchen.

Greta introduces herself next. "I'm Greta Walmsley." A flutter of clapping ripples through Stella's living room. "As you know, I write self-help books.

With two published, I'm working on my third. I'm not from Nova Scotia but make my home in Halifax now, because my publisher insists that I reside nearby."

Stella hears Cavelle whisper to Trixie. She has read both of Greta's books and considers them bibles of self-help.

"Damn! Let's move on. I'm Elsbeth Strauss."

"Please, Elsbeth. Try to contain your language. We don't appreciate your curses."

"Button your pie hole, Frances. I'll say what I damn well want." Her white hair flips from side to side as she declares, "I write murder mysteries." The subdued lighting in the room enhances her aging but beautiful face.

"Good evening, everyone. I'm Hope Carlyle. I own the weaving shop in town and am pleased to present Mayko Doan, who will stay with me until Sunday." She points toward the author.

"How do you do? I wrote a memoir describing my experiences before and during my escape from Vietnam."

"You are famous. I am excited to work with you tomorrow. Your dog is cute."

Mayko pulls Tanchau out of her airline bag, and hands him over to Hester.

"I am Hester Painter. I want to write a memoir. I love dogs." She scratches Tanchau's ears. "My cocker spaniel is named Angel. I will read a poem for you tonight." She points at Cavelle. "And please meet my sister, Cavelle, who is not a writer but drove me here because I cannot drive."

Cavelle nods.

Bryce Blanken remains focused on Greta and misses his cue. Cavelle nudges him. "Oh. Bryce Blanken here. I write western romances. Two published already. No big deal. I'm stayin' in the park, courtesy of Stella, here." Stella doesn't miss his wink aimed at Greta.

Naomi and Greg touch shoulders on the couch. She answers. "We are Naomi and Gregory Whittleton. We compose travel and adventure books. We are staying here in our trailer, home for many months out of each year. We enjoy drinks by the campfire after supper and have made the acquaintance of the charming Mildred Fox, who accepted our invitation to accompany us tonight."

Mildred coughs and her beer rolls around inside the tall glass. "I'm a regular here in the park. Old friends with Stella, right? Too bad you ain't got no lemonade," she cackles. "Shoulda brought ya some."

"Nice to see you, Mildred. Happy you were persuaded to change your mind." She forces a patient smile. The woman never misses a chance for a free drink.

Aiden has settled into one of the leather chairs by the darkened fireplace. "Good evening, everyone. I am Aiden North, an old friend of Stella's and I keep a trailer in the front, near the cliffs."

"We're Curtis," he says, as he nudges Elroy.

"And Elroy. From northern Ontario, we live here at Shale Cliffs every summer."

"Bringing up the rear, as usual, I'm Trixie Kirk, Stella's untalented sister and a third partner for now. I came to deliver the shrimp."

Stella settles for the hostess approach in her struggle to find a suitable and supportive response. "Thank you, Trixie. With everyone introduced, who wants to read first?"

Frances leans across Edward's lap to poke Elsbeth on the knee. "We are graced with two amateurs tonight." She gazes around the room. "I guess we intimidate the less experienced," she titters. "Anyway, Elsbeth, I gather from our conversation earlier, you will begin? And Elsbeth, try to keep your language under control, okay?"

"Dammit, Frances. Let me read Chapter One, Scene One from my god-damned latest novel. See what you people think." After shuffling through a pile of loose-leaf on her lap, she begins with the line: "She didn't notice the blood at first."

Catapulted back to the day she found Paulina, Stella swallows to maintain control. The prose draws her in. Elsbeth's work makes her want to hear more.

Owen is next. He states simply, "I will read the beginning of a manuscript I have worked on for two years." He describes a bludgeoning, a decapitation, and floors slippery with the entrails of a child. The screams are not of fear or loss, but of jubilation. The smells are not of death, but of freedom. A thirteen-year-old girl, with the help of her nineteen-year-old boyfriend, kills her parents and her seven-year-old brother. The small group sits in stunned silence while Frances claps.

Hester rises. She turns to Mayko and gives her a solemn nod. "I want to write a memoir. Right now, I wrote a poem which I will share." She closes her eyes and recites.

"The forest fears the fire
Flowers cry when sacrificed to bouquets
Weeds struggle to overcome their lot in life
Every animal has a soul
I am but a child of death
On a return journey to find my reason
My losses are many and I ceased to grow when my mother died
Angel listens
Accept me as a creature of the universe"

Without a nod or glance toward the group, Hester returns to her seat.
Cavelle and Stella lock eyes for a moment.
She senses the feather touch of Nick's hand on hers.
The room explodes into applause.

CHAPTER 3

The Retreat is Over

Sunday, September 27, 1981

"Broken neck," Aiden points out with unnecessary abruptness. He offers Stella gloves. "Go for a closer look if you want but put these on—and hold the handrail for God's sake!"

Parlour Antiques displays an extensive collection of Victorian dolls. When she touched one last week, thinking of her great-niece Mia, the limbs were disjointed at the knees, elbows, shoulders, and hips. She thought it had fallen apart in her hands. Mercedes Savioli, the proprietor, reached for the doll, lifted its skirts, and exposed the wooden appendages held together with cord. Owen lies crumpled at the bottom of the red-painted cement stairs. His countenance reveals his shock.

She's shaken by what she sees below her. "He fell?" *Why do you need me here?*

"Looks like he did, but forensics and the coroner will sort out how. The caretaker found him—a fellow named Valentin Reguly. Ring a bell?"

"Yes. He's worked here for years."

"We assume the fall took place last night." He starts to descend. "I want to examine why the hall wasn't secured after activities ended. Who might have been here with him? Where were Frances and Edward? Did he plan to meet a friend after the workshops finished? Didn't his folks wonder where he was?"

"His poor parents," she whispers in a sudden rush of clarity. "We need to tell them before they arrive."

"It's possible they'll appear on your doorstep to use your phone since their son never came home. Will you call Nick and ask him to keep them at the park?"

"Sure." She has no interest in following Aiden down the stairs. "Today is the final day, with classes in the morning and an author question and answer after lunch. Farley must be informed so he can find an alternate spot for people to congregate." Anxiety builds. No one should see the scene. "I imagine participants are scheduled to be here in an hour. I'll use the office to call both Nick and Farley. Gloves will stay on," she adds, in response to Aiden's frown. She hopes he doesn't expect her to examine Owen's crumpled form.

"Hi. Please go to the cottage and ask Frances and Edward to remain where they are. Report the hall is closed because of an incident, and Detective North is on his way as soon as possible."

"Can't Aiden meet them now?"

"No." Her voice shakes. She's aware she sounds like a police station receptionist. "We need to wait for forensics, but his folks will be worried. Tell them to stay put. Further details are forthcoming."

"Okay, but Frances came to the house earlier, to see if he was here. I guess she expected, since he was so late, he just collapsed on the rattan sofa on the veranda rather than disturb them. She said he was supposed to receive a lift back to the park with a guy Owen referred to as Jacob. She was frantic because Owen wasn't here. I hope they haven't left for town."

"Oh God. Invite them for coffee if necessary and wait. I need to speak with Farley and have him herd participants over to the café, or the hotel—away from here. Aiden has an officer on the door." She stops to catch her breath. "He likely fell, but why was he still at the venue when everyone else had finished for the day? And why Jacob?"

"Call Farley. I'll do my best from here."

"Hi, Stella. I know I'm late. Give me twenty minutes. Do we have a problem?"

"Yes, as a matter of fact, we do. There's been an incident. I can't say more, but you need to hurry over to the hall, stand at the door with the police officer, and direct attendees to the café or the hotel to regroup. Are you able to pitch in and help?"

"With no more information except there's been an 'incident'? If the cops are in attendance, and you're involved, somebody's dead. Who died, Stella?"

"I'm not at liberty to say more." She hates the sound of herself in this moment. "We want you on site before others start to arrive. Ten minutes, Farley. Will you be at the front door of the hall in ten minutes? I'll call Tiffany and suggest she pull every croissant she has out of the freezer."

"On my way."

"Cocoa and Café. How may I help you?" Tiffany Blair's sing-song voice floats through the phone line.

Added stress heats her flushed face. "Hi, Tiffany. Stella here. There's been an incident at the hall and attendees won't be able to take part in scheduled workshops or access the building. If Farley drags a gaggle of them over to your place, will you host, say, thirty plus people?"

"What? Stella, what's happened? What's going on?"

"Too many 'what' questions, Tiffany. I can't share more. Can you help?"

"Certainly. Tell Farley to send over whomever he wants. We'll do our best. With the morning warm and sunny, I'll run outside and wipe off the deck furniture. Andrew is here with me. No problem."

"Thanks, Tiffany. Your support is invaluable. See you later."

She rounds the corner to find Aiden in the foyer with his back to the front door. "Forensics arrived. They confirmed he's been dead for hours. Let's go have a word with the caretaker."

Valentin Reguly sits folded into a seat inside the theatre space. He could well be hung over.

"Good morning, Mr. Reguly. I'm Detective North and you know my consultant, Stella Kirk. We will meet with you at the police station for a complete statement later, but we need answers right now." Stella chooses a spot immediately ahead of Valentin, and Aiden sits in the row behind.

Nicotine-stained fingers scrape through dark and oily hair. He reminds her of one of the Everly Brothers on an off day. "Sure," he mutters.

"Can you tell us why a person remained inside after you locked the hall last night?"

"The place wasn't locked, Sir. My brother-in-law called me. I left early and went to sit with him and my sister."

"And you didn't return to complete your duties? I expect you were required to perform other tasks—garbage, floors."

"We drank. Mallory is much worse, and Ted wanted company. I walked home and never came back to the hall until this morning."

"Mallory, Theodore Gorman's wife, is suffering a bad patch," she states, for Aiden's benefit. "Valentin, I *am* sorry." Stella twists forward far enough to pat him on the arm.

Unruly strands of white hair dust Aiden's brow when he tilts his head in Stella's direction.

"Theodore Gorman owns the local print shop. He's married to Valentin's sister. Her declining condition means Mr. Gorman has been unable to help out with the retreat, although he provided advertising materials."

"Thanks, Stella." He turns toward Valentin, who continues to rake his thick hair. Tiny white flakes settle on his green caretaker's coveralls. "We have an open hall and a victim with access. Did you see anyone else here before you left?"

"Three of the authors were still in their classrooms. I told them I was on my way out and to please lock the door with the inside knob. I intended to pop in later and set the deadbolt. I figured I'd clean this morning."

"Your clarification helps. We'll conduct a more detailed interview in due course, Mr. Reguly. Notifications must be made first. For now, don't discuss the incident with anyone."

On their return to the foyer, Aiden is quiet.

"I spoke with Nick. Frances walked to the house earlier to see if Owen slept out on our veranda or called. Tiffany is on board and Farley will move people over to the café."

"You can mobilize folks, often an advantage because the locals trust you." His hand brushes her shoulder. "Thanks. Let's drive to the park right now. I'll follow you."

Her thoughts remain with Frances and Edward for the duration of the short trip. She knows her speed won't be an issue. How does Aiden plan to tell them their child has died? She hopes the forensic team and the coroner determine his death was an accident. But what was he doing in the hall so late? And why was Jacob expected to deliver him back to Shale Cliffs?

****

As she parks the Jeep, Nick steps out on to the veranda. "I did as you asked. They're still in the cottage from what I can tell, although worried sick. Will you go with Aiden?"

Stella watches the detective park. "I expect so."

Nick's frown speaks volumes.

She trudges up the stairs.

"There's no need for you to put yourself through another painful experience." Nick's hushed voice brushes her ear. "He's the cop. Let him handle the chore," he mumbles. "You've been involved in enough trauma over the past summer." He wraps his arm around her shoulder and pulls her close.

Aiden leans against the unmarked Caprice, arms folded, legs crossed at the ankles. She will go with him. "Aiden needs to return to town after the notification."

"And you'll stay here?"

"I'll assist with interviews, but not right away. We'll see." She reaches to touch his cheek with her lips before she gives Aiden a limp wave. "On my way."

On the walk along the narrow and rutted road to what used to be the manager's cottage, Aiden and Stella discuss the circumstances in quiet tones. "Nick says they're upset."

"Their son didn't return home last night. A police officer is coming to talk to them. In my experience, they already fear the worst." He focuses on the single lane. Tufts of grass and potholes blotch the two-tire pathway. "You need to fix your road. A guy could break an ankle."

"Your criticism will be taken under advisement."

She turns to catch a sliver of his momentary smile.

"A death notification is the absolute hardest part of my job, Stella." They stop, taking deep breaths in unintended unison, before they navigate the one step to the small veranda.

There is no need to knock on the screen door. Frances and Edward stand in stoic silence, distorted by the mesh. They are holding hands.

Stella pulls on the metal handle. To her surprise, Edward reacts first.

"Is our son dead? Have you arrived to tell us Owen is dead?"

"Mr. and Mrs. Thomas, I am Detective Aiden North, an investigator with the RCMP. We met Friday evening. I regret to inform you your son, Owen, has died. Our office continues to investigate the circumstances. May we come in?"

Until this moment, Frances has remained quiet. Her silver-streaked hair hangs in a single braid. A dark blue velour track suit, two sizes too big, swallows her frame. "Please, sit." She gestures toward the chairs at the little kitchen table. Tears flow in a waterfall of emotion, wetting her chubby cheeks.

"Let's talk." Aiden's soft and kind voice reaches out to them.

Edward controls their side of the conversation. "How did Owen die, Detective?"

Aiden perches on the edge of a chair, hands clasped on the old table. "Valentin Reguly found your son at the bottom of the stairs in the Shale Harbour Community Hall and Playhouse. Our forensic investigators will determine the exact cause of death, but right now we assume he died from a fall."

Frances covers her mouth in a vain attempt to muffle her sobs. "He said he wanted to meet with another attendee to discuss their work. He planned to receive a drive home from them. He said he would eat an early supper with her at the café and return later. Why was he still at the hall?" She points to a camp cot in the corner. "When we woke this morning, he wasn't here. I assumed, because he was late, he stretched out on your veranda." She blubbers toward Stella. "When I went to find him, he wasn't there."

"We have no further details right now."

"Excuse me, Detective," Stella interrupts. "Frances, did you tell Nick a man named Jacob was to drive Owen home?"

"Correct, but I have no idea who he is." Her blubbers continue.

Aiden meets Stella's eyes. "Hester Painter came to the reading on Friday night."

Frances sniffs in a flushed attempt at graciousness. "Her poem moved me."

"Jacob is Hester's brother. No doubt he planned to meet with Hester, who doesn't drive, so Jacob offered to deliver them both home. Did he mention Hester?"

"No. Could one of them have hurt our Owen?" Edward's guise clouds with intensity.

"For the moment, we consider your son's death to be accidental, although we want to examine every avenue of inquiry."

"May we see him?"

"I will call the park office and tell Nick or Stella when you're needed for formal identification. I appreciate your time and am sorry for your loss."

Edward nods, and Frances plunges into another episode of tears.

Stella forcibly calms her voice. "Please visit the house whenever you like. Nick and Duke are both around."

"We want to go home to Port Ephron. May we remain there once we see Owen?"

"I expect you feel isolated without a phone. I plan to gather the workshop attendees and leaders together later today. I've organized additional investigators to come from Port Ephron, so we can question each person in a timely manner. Stella will be apprised of the progress of our investigation and she or Nick can provide any pertinent information to you. I imagine, after identification, you may return home, but please stay on site until I call."

They stand in the doorway when Stella and Aiden leave. She senses the pressure of the couple's eyes on her back while they navigate the narrow roadway toward her house.

****

"Jewel Winslow rang when you were at the cottage. She said to contact the farm because Hester wants to talk with you. How were they?"

Aiden departs the driveway and Stella plunks into a rattan chair on the deck. "As expected, I guess—distraught, in disbelief. Aiden told them to stay put until he calls. They'll go to the morgue in Port Ephron and identify Owen, although merely a formality. I expect we'll meet with everyone later today. Frances and Edward might well appear on our veranda before the morning's over."

Nick, seated in the chair opposite, analyzes her with concern in his eyes. "I'll check on them."

Her brain charges forward as she nods absently. "From what I can gather, Owen promised to eat supper with Hester last night. Frances said he planned to meet a new friend, and a person named Jacob would drive him home. Hester needs to be told what happened." She stands.

"Duke will be here for lunch. He's off on rounds. I promised to scrounge us a bite at noon. I'll make enough for Edward and Frances—and you, too."

She leans over, plants her hands on his shoulders, and kisses his forehead. "You are my rock. I hope you understand I appreciate you."

He pats her hand. "You couldn't manage without me. I planned my role—to be invaluable."

"You did, didn't you?" She hugs him, knowing her voice sounds sadder than necessary, and turns toward her office.

"Hi, Jewel. I hear Hester wants to talk with me. Do I need to come out to the farm, or will she have a phone conversation today?"

"I'll find her. She's real upset, Stella."

Ideas and fears fly through Stella's mind. *Did Owen and Hester have an altercation? Might Hester be implicated in Owen's death? Is she even aware?*

"Hello."

"Hi, Hester." Before she provides a notification, she asks, "What's on your mind, my friend?"

"You have encouraged me to expand my horizons, your words, and meet people. I followed your advice, enrolled at the retreat, and met Owen. He acted nice enough. After we both read at your house Friday night, he invited me to have supper with him when the workshops were finished yesterday."

"Go on." Stella has figured out the rest of the story but lets Hester finish.

"I waited at Cocoa and Café for two hours and fifteen minutes. I sat at a table by the window and eventually accepted my error in judgment. I asked Tiffany to call my brother to come fetch me. Jewel made me scrambled eggs and cinnamon toast."

"What time, Hester?"

"Jewel served my supper at six-forty-five, which is late for me."

Patience is a virtue. Hester's communication style is exacting. She remembers every detail. Sadly, she will make an excellent witness if needed. "Hester, when did you wait for Owen and when did Jacob come to retrieve you?"

"Owen and I scheduled a light meal to take place at four o'clock. We planned to discuss our projects. Jacob instructed me to ask Tiffany to telephone him at six o'clock. Owen disappointed me and I do not expect to follow your advice again, except in special circumstances. Why are the workshops cancelled?"

"Hester, there's been an accident at the hall. Can you tell me the last time you saw or talked with Owen?"

"Yes. At two-thirty tea break, he reminded me of our rendezvous at four. Are you able to reveal what has happened? Will you drive to the farm? I want to hang up now."

"We won't talk for much longer, but you need to be aware Mr. Reguly found Owen at the foot of the stairs early today. He's dead." She waits for a response.

"At least he didn't forget our supper. Is my personal remark inappropriate? A volunteer called to cancel the workshops. She didn't say why."

"Detective North has told Owen's parents who, understandably, are unable to continue with the retreat. Now he's on his way to meet with Farley and his sergeant. Everyone is currently being informed they are required to make a statement and give their contact information to the RCMP before they leave

for home. I'll take you to the police station this afternoon for an interview."
Aiden will want to hear her statement.

"The retreat is over."

"As a matter of fact, yes. The hall is a crime scene. The son of the organizers is dead. May I pick you up after lunch?" Bluntness is best.

"Hopefully, no one hurt Owen."

"What makes you wonder if another person was involved?"

"He acted nice enough, as I said, but people with experience interacting with him in the past actively stayed away from him. I expect their dislike is the reason few amateur readers attended your party on Friday. Everyone knew his parents would be in the group and he would be reading so they avoided the gathering. I have overheard many conversations, Stella. I have excellent hearing."

"Give me an example of what people said about Owen."

"Okay, but I need to stop talking soon, have my lunch, and prepare for your arrival."

"Fine."

"One girl emphasized she never intended to read in front of him again, because the last time she attended a class and he was present, he took her journal when she excused herself to visit the washroom. Others told her later."

"Did he copy her work?"

"I have no firsthand knowledge. I was determined to make my own judgment, although I heard many negative comments whenever he entered a room. My story will be a memoir, and no writer would describe my life and pretend my losses are theirs. Ridiculous. He took my special pencil, though, and I expected to ask him to return it last evening."

"I'll fetch you at one o'clock, okay?"

"Try to be punctual, please. As you now understand, I have lost patience with waiting for people who do not appear. I guess I can make an exception for Owen, given the circumstances, but you are often tardy. I hope Detective North will retrieve my special pencil for me." She hangs up.

CHAPTER 4

Could Hester Be Mistaken?

"I'm not finished my tea. Please sit and Jewel will pour you a cup." Hester pats the seat beside her. "Don't tell Opal, but Jewel's tea tastes good, if not better." Hester giggles and sips.

Stella pulls out a chair and nods to Jewel. Tea sounds perfect because she skipped hers at home to arrive at the Painter farm on time. "May I ask a question?" Hester has remained quiet while Jewel putters around the sink washing Mason jars. Her attention remains on Kenny, who sputters away in his playpen.

"Yes."

"I hope you'll provide Detective North with straightforward answers today, or shall we expect to be challenged to phrase questions in a particular way?" She nods to Jewel who places a cup at her elbow.

"My responses will be forthright and honest, and I will volunteer information." She slurps the last of her tea. "Owen and I are not related. I possess no vested interest in the outcome of your investigation." She fiddles with the buttons on her grey blouse, a garment that does little to enhance her mottled complexion. "If Owen was murdered, and I'm certain such is the case, then I expect to play no part except for my detailed report of the circumstances I provided to you in our previous conversation." Hester makes eye contact with Stella for the first time.

"Fair enough. Detective North will be relieved. Are you ready? He expects us in half an hour."

Hester rounds the corner to retrieve her coat from the back closet, and Stella turns to Jewel. "Thanks for the tea. You and Ken are the perfect match for this family."

The young woman, who Stella knows has slept in her car more than once and who ran the risk of becoming homeless with a newborn last winter, glows in response to the compliment. "Ken and me, we couldn't be happier. We love the house next door. We thought, at first, Jacob would be troubled." She lowers her chin in appeared reverence to the circumstances of Lucy Painter's death ten months ago. "He's bin real good; gives little Kenny lots of attention. Jacob's a kind man." She leans closer to whisper in Stella's ear. "We told him if he ever wants the bungalow back—if he remarries—we'll move in here with Hester and Cavelle, so long as we can stay." She stands straight at the sound of Hester's footfalls in the hall. "The best place ever," she finishes, with a swing of her arm.

Jewel has never been talkative in the past. She's safe and happy. She carries her new-found status as a badge of honour.

"Ready, Stella—and Jewel—you make excellent tea. Thank you."

Stella swallows her shock. Hester is never magnanimous.

Their drive into town will consume thirty minutes. Stella steels herself to review Hester's observations with her again in the car, but Hester begins with a different discussion topic.

"I've written to Opal."

"What?" Stella takes her eyes off the road long enough to see Hester's face disappear behind a curtain of mousy hair. "Jacob and Cavelle gave you strict instructions. No contact."

"True, but I sympathize with her."

"How did you send a letter?"

"Jewel took it with her when she drove into town to the Groceteria. She likes me best." The shadow of a smile curves her lips. "There has been no response. I check our mailbox every day."

"You won't hear from her. Opal murdered your parents and Jacob's wife. What do you expect?"

"I want her to forgive me since I am to blame for revealing her secret. Humans need forgiveness, even me."

A cotton wool silence fills the Jeep. Hester remains quiet for the remainder of the journey and Stella ponders what to say to her complicated friend.

She parks at the back of the tiny detachment in Shale Harbour. Cars line the street out front. Sergeant Moyer, frazzled in his salutation, waves them toward Aiden's office while he answers the telephone.

"Come with me. The detective must be busy."

On the way along the cement block corridor, Aiden flies out of the interview room. "Make yourselves comfortable in my office. I have to instruct the investigators before they take off for the Presbyterian Church."

"Church?" The station has all the characteristics of a madhouse. Aiden said he needed additional personnel from other detachments. She counts six unfamiliar faces around the big table.

"Give me five minutes." He dashes off toward Moyer.

Hester assesses Aiden's office. "The space is sparse."

"Detective North is posted in Port Ephron and travels here when there's a case."

"After three murders—five, if you consider my parents, and now there's Owen's suspicious death, he should consider working here full-time."

They perch on wooden chairs in front of his battered desk. "You need Opal's forgiveness?" Stella chances a return to their previous conversation.

Hester clasps her hands in her lap, on top of her tied cotton bag, and once again curtains her face with her hair by bowing her head. "Yes."

"Jacob forgives you."

When Hester looks up, her eyes are brimmed. "My brother is heartbroken."

"Your brother is a kind man and understands. You tried your best to protect Lucy."

"I want Opal to forgive me."

"Don't be surprised if she never does, Hester."

"Good afternoon, Hester. Hi, Stella. It's a crazy day. Our meeting needs to be brief, but Hester?" Aiden pauses to ensure the woman's full attention. "We'll find time to talk again if necessary. There are twenty-eight other attendees scheduled to be interviewed today."

"The interview can be rescheduled, Detective, but Stella has been kind enough to drive me here now. I wish to tell you the details of my experience last evening and will attempt to be succinct. Did you find my pencil?"

"Staff found a mechanical pencil with the body, and I'll see that you are given an opportunity to identify it later in the investigation." Aiden doesn't miss a beat and makes no eye contact with Stella. "You were to meet Owen after the last workshop yesterday?"

"Thank you and correct." Over the next fifteen minutes, Hester repeats her experiences with Owen in minute detail. Aiden doesn't push. Stella keeps her eyes trained on Hester.

"You think the participants, for the most part, were not keen on Owen. Therefore, any one of them could be a suspect?"

"Detective North, I assume anyone at the retreat who knew Owen from other events did their best to avoid him. Stella's party illustrates my point, where the single amateur reader to attend, besides Owen, was me." She leans over in an uncharacteristic show of affection and pats Stella on the knee. "I felt sad for you. Such a nice gathering and a lot of work by you and Nick."

"We were okay." Overcome by Hester's unexpected empathy for the second time, she adds, "Your poem was beautiful, and the evening provided you with an opportunity to read."

"Hester, please wait here in my office for a few moments. I need to confer with Stella in the hall."

Aiden leans against the wall and taps his foot with impatience. "I spoke with Farley Tompkins and Valentin Reguly earlier. I learned Reguly performs janitorial services for the Presbyterian Church. Between him and Farley, they've opened the premises and gathered the participants to be interviewed by six investigators I've managed to haul in from other detachments."

"Wow. You've been busy."

"People want to leave for home, and I can't blame them. Each one will be questioned as to their whereabouts at the time of the death, and we'll collect their contact information. The authors were asked to stay for another couple of days."

"How can I help, besides inviting you out to the park for supper?"

"We should interview both Farley and the caretaker again. I don't consider them directly involved, but I need the benefit of their observations. Will you take Hester home and come back to the station? I requested Farley be here at three and we'll meet Valentin at four." He touches her arm. "Our evening may be spent reviewing the investigators' reports. Are you ready for the task?"

"Whatever helps. We can work after supper. What's the plan for Frances and Edward?"

"Formal identification is scheduled to take place tomorrow, after which they'll be able to go home. I'll organize a time to talk with them later in Port Ephron."

****

"The story Owen read proved to be both unpleasant and vaguely familiar. Did you find the content horrible, too?" Hester breaks her silence as they pull into the Painter farm driveway.

"We've spent months in detailed murder discussions. I found Paulina dead in her chair last May. But I agree with you. His reading was gruesome, although no one killed him because he was annoying or a writer of gore, Hester."

"You're correct. And murders aren't committed over plagiarism, either." She turns to Stella and scrapes strands of hair off her face. "It's still possible you and Detective North will discover Owen's death was, in fact, a case of misadventure." She does not sound convinced.

Stella speeds off the Painter property and hurries home to touch base with Nick. "Hi. Quiet?"

"Yes, except for a steady stream of authors who want to use the phone. I told everybody tonight and tomorrow night will be no charge. People complain, but at least extra costs won't be one of the reasons. And you, my love? Time for tea?"

They stand on the veranda. "No, thanks. I promised to take part in deeper discussions with Farley and Valentin." She explains the schedule and the need to scrutinize attendee interviews. "I invited Aiden out here. Rosemary remains in hospital and he's worried. I thought we could enjoy supper and talk about participants."

"Great. I'll figure out the meal. By the way, suggest he drive his own car. We don't want any of our writers to discover the detective is in our living room."

"Good idea." She stands, wraps her arms around his neck, and plants a warm kiss on his lips. "I *will* be back." She races down the steps to the Jeep.

****

"Go right in, Stella. Farley and Detective North are in his office." One of Sergeant Moyer's ears remains glued to the phone.

"Hi. Am I late? I took Hester home and cruised past the park to check in with Nick."

"No, we're good."

"Hi, Farley. What a mess, eh?"

"Yes. I'm afraid our little retreat started off on the wrong foot and has stayed firmly planted there." He nibbles on his lower lip. "Meredith could plan, not me."

"You didn't have the power to prevent this situation, Mr. Tompkins, but if we discover a crime has occurred, you may be pivotal in its solution. Explain your role and duties, please. You said you were the organizer." Aiden leans across his desk and plants tweed elbows on the blotter.

"Edward and Frances managed the creative side—the authors, the design of the workshops, and the schedule of events. I spent most of my time dealing with registrant and venue issues, although I checked with each author before their workshop to ensure necessary supplies were available. I ran late to whatever class I wanted to attend."

His whining is unnecessary, given the current circumstances. Stella glances at Aiden before she jumps in. "I'm sure you observed a few interactions of interest, Farley."

The owner of Grey Cottage Realty settles deeper into his chair. "Well, Bryce Blanken, the cowboy author—he has the hots for Greta Walmsley. He couldn't take his eyes off her. Oh, and Greg Whittleton comes across as a nice enough fellow on the surface, although I found him in a lip-lock with a giggling young woman in the janitor's closet when I tried to catch Valentin because the Gents ran out of paper towel. I asked her later if Mr. Whittleton harassed her, and she laughed in my face. Women!"

"What were your observations of Owen?" Aiden prods.

"Owen lurked. Every time I turned around, I saw him posted too close to some group in casual discussion. He trolled the halls while the workshops were on. I understand he's dead, and I'm sorry, but he was weird. Of the thirty people who came to the retreat, twenty-two of them were women and I bet each one did her best to avoid him."

"Any comments on the eight men?" Aiden pushes harder.

"No, Detective. The guys are older. He showed no interest in them or them in him."

"Did you have occasion to return to the hall after the workshops ended Saturday afternoon?"

"At the risk of repeating myself, no, Detective. I raced back to Grey Cottage to give Cavelle a break." He purses his lips. "To be honest, I depended on Valentin to stay behind and lock the place."

"Mr. Tompkins, our conversation has been a great help." Aiden stands to shake his hand after he jots a few notes. He rattles off the familiar refrain. "As usual, please don't discuss the case with anyone, or disclose the content of our interview. I assume we can call on you again if necessary?"

****

Their follow-up visit with Valentin Reguly is scheduled for four o'clock at the community hall. They enter the cool foyer via the unlocked door. The registration table and chairs are gone. The cranberry cement floors glisten. Forensics released the scene back to the volunteer committee who runs the facility, and appearances suggest Valentin has cleaned since midday.

"Be careful on the stairs, for God's sake. He took the polish to them."

Stella holds tight to the handrail while she descends. "Anybody home?" Her voice echoes along the dimly lit hallway. Although the wall sconces are on, they create a shadowed and creepy atmosphere. She steps around the general area where Owen's body was discovered.

"I'm here." Valentin pops out from the vestibule, which leads to the Ladies. "Tryin' to clean. I've been hard at work since Sergeant Moyer called the church and told me I could come back." He throws the piece of paper towel he used to wipe his hands into the garbage can near the foot of the stairs. "You want to sit in the office upstairs? More comfortable."

"Sure." Aiden starts the return trek to the foyer.

Stella swallows a mutter and follows.

They muddle around the chairs in the tiny space occupied by the committee secretary on occasion. In the end, Aiden assumes the position of authority and chooses the wooden relic behind the desk.

"We need to clarify a few important details related to the time you were in the hall after the workshops finished on Saturday."

"Ask away, Detective."

Although dressed in bottle-green shirt and pants—work clothes common to cleaners—his hair is combed and he's sober. Valentin might make a better witness than she first surmised.

"Who were the authors who remained behind after people left yesterday? You said three, if I recall." Aiden flips through his notes, compiled on a tiny pad he keeps in the inside pocket of his jacket.

"Kinda vague on names, but a tall and skinny lady was still here, and I interrupted a noisy argument. I didn't hear much, but she was not happy with him. Owen was here, too. I talked to the skinny lady first. Once they noticed me, I made sure the couple got the message about locking the hall—and I told the dead guy."

"So, there were four people left in the hall when you took off. Where was Owen?" A theory has begun to percolate in her brain.

"At the top of the stairs. I assumed he was waiting for one of the authors still here. He seemed in a hurry."

"Why do you believe he was in a hurry?"

"He asked me for the time, and when I said five past four, he started to shuffle back and forth. He was twitchy, like he was gonna be late."

"You left after you spoke with Owen?"

"I did, Detective. I found the door open in the morning and the guy at the bottom of the stairs. I called the detachment."

"Stella, any questions for Mr. Reguly?"

"Yes." She swivels in her chair to make direct eye contact with Valentin. "Did you overhear the topic of conversation between the couple?"

Valentin runs stubby fingers through his hair—a habit Stella has come to recognize as nervousness. "He likes the young girls, I guess. She yelled at him. He told her *it*, whatever *it* was, meant nothing."

"What else did you overhear?"

"When I interrupted, they shut up, but she cried, and his face turned beet red. I said my piece, repeating the same message I told the skinny lady, and took off up the stairs where I ran into Owen."

Aiden stands. "Thanks, Mr. Reguly." He shakes the janitor's hand. "Your information has been a big help. Please do not discuss the interview, or the case, with anyone. We appreciate your discretion."

On the walk back to the station, Stella presents a theory. "Gregory was caught kissing someone other than Naomi. We know this from Farley. Besides Frances and Edward, the Whittletons were the only authors working as a couple at the retreat. They probably were the people Valentin overheard. I bet Owen, the lurker, saw Gregory and threatened to tell Naomi. Gregory got the jump and told her, but he then had a bone to pick with Owen."

"If you're right and the Whittletons have motive of some kind, then Greta Walmsley—I guess she's the other author who remained in the hall—left first. Both the Whittletons are compromised because, if one of them pushed him, the other will be aware. There may have been a fourth person who arrived after the authors exited. Reguly said Owen acted anxious and in a hurry."

"Did he assume Hester was to meet him in the foyer after classes? She told us they planned for an early supper in the café at four, but maybe he misunderstood."

"Could Hester be mistaken?"

"Not a chance. If he confused the time or place to meet Hester, then a case of misadventure is a good possibility."

"The others left, and he remained since Hester hadn't shown up. Hence the unlocked door."

They stop in front of the detachment. "What time shall I arrive tonight?"

"Around six-thirty, if that works. Nick will make supper and the menu is his department," she adds in response to his raised brows.

"I'll collect the attendee interviews and be there."

"And Rosemary?"

"I called Toni and told her we were deep into a death at the hall. She said she and Mary Jo could manage visits for the time being." He turns toward the building. "She never wants to see me, anyway. A few days won't hurt."

"Oh, Aiden. What's the plan?"

"Nothing firm. They pulled her old medications and now she's on a complicated anti-psychotic cocktail which transforms her into a zombie. Her sisters are as worried as me. They've researched a bunch of different facilities in Ontario. We'll move her to a location with more specialists and expertise soon."

Stella is lost for words. Sympathy is useless. She cannot help and her frustration bubbles. As a last resort, she pats his sleeve. "See you at the park."

❦

CHAPTER 5

What a Ridiculous Question

"Jewel, Stella here. I know she won't be happy, but may I speak to Hester for a second?"

"Sure. She's upstairs. I'll go fetch her."

The receiver clunks on the counter. Stella drums her fingers. Kenny's baby-gurgles rumble in the background. He must be in his playpen beside the phone.

"Stella, is your call necessary? I have been busy with my research."

"Yes, for a moment." She employs patience. "Are you able to repeat the exact conversation you had with Owen when you made arrangements to meet at the café late yesterday afternoon?"

"What a ridiculous question."

She hopes Hester won't hear her teeth grinding and adds a further prompt. "Your information is important. I know you can recite the exchange word for word."

"Indisputably. He asked if I wanted to talk with him regarding memoirs and my poem. He hated Mayko Doan and wondered why I was fond of her."

"Go on."

"We agreed to meet after the last workshop, and he suggested we eat together. Do you want every word, or will my summary suffice?"

Stella senses her impatience. "A summary will suit for the moment."

"When he mentioned the idea, I recommended Cocoa and Café because they have yummy soup. He acquiesced. After my session ended, I walked to the café, chose a table, and waited. Has my interaction with Owen prior to our failed supper become important?"

"Possibly. Might he have misunderstood and expected to meet you at the hall?"

"Yes, I suppose. I admit to a modicum of nervousness. I assumed he would come to the café."

"Much appreciated, Hester. You have been a huge help."

The phone bangs in Stella's ear.

****

Before she sees Aiden's car, she hears the Citation pull into the back lot. She's been home for an hour, and reception has been mercifully quiet. Nick concocted a meatloaf while she prepared potatoes and a salad. Their comfortable camaraderie in her—soon to be their—farmhouse kitchen warms her soul.

The day has been summery for the end of September. Nick, in his standard uniform of park T-shirt and khaki shorts, never fails to tempt her. She wanted to wrap her arms around his waist, but Aiden was on his way.

"Come on in," she hollers as she holds open the screen door. Aiden balances a stack of manila file folders. She guesses two dozen.

"Let's put those over here on the big table." She points to the formal dining room set on the far side of the living room. Under normal circumstances, they eat in the kitchen. On cold nights, they often drag the heavy mahogany drop-leaf nearer the fire. The furniture also comes in handy when they host a crowd. Stella's thoughts race back to the search and rescue operation headquartered at Shale Cliffs when Lorraine Young, one of her seasonal residents, disappeared more than a year ago.

"Thanks. I have twenty-eight individual reports." He responds to her lifted brows. "I didn't include Hester's file, and Owen's makes thirty in total."

"We might need to add to the information on Hester. I spoke with her again."

"What?"

She moves toward the kitchen. "I'll tell you what she said. A witness with the precise recall of Hester is advantageous. Wine or beer?"

"Hey, Nick. Supper smells good."

"Meatloaf. An old family recipe." He lifts his beer glass. "Can I interest you in one?"

"By all means."

"Have a seat. We'll eat in ten minutes."

Aiden drapes his jacket on the back of an oak chair and accepts a frothy brew. He puffs his exasperation. "You might as well know, I encountered six bored investigators after you left. The participants have been freed to return home but, from my scan of the various verbal reports, each woman thought of Owen as a weirdo."

"And the men?"

"As we assumed—indifference, for the most part." He sighs again as Nick serves their plates. "We'll examine the files after supper, okay?"

Nick nods his understanding and Stella acknowledges the pressure she considers they're under. "Today has been exhausting, but a review is necessary to see if any clues float to the surface. I want to report my conversation with Hester, too. I'm not sure she provided any clarification."

While they enjoy the meal, Nick discusses the park and their plans for the winter. "I've been on the horn to an engineer, and I hope," he pats Stella's hand, "we'll be able to install septic before spring."

Stella pastes a blank look on her face. She prefers not to share her concerns in front of Aiden.

"Expensive, although attachments for water, power, and septic in a seasonal park make life easier for everyone." He sounds morose. "And if I sell, the trailer will be more attractive to a potential buyer who wants to keep the lot at Shale Cliffs."

"Sell? Are you certain?" Nick digs into his apple pie.

"Rosemary isn't good. All of her doctors agree I made a poor decision when we purchased a summer spot near the individual they describe as her nemesis." He frowns while he scrutinizes Stella.

"I am not Rosemary's nemesis." Her thoughts swirl. To think psychiatrists support the idea she and Aiden are an item. They were involved back in high school, for God's sake. Rosemary is sick. She realizes the blame doesn't lie with her but accepts the burden regardless. Perhaps the best plan for Aiden will be to sell his trailer.

"No, although in her mind, you are her archenemy and biggest threat." He turns to Nick. "Septic systems are expensive. Did you guys come into a windfall? Business has been good for you this summer, but...."

"Shall we tell him?"

"Aiden can keep a secret." She faces the detective. "The plan isn't finalized yet. No one knows except Trixie and Nick's folks."

"Tea?" Nick plugs in the kettle and starts to tidy.

"Sure. What's your news?"

Nick leans against the counter while the sink fills with soapy water, his slim frame shadowed in the now dim light from the kitchen window. "Trixie has agreed to let us buy her shares. Once we finish the deal, Stella and I will be fifty-fifty. Instead of a thousand bucks a month to Trixie, we can pay the bank loan for a sewer system. What do you think?"

"Has Trixie moved to Yellow House with Brigitte?"

Stella gives him a direct answer to his seemingly unrelated question. "She left her rental, quit her job except for the odd shift, and settled into Yellow House mid-summer. She helps with Mia. Why?"

"She might want to buy my trailer."

"Trixie hates spending time out here." She grabs a tea towel from the kitchen drawer.

"Right, but if she's no longer an owner, Shale Cliffs becomes a vacation place where she can bring Mia for a few days."

"Faint hope, but if you decide to sell, ask her." She has her doubts. "Shall we review those files after we finish dishes?"

****

"From a cursory glance at the interview sheets, almost everyone who attended your retreat disliked Owen. Let's go through them and see if a detail pops out."

Stella checks basic information and sorts the pages into piles. "There are two groups of four women who travelled in on the bus, average age over fifty. I've found another foursome. They are younger, with a trailer out here. Plus, nine more women and Hester. Four travelled in two pairs and the remainder came solo. One of those individuals camped near the trailer in a small motor home."

Aiden digs through the male attendees. "Of the seven males, two were able to comment on the victim's behaviour. The other five didn't pay any attention to him. It appears they all travelled to Shale Harbour on their own and stayed at the hotel."

"What did they say?"

He rifles through the sheets. "Investigators need a lesson in handwriting," he mumbles, as he peers at a page covered in a child-like scrawl. "One said he was opinionated in the memoir class with Ms. Doan. Let me see. Oh, here.

The other described him as unpleasant to Ms. Doan because of her dog. The guy figured Owen feared her—in his words—'itty-bitty fluff-ball,' and left the room before Mayko completed her workshop."

"Owen detested Mayko and her work, I gather. Hester used the word 'hate'. I know he had an aversion to Tanchau because of his response at the reading on Friday night."

"We'll interview the parents and explore his fears later tomorrow after they come to the station for a formal identification."

"You expect the autopsy results then, too?"

"Tuesday morning. They completed a preliminary report today because we needed answers and people wanted to go home. They have no definitive cause of death yet. And the female workshop participants?"

"Oh." Stella shuffles more loose-leaf. "Let's see. Each of them remarked on Owen in a similar manner. I'll read you the comments noted by investigators. 'Creepy,' 'lurker,' 'eavesdropper,' 'scary,' and 'pushy,' were the words repeated over and over. They said he disrupted workshops because he popped in and out of classes. One mentioned he acted as if Mayko Doan couldn't write. He unapologetically criticized. He made fun of Bryce Blanken behind his back and told people he was a fraud—which I don't understand. He trashed Eliza Strauss' work as cheap dime-store paperback fiction. A female attendee summed him up when she said Owen sat in a class long enough to make a condescending or argumentative remark and then left. Each participant in one of the older groups complained Owen was extremely disrespectful to both his parents. He ridiculed his father in public and walked the other way when his mother appeared."

"If someone pushed him down the stairs, an amateur writer didn't do the deed." Until now, Nick has been quiet as he sat in a leather chair near the fireplace.

"I think you're right, although the investigators told me every female found him irksome, but they avoided the guy—or ignored him."

Stella agrees with Nick. The perpetrator isn't an amateur writer. "Our first assumption is probably correct. He misunderstood Hester and waited for her in the foyer. Somehow, he fell down the stairs. The poor kid. He might have decided to check the washroom for Hester, and the stairs became the end of him. I told Hester nobody's murdered because they're a bad writer of gore or killed because they're annoying."

Aiden shuffles more paper. "Speaking of Hester, what did you find out?"

"Right. Employing her perfect memory, she described her conversation with Owen earlier in the afternoon and agrees with the possibility that Owen could have misinterpreted the arrangements. He may have been hanging around the hall by chance."

"Hopefully, the autopsy will provide answers. In the meantime, I need you to meet me at the Port Ephron station tomorrow after lunch. I want to interview Owen's parents once they return home. One of them is due to confirm identification at eight-thirty in the morning. I asked Sergeant Moyer to drive out and deliver the notification in person. I assume he did."

"Yup. He parked in the lot this afternoon and walked to the cottage." A thump on the veranda startles them. "Did you guys hear a knock? Hold on." Nick takes two long strides over to the back door.

He turns toward Aiden and Stella. "Edward and Frances. Come in, folks. What can we do for you?"

Frances appears muddled and untidy. Her sweater and skirt clash. Her braids have unwound from their halo. Her face is puffy.

Owen's father shuffles into the room and directs his remarks to Aiden. "We came to the house to use the phone to call our neighbours. They need to know what has happened. Your sergeant said we can go home tomorrow, after...."

With Edward's hesitation, Frances collapses into a fit of sobs. He strokes her arm in the way one might sooth a fretful cat.

Aiden approaches the pair. "We want one of you to come to the Port Ephron station tomorrow. Following identification, you may go home. Stella and I will visit in the afternoon. The other writers are required to stay in Shale Harbour or here at the park. Their interviews are scheduled for Tuesday and maybe Wednesday."

"Yes, the nice sergeant explained. I want to call our neighbours."

Stella nods. "Use my office. You can close the door." She leads them off.

****

On Monday morning, she awakens as exhausted as when she collapsed in bed. She rolled into Nick's arms and can't remember if she said good night. He's downstairs. She hears Duke and squints at the clock radio—nine o'clock. *Lordy!*

"Give me a few minutes," she hollers from the top of the stairs, as Nick materializes at the foot, cup in hand.

"Here's coffee. Take your time. Duke and I have the place under control."

"You are too good to me. A quick shower and I'll join you guys."

Clouds rest heavy on the horizon, holding the promise of drizzle. She shivers. Thanksgiving approaches. The park closes soon for another winter, and the pressure begins. She must figure out a way to purchase ten percent of Trixie's share, and work through the idea of septic infrastructure and how the upgrades will change their maintenance and workload around the park. Her racing thoughts are scrambled with information related to Owen's untimely death. Dressed in soft, baggy blue jeans and a bulky beige sweater, she rumbles down the stairs, empty cup in hand.

"Good morning, Duke, Kiki. Any more coffee, Nick?"

"Fresh pot. I can't work much outside today. Duke plans to do his inspection run, though."

Addressing her comments to both men, she asks, "Do you have time to tour the park and see which seasonals will be here for the potluck and what they plan to contribute? With a meeting in Port Ephron after lunch, and the cottage to clean, I don't have enough time. The party is scheduled for this Saturday."

"We'll help, won't we, Kiki? We can clean the cottage. You cover the office."

Duke sounds enthusiastic. Stella understands his heart remains here at the park and he would endure the winter in his trailer if given the chance. The days must be long in his efficiency motel unit. Free cable doesn't equate to family and friends. "You still see the lady over at Port Ephron RV?"

His frown declares volumes. "Off and on. More off. Shoulda stayed for the readin'."

"Sorry to hear. Invite her to the end-of-season bash. The Port Ephron RV party isn't the same night, is it?"

"Nope. I can ask her." His voice doesn't signal confidence.

****

The RCMP station in Port Ephron is quiet. She doesn't come to this location often. The surroundings are unfamiliar. A civilian receptionist asks her name and if she has an appointment, then points to a green institutional-style chair across from the counter. Stella waits for ten minutes before Aiden appears.

"Hi. I told them to send you through, but the detachment sticks to strict protocols. No civilians permitted to 'wander' the halls unattended. Let's have a wee visit before we drive over to the Ellis-Thomas residence."

Once settled in his office—and Hester would note his space in Port Ephron is as austere as the one in Shale Harbour—she asks him to describe the identification process.

"They viewed Owen's remains together, which surprised me. I expected one of them to take the lead. Tough morning."

"When did they leave for home?"

"Near ten. They should be settled enough by now. We can drive over."

"I'm interested in whether they were aware of Owen's socially inappropriate behaviour."

"Socially inappropriate," he repeats, as if experimenting with the syllables on his tongue one at a time. "Owen fits the description if we refer to the remarks made by attendees. I want to see his room."

They locate the Ellis-Thomas' nondescript brick bungalow in a lower-middle-class area of the community, where car parts and motorcycles litter driveways, lawns are unattended, and garage doors are broken. Although their residence has seen better days, the couple has managed to maintain a modicum of curb appeal despite the low bar set by their neighbours.

Edward waits behind the aluminum storm door as they pick their way along the cement block path.

"Hello, again," Aiden remarks when Edward opens the bent contraption with its scrolls of dented metal. The screen has a small tear.

"Hi, Edward. Happy to see you're back home."

"Welcome, Stella, Detective North. Frances is in the kitchen. Coffee? We thought we could talk in the living room."

Stella notices, at the far end, a brick fireplace closed off with plywood.

"Please sit," he instructs. The choices are a low, flowered sofa or one of two fragile upholstered side chairs.

They both choose the sofa, a decision Stella, with her long legs, regrets the moment she lowers herself onto a faded cushion.

Frances enters with a tray of mugs, cream, sugar, and spoons. She bustles off to retrieve the coffee pot after a quick and silent bob to her guests.

Once settled, heavy mugs with decals of antique cars in hand, Aiden begins. "I expect the final autopsy report to be available tomorrow morning. Our questions, at this moment in time, are based on protocols put in place for a sudden death. Don't make any assumptions, okay?"

The couple nods in unison.

Stella speaks after Aiden has set the stage. "Please describe your son as you see him. We know he was twenty, lived here with you, and you mentioned he wasn't attending college or university."

Edward clears his throat.

Stella suppresses her surprise since she expected Frances to speak first.

"Owen's differences were distinctly special. Others bullied him in public school. We couldn't afford a private option, therefore taught him ourselves. Because his mother and I are both writers, we work at home most of the time. We became a close-knit trio. Our son was a loner outside these four walls." He turns to make eye contact with Frances. "He didn't respect many people. We were pleased to learn he admired Hester Painter, after they met at your house, Stella."

Their description sounds like an apology. "Horror fascinated him." She makes the statement in the hopes one of the parents will respond to the remark. "And he exhibited a fear of dogs," she adds.

Frances jumps in. "Owen possessed talent as a writer. He learned well at home and was self-educated about many topics of interest to him. He followed the news and devoured books on crime fiction. He burgeoned with aptitude, and we expected him to follow in our footsteps." She collapses into tears. "We bought him a puppy when he turned six. We didn't realize he hated dogs. He carried her outside and came back in alone. A car hit the little creature before we realized he'd left her in the street. He was complicated and showed no sympathy. Sometimes, I thought he only felt indifference." Her shoulders heave.

Edward rises from the rickety side chair and places his arm around her as she remains seated. "We understand how Owen was often a challenge in groups. His behaviour made people—women—uncomfortable. He held impeccable standards. He told us from the outset he thought the authors at the retreat were not of a high calibre. We tried our best." His facial muscles tremble.

"May we see his room?" Aiden stands.

Edward acquiesces at once with a nod while Frances bites her lip.

"It's necessary to formulate a clearer picture of your son, Frances. We won't touch his possessions," Stella adds as a means of consolation.

The grieving father leads them into the basement. Owen's personal space is a box framed into a corner. Cheap dark wood paneling covers the walls, producing a cave-like sensation. Stella can find no bathroom downstairs. A single mattress, in the middle of the floor, supports a rumpled green sleeping bag in a heap on top. There's a relatively new recliner in front of a bookcase in disarray.

"Owen preferred his privacy," Edward mumbles from the doorway.

Posters and newspaper clippings comprise the décor. The posters represent various horror classics. Stella notices *Phantom of the Rue Morgue*, *The Mummy's Hand*, and *The Hunchback of Notre Dame*. There are more. The newspapers reflect gruesome murders from around the world. They date as far back as the 1940s.

After a cursory glance, Aiden makes himself clear. "I will send a forensics team in for the posters, newspaper articles, and his writing. Please close the door and leave your son's room as is. Allow no one entry."

CHAPTER 6

Romance and Business Need Paperwork

She harbours no doubt. Shale Cliffs RV Park has blossomed under her stewardship with Nick's assistance. Her staff are reliable. Renovations have brought the old family home out of its 1950s doldrums. She hasn't missed her journalism career for months.

When her father called in late 1978 and asked her to return to Shale Harbour and help him operate the park, she was shocked at how far along the road to dementia he had already travelled. Finances were her biggest concern. The emergency fund was a GIC locked away for five years at seven percent. It came due in 1980 and she managed to find a three-month revolving term. With interest rates the way they are now, it has made money.

At the time of her move, though, she sold her car and used her savings to fix the truck and the front-end loader. The premises were derelict. Over the first winter, she had her father assessed, and he moved, with little resistance if the truth be told, into Harbour Manor. He was relieved, but she was left with no choice except to lift the business back on its feet. Although selling was possible, the idea of letting the property go broke her heart. Trixie offered minimal support. She worked at the fish plant and supported both her daughter and granddaughter. With the expertise of Stephens and Stephens, the local law firm, Shale Cliffs RV Park's proprietorship was turned over to the two of them. Trixie did not want to participate. Stella thought her sister's attitude was probably advantageous. The agreement stated Shale Cliffs would pay Trixie one thousand dollars a month, year-round, in exchange for fifty percent ownership and no engagement.

Stella desperately needed help before the 1979 season started. She advertised. Nick appeared on her doorstep. He worked his ass off. He cleaned the property, fixed power connections, changed water filters, and helped her hire staff. When Duke, the one previous employee, returned in May, he was amazed by the transformation. She admonishes herself that she didn't pull out the ledger to be inspired to take a trip down memory lane earlier. How can she dig up the money for those last five shares?

In 1978, she loaned the park more than ten thousand dollars from the sale of her car combined with a portion of her savings. If the business were to pay her back, the money to purchase five percent would be covered. She stares at the last bank statement. The little emergency fund GIC has grown to nearly fifteen thousand and will turn over again in December. The answer was sitting right in front of her. Too many other issues have occupied her mind.

Nick rustles around in the living room. In time, she expects she'll trust the solidity of their relationship, but she learned years ago to guard against the possibility that an entanglement can change on a moment's notice. They will have their fifty-fifty partnership after a lawyer draws up the agreement. If one wants out, the other has first dibs to purchase. Trixie receives her thousand a month through December and will then pocket the lion's share of her buy-out the end of the year—done deal. Stella's practicality emerges. Romance and business need paperwork.

"Nick, are you busy?" Her office door has been ajar, but she wonders if he hears her shout.

"I'm right here. Didn't want to disturb you. Figured you might be working on the case."

"No, although Owen's fascination with gore troubles me. Tomorrow's a big day. The final autopsy report will be available, and I hope they say more than 'cause of death undetermined' the way they did in the preliminary. We're scheduled to interview authors too, but, no, the investigation isn't my focus."

Nick doesn't pry.

"I needed to resolve the whole idea of our purchase of Trixie's shares."

His eyes are full of love. "If you're uncomfortable with a gift of ten grand, I understand. We want to keep *us* as a couple separate from *us* as business partners."

She's unprepared for his reaction. She expected him to tell her that her money concerns were unnecessary. "It's fine?"

"Yes. You need to do what you need to do. I assumed you might talk to the bank and take out a personal loan. You could pay it back out of your salary.

We're in good shape. You can borrow funds if you want."

"My idea involves cashing out Dad's little GIC in exchange for the money I dumped into the business when I took over."

"You spent that much of your own money?"

"Yeah. Even sold my car and liquidated my savings bonds. The total comes to more than the ten I need."

"Funny, I examined the books when I invested the first ten percent but didn't realize your contribution." He stands, rounds the desk, bends, and plants a firm kiss on her forehead. "Problem solved, my love. If I want to give you a gift, I guess a more romantic present will be in order."

"We have a sanctuary upstairs. You've done more than expected and I appreciate it." She produces her warmest smile. "When it comes to the business, I insist on independence."

"Understood. I admire and respect your work ethic." He reaches to touch her hand. "Enough for tonight? Wine or tea?"

"One more complication. I want us to find time to meet with the lawyer to write wills, too. Do you have a will?"

He frowns. "No, I do not, as a matter of fact."

"They're necessary. If one of us dies, the other needs to inherit the shares. You don't want Brigitte to be your partner any more than I want your parents to be mine. We aren't married. Therefore, the paperwork has to be our priority." She worries she sounds too blunt. She's been absorbed in the share dilemma for too long.

"You're pragmatic, but correct. We'll make an appointment as soon as the park closes, okay?"

They are both startled by the ring of the reception bell. "Damn, Nick. I forgot to lock the office. It's after eight."

"So much for a glass of wine and a quiet night. I'll go." Nick strides toward the front.

"Anybody home? The lights were on and the door's unlocked."

The bellow comes from Bryce Blanken. *What does he want this late in the day?*

"Welcome. Bryce, am I right? I'm Stella's partner here at the park—Nick Cochran. We met on Friday evening. And you're Greta, correct?"

Stella hears the interchange from the entry to her office and rounds the corner to greet their guests.

"Yes. Nice to see you again. Oh, hi, Stella."

"Come have a seat in the living room. What can we do for you people tonight?" *Farley's gossip must be true.*

Bryce takes the lead and, in his best western vernacular, explains. "The little lady and I were cuddled round our campfire and tradin' stories." He pats Greta on the knee. "We decided to take a walk to the cabin and have a chinwag with Eddie and Fran. The place was locked tighter'n a drum. We stopped here to see what the story is. Right, Sweetie?"

Greta squirms. Stella assumes it's because Bryce has acted too familiar in front of them. She readjusts her long, T-shirt cotton, dress, tugs on her knitted vest, and moves his hand from its position on her knee. "We're worried, Stella. The authors are scheduled for interviews tomorrow and we're wondering where Frances and Edward are."

After a quick glance toward Nick, Stella satisfies their obvious curiosity. "They returned home to Port Ephron today."

"Oh." Disappointment crosses Greta's face. "We are sad for them and wanted to express our condolences." She turns to Bryce. "I suppose we could call them. I imagine you have a number, Stella?"

"Perhaps the best course of action is to wait until after your interviews tomorrow before you contact Owen's parents."

"The kid was a scumbag, but I'm sorry he fell." Bryce cracks his knuckles and focuses on the hardwood floor.

"May I pour you folks a glass of wine?" Nick stands.

"Why, a glass of wine sounds fabulous." Greta relaxes on the sofa beside Bryce. "I must admit, as much as I've enjoyed my time out here at the park with Bryce, the evenings are cool."

"Now, now, girlie. I made a big fire, and you were curled in my favourite blanket. No complaints from you, now." He leans over to rub his shoulder against hers.

"It's back to the hotel for me, tonight. My interview is at nine tomorrow, and I want to be fresh and alert to meet Detective North." She wiggles her shoulders. The motion reflects her less than subtle effort to avoid Bryce's touch.

Stella doesn't tell them she'll be in attendance. "Here comes Nick."

With wine delivered, Nick settles in one of the two leather chairs which flank the fireplace. Stella occupies the other, while Greta and Bryce remain side by side on the couch. Bryce gulps the white wine. She suspects it isn't his favourite beverage.

"You must be friends with North. He attended your party on Friday." Bryce pauses for another mouthful.

"Yes, I am. We went to school together. He and his wife have a trailer here at Shale Cliffs."

"And you, Nick? How did you end up here? Cochran isn't a Maritime name."

His statement sounds accusatory, but Nick has Bryce figured out. "I heard Stella needed a hand and knocked on her door," he answers. "I was the homeless dog she took in. I make myself useful."

Bryce guffaws. "I bet you do. You're younger." His eyes dart between the two of them.

Greta intervenes before the smart remark, poised to leave Stella's face, flies past her lips.

"Be nice." She meets Stella's gaze. "He can be too blunt."

"Did anybody else think Owen was a weirdo?"

Greta doesn't let Nick or Stella respond. "He made nasty remarks and spread idle gossip about each of us, Bryce. Don't make too much out of his behaviour. He's dead now."

"The guy was an ass, and his parents couldn't control him. The way he talked to his father...and he treated his mom with no respect. Eddie and Fran are good people. I can't imagine them livin' with that creep in their basement."

"What makes you assume Owen lived in the basement?" Stella asks the obvious question.

"Doesn't every creep live in the basement? I'm guessin', but a twenty-year-old...well, he's the kind of guy who imagines axe murders. He admired psychos."

"Did he spread specific gossip about you, Bryce?"

"He said stupid stuff, like I'm a phony and pretend to be a cowboy. He told people I didn't know dick when it comes to livin' out west."

"Bryce, the kid was troubled. Don't concern yourself with a dead boy. He was riddled with problems." Greta's tone insists more than comforts.

"How did Owen refer to you, Greta?" Stella doesn't avoid a quick glance at Nick. She can't help herself.

"Well, it was obvious he didn't read my books. Have you read my books?"

"I have, as has my sister." Her response remains noncommittal.

"He told people I lie and I'm older than twenty-six. Not true. I have a legitimate birth certificate. He whispered to attendees that my slimness is because I go to the bathroom and throw up after I eat." She pauses for a moment and meets Stella's gaze. "I am naturally svelte." She sits straighter and smooths her dress for the umpteenth time.

"When's your appointment with Detective North, Bryce?"

Stella knows Nick will want to have check-outs sorted as early as possible.

"After Greta—coffee time. Gonna settle finances with you and go into town. I'll park the trailer at the Groceteria. A feller can walk to anythin' in a place the size of Shale Harbour." He stands. The heels of his boots scrape the wood. "Let's be goin' back, darlin'. I wanna see if I kin talk you into stayin' a while." He leers at Nick.

Once they leave, Stella and Nick lock the doors and make their way upstairs. "You never told them you would be present for the interviews tomorrow."

She smirks. "Nobody asked. I wonder if Bryce returned to the hall to fetch Greta."

****

"You realize you have interrupted Nick and me." She tries to lighten her tone. "We watched a magnificent sunrise and were drinking my favourite coffee. Now here I am in my office, on the phone with a cop."

"Sorry. I wanted to catch you before you came into town."

"And what makes you think I would drive into the detachment at seven-ten in the morning?" She snickers. "I was under the impression interviews start at nine."

"Yes, but I expected you might appreciate autopsy information, in particular because of the contents of the report."

Stella gulps. She takes a quick sip of her coffee. "Was Owen murdered?"

"The account is inconclusive. Let me summarize. You can read the whole document before the interviews."

She hears paper shuffle.

"Bruises on the throat may be ante-mortem. He broke his neck in the fall—considered the cause of death. He suffered a dislocated shoulder, and both a fractured skull and ankle. There's the distinct possibility he was partially strangled before he fell, but no way to know for certain if another person first tried to choke the guy and then pushed him."

"Crap."

"Right. After our review of the attendee interviews, it's obvious mostly everyone disliked him...a lot."

"And they were graced with opportunity because the door to the hall was open." She sips her coffee.

"Three other people, still on site after the caretaker took off, add to the equation."

"One of those potential suspects—Greta Walmsley—was here last night with Bryce Blanken."

"Why were they at your place? Greta is booked into the hotel."

"Remember what Farley said? Bryce is enamoured with Greta. When they left, he seemed determined to persuade her to stay in his trailer. He didn't pull his punches when he described how much he loathed Owen, either."

"Because Owen poked fun at him?"

"Yes. He was perturbed when Owen called him a phony. I'll be interested in how he describes his anger in the interview. Greta attempted to pacify him."

"Did you tell them about your involvement with the police?"

"Nope. Wanted to save the surprise for today."

"I've scheduled six interviews, placed an hour apart. The day promises to be long."

"Six?"

"We'll talk to Naomi and Greg Whittleton separately. Good idea?"

"Excellent. Before you go, what's the latest with Rosemary?"

"Mary Jo has engaged a private psychiatric facility in Hawkesbury, Ontario. The town is east of Ottawa. They secured a bed, and final arrangements to take her are almost complete. Mary Jo says she'll drive the distance in one day." He stops for a moment to clear his throat. "I'm not included in the trip. Her sisters claim the circumstances will be better controlled if I stay home."

"So sorry her condition has progressed. Can Nick or I help?"

"No, afraid not. Focus on author details. I asked three of the investigators to complete background checks on each of them."

She's aware of both his abrupt and successful avoidance of further discussions related to Rosemary. She glances at the clock in her office. Brigitte might be awake. "Let me find a bite of breakfast. See you in a while."

When she hangs up, she sees Nick standing at the door, hair tussled, in a T-shirt and boxers. "Aren't you the picture?"

"I heard the phone after you came down for more coffee. Aiden?"

"Yes. The autopsy was a bust—inconclusive. They hypothesize the bruises on his neck occurred before the fall." She walks around her desk and hooks her arm in his. "I need another cup of coffee and a piece of toast." She squints at him. "Can a person bruise their throat when they fall?"

"Not likely, but if he was pushed, you and Aiden will need to ferret out a motive."

"Time to read a few books?"

"No, but sure...."

"I'll call Brigitte before I drive into town. She said she wanted to purchase stock of each of the authors' publications for the business. I expect I can snag us copies." She answers his unspoken curiosity. "How and what a person writes speaks to their personality."

"Okay. Will you make a fresh pot of coffee? I'll run upstairs and put on pants before Duke arrives."

As she scoops coffee into the filter, she decides to call Yellow House. If they don't want to answer, they'll let the machine kick in.

"Hello."

"Trixie, hi. Sorry for the hour. May I talk to Brigitte for a minute?"

"Sure. About the dead guy?"

"The investigation into Owen's death continues, I'm afraid. Brigitte said she ordered books written by each of the authors and I called to see if I might borrow a set."

"Here she comes."

"Hi? Aunt Stella? Thanks, Mom. Will you help Mia with her juice?"

"Brigitte, is your mother anti-social to everyone?"

"Yes. What can I do for you?"

Stella understands Trixie is nearby. She repeats her request.

"I have every title available."

"I'm investigating with Aiden, and I want to skim their work. It might illuminate the little dark corners of their lives. One never knows. We have interviews scheduled with each author today. May I pick up the books around noon?"

"Stay for lunch. Whatever I can do to help, Aunt Stella."

❧

CHAPTER 7

My Life Is an Open Book

The detachment is calm compared to the last few days. Stella nods to Moyer, who is on the phone, and navigates along the familiar corridor, past the empty interview room, to Aiden's office. She stands at the door and watches until he tears his eyes away from a file and places it on top of a stack of similar folders.

"Hi. Come on in. Take a seat. I wanted to read through the forensics report again before you arrived."

Stella collapses into one of the wooden chairs in front of his desk. "I gather we aren't enlightened."

"No. I spoke to the pathologist briefly. He prefers not to speculate, but he's convinced the bruises under Owen's chin didn't come from the fall. He suspects an altercation prior." Aiden tosses the report over to Stella. "Have a peek, but the bottom line is 'maybe he was grabbed by the throat and thrown or pushed; maybe he was grabbed by the throat in a scuffle and then fell by accident.' A broken neck caused his death, which occurred between late afternoon and early evening, no later than ten. The rest is hypothesis and conjecture." He puffs his dissatisfaction in her direction.

Stella peruses the report. "In summary, this is the preliminary autopsy plus a few possibilities. In your opinion, was he pushed?"

"Judging by what the attendees described, the likelihood exists, although none of them possessed much of a motive besides the fact he was a weird dude with poor social skills."

"Interviews with the authors will tell the tale. From my brief interaction with Bryce, he considered Owen a secret-gatherer; and you and I both know Farley thinks the guy lurked in the shadows." Aiden's silence suggests additional clarification is needed. "Owen discovered dirt on people and threatened to use his information against them or spread harmful gossip. Greg believed Owen intended to reveal his indiscretions to Naomi, as one example. Exposure of one's secrets is motive, right?"

"Did Bryce or Greg grab Owen by the throat and push him down the stairs?"

She squints. "No idea. Let's hear what the other authors share. I want to find out the exact times when Greta and the Whittletons left the hall. I wonder if they took off separately." She glances at her watch. "We're still early. How's Rosemary?"

"I was abrupt on the phone, and I'm sorry."

Stella lifts her hand and waves away his apology.

He continues. "Her sisters will drive her to the private hospital in Ontario tomorrow. They instructed me to leave Rosemary in their capable hands, and as I stare at this stack of files on my desk, I have little choice."

"You could turn the case over to another detective, Aiden. There were enough of them here over the weekend." She hates the idea, but her support of him is important.

"Indeed, and I discussed the matter with Toni and Mary Jo. They are both intent on caring for their sister. To be honest, I imagine they figure I can't do the job they do." He leans back in his chair. "Toni told me they managed her even when they were children. She said their parents would have dumped her into a psychiatric hospital at twelve-years-old, if she and Mary Jo hadn't stepped in."

"Aiden, how sad. I guess her sisters hold her well in hand."

"Yes, and I'll travel to Hawkesbury once we wrap the case. Let's go into the interview room. Greta Walmsley is first."

****

Dressed in a floor-length white cotton jumper paired with an amber T-shirt, Greta arrives at the door with Sergeant Moyer. She presents as both angelic and waif-like. Her long-waisted garment doesn't disguise her gaunt frame.

Greta fails in her valiant attempt to mask puzzlement with a broad and shallow smile. "Stella Kirk. Why, in heaven's name, are you here?"

"Stella consults for the department, Miss Walmsley."

Leaning across the table, she delivers a warm and affectionate simper.

"You may call me Greta, Detective."

She's flirting. "Good morning, Greta. You met Detective North at my party on Friday."

"Oh, I could never forget the fabulous Detective North."

"Let's begin, shall we?" Aiden has begun to fidget.

Greta adjusts herself and plants a blank cast on her skeletal face.

"I wish to start with your biography, Miss Walmsley. My detectives learned you reside in Halifax and you're twenty-six years old, correct?"

"Yes, Detective. With two titles published, my life is an open book." She titters at her own joke.

"You attained no higher education?"

"A circumstance I regret. My parents were killed in a car crash when I was thirteen. Social Services shuffled me from one foster home to another until I aged out at nineteen." She turns toward Stella. "I learned simple changes in a person's life can make a huge difference in their success or failure. Many young people, with a similar background to mine, end up on the street, addicted to drugs, pregnant. I wanted none of their choices. I started to write."

"Your books are commercial successes, Greta. Congratulations to you."

"Thank you. You should read my work, Stella."

"I have." She attempts to sound impartial but knows her enthusiasm for Greta's writing will show on her face. The fact Greta doesn't remember she's already admitted to being a fan helps.

"If you don't mind a recommendation, I advise you return and review *Improving on Self.* I suggest to my readers how a huge attitude adjustment can occur if basic attention is paid to one's wardrobe. You might benefit from a re-read of that particular chapter."

Stella discreetly assesses her wrinkled linen pants and oversized blouse. Before she formulates an answer to Greta's personal slur, Aiden interrupts.

"Greta, what time did you leave the community hall on Saturday afternoon?"

"Let me recall." She pauses and glances toward the ceiling. "Around four."

"Can you be more specific? Valentin Reguly, the caretaker, said he spoke to you at four."

"Oh, right. Well, perhaps five past. He came in to find me as I packed my notes—mentioned a sick sister? He kept raking one hand through his greasy hair and wanted me to lock the door if I was last to leave."

"Were you?"

"No. Owen was in the foyer and the Whittletons were still in their classroom deep in an argument. I had a rendezvous with Bryce Blanken." She faces Stella. "A woman needs to take advantage of a handsome man who offers to buy her a meal. I was excited to return to the hotel and freshen up. I expected him at five-thirty. We drove to the Purple Tulip in Port Ephron. What else might interest you?" Her eyes hold Aiden's.

"Stella?" He flushes and turns to her.

"Did Owen threaten to reveal any secrets of yours? Bryce mentioned, when you were at my home last night, Owen's near universal dislike by others related to threats toward authors; exposure of their personal information."

"Not me, in particular." She sits straighter and frowns. "I left my journal on the desk Friday afternoon. I returned to the classroom, and he was absorbed in the contents. I hate to admit I was unpleasant with the little sneak, and I also told Frances right away."

"Greta, what observations can you share in regard to your fellow presenters?"

She relaxes in her chair and makes eye contact with each of them in turn. "I am much younger than Edward and Frances, although I deeply respect them as hard workers and excellent writers. Elsbeth Strauss is a crank-puss. She's a woman who has lived far too long inside a murder mystery."

"You travelled from Halifax with her."

"I tolerated her for the drive. Frances asked her. I don't own a car." She picks an imaginary piece of thread off the skirt of her jumper.

"And the others?"

"Well, Naomi and Gregory produce stunning coffee-table books. I can't imagine the two of them tramping around cathedrals in Europe. They must stay together because of their success."

"Why?"

"They fight like cats and dogs. Bryce told me he heard them in their trailer. He said they're forever in an argument over one issue or another."

"And Mayko Doan?"

Greta flutters her hand. "She's a skittish little creature. Her dog is more relaxed. I often wonder what her true background might be. I've never engaged in a real conversation with her." Her spontaneous revelation produces a second of momentary amazement on her pretty face.

"Thank you for your help today, Greta. We request every author stay in town for now."

"For how long, Detective?" Her voice becomes pitchy. "I have responsibilities back in Halifax. My third book is deep in edits and due to be released in a few short months."

Stella can't disguise her surprise. "My park authors expected to check out today."

"We need them to remain for another day or two at least."

After Greta flounces out with Moyer, annoyed but seemingly cooperative, Stella calls Nick. "Hi. Yes, I expect the interviews will be a grind. I imagine Bryce has left and is on his way into town, but please find the Whittletons and tell them to stay put for an additional couple of days, as ordered by Detective North. We'll explain to each author when we interview them."

"Are you okay?"

"Fine. Caught off guard, I guess. I want to call Hope Carlyle and the hotel, to advise people not to leave yet. I'll be home by five. You decide on supper. Since you've been in charge, you choose."

As she hangs up, she faces Aiden. "The guy's a gem."

"Why the guilt?"

"Because he runs Shale Cliffs by himself when I become involved in a case with you."

"Soon half the park will belong to him, right? I wondered if you felt guilty for another reason." His words hang as a question in the air between them.

Flushed and with her thoughts scrambled, Stella attempts to take control. He sits on one of the chairs opposite his desk and studies her. *Focus.* "What's your assessment of Greta?"

"I'm troubled we can't find any records relating to her. I suppose the foster care system swallowed her and those details are sealed. She acted straightforward enough," Aiden admits.

"We need to talk to her publisher. I checked her books at home and noted the name. Sailboat Publishing, in Halifax, managed her first two manuscripts, and from Greta's own report, is involved with her third."

"I expect our task will be to dig deeper into everyone, before we let them leave town." He crosses his legs at the ankles. The muscles in his face relax. "Let's finish the notification calls and then interview Blanken."

****

No introduction is necessary. The forceful thud of heeled cowboy boots invades their space before Bryce Blanken, accompanied by Moyer, materializes.

"Well, little lady, to what do I owe the pleasure? Didn't realize you were a cop."

"She's a consultant for the police department, Mr. Blanken. Take a seat."

"I'm hitched and ready to leave your quaint village. Time to git home to my lovely wife, if ya git the picture?" He winks at the room in general.

"Wife? Are you serious? Last night, you acted interested in Greta." Stella fights to keep surprise out of her voice but knows a thread of challenge remains.

He's unable to suppress a full-bellied guffaw. "Do you buy my bull, Detective? Stella, here, does."

"Sir, my colleagues did the research and found out a few details about you. You're forty-five and have been married for twenty years to a professor of microbiology at Laval University in Québec City where you both make your home." Aiden takes a breath. "Care to enlighten us about your youth and career choices?"

She muffles her surprise while observing the interaction between the two men. Aiden crosses his arms and lifts his chin. Stella knows he has a few more answers but wants to hear them from Bryce.

"Sure. I'm not what you thought." The cowboy act rolls away—tumbleweed across the prairie. "Born into a family with an English father and French mother. Dad worked in French for the province of Québec. He was perfectly bilingual—no accent in either language—and he expected us kids to develop the same skill." He repeats himself in perfect French. "Né dans une famille de père anglais et de mère française. Papa a travaillé pour la province de Québec en français toute la journée. Il était parfaitement bilingue—aucun accent dans les deux langues—et il s'attendait à ce que nous, les enfants, ayons les mêmes compétences."

Stella and Aiden can't prevent the exchange of a quick glance.

Bryce continues. "I began my writing career as a translator for Harlequin Romances. I read stacks and decided I could write one myself. I wrote a dozen under the pseudonym Penny Luckett. Get it?" He roars with smug amusement.

"I tired of Harlequin. They don't pay much. I took a chance and forged out a place in western romances." He sits straighter and puts his arms on the table. "This," he spins his hands around his person, "is a facade for the readers."

"You play the role of Cowboy Bryce." Stella remains dumbfounded, although no longer shocked. "And what of Greta Walmsley?"

"Oh, for God's sake." He holds his palms like two stop signs. "She's a child. Doesn't possess the brains God gave lettuce. Part of my act."

"Is she aware?"

"Jeez, I'm doubtful, but creepy Owen figured my story out."

"What did Owen say, Bryce?" Aiden scribbles in his book.

"Owen pointed out I was a fake, lived in Québec, and spoke French. He threatened to tell people my work was fake, too."

"His intimidation made you mad," Aiden suggests.

"Detective, I know what you must think, but I wasn't involved in the little worm's death, whether he fell, or somebody pushed him. I left the venue before four, drove back to the park long enough to change clothes, and returned to town. I checked the hall for Greta, though."

"What time?" Aiden remains stern and pinched.

"Around ten to five—early. I planned to meet Greta at the hotel at five-thirty, but she dawdles. I figured she could still be at the venue."

"Tell us what happened when you arrived."

"I assumed, since the place was open, she might be delayed. I stood on the threshold and hollered as loud as I could but heard nothing. I closed the door. With time on my hands, I walked back along the sidewalk to Parlour Antiques and bought my wife a piece of the Ridgway pottery she collects. Afterward, I moved my truck up the street to the hotel."

"When did you shop?"

"Around five. I wasn't long at the antique store. Found what I wanted the minute I scanned the place, but I had to wait for cranky Elsbeth to finish buying some ugly vase she insisted was old. The proprietor tried to clarify it dated from the mid-twentieth century, but she refused to listen. When I arrived at hotel reception at five-fifteen or so, the girl called Greta's room. She was still not dressed. I waited for her on the veranda. We drove to the Purple Tulip over in Port Ephron for supper."

Bryce stops for a moment, as if he's reviewing his previous words. "A person can't see the stairs from the door of the hall. They're around the corner.

Was the kid at the bottom when I dashed in?" He removes the Stetson, places it with care on the chair seat beside him, and rubs his forehead. "I hope he wasn't still alive and me, preoccupied with my fake date, didn't check inside."

"I'm doubtful, Mr. Blanken."

"To be honest, the place was spooky. I left right away."

"Understood," Aiden replies.

"I've already checked out of the park. Did I understand your sergeant? He mentioned authors need to stay."

"Yes," Aiden answers. "We want you available for a day or two. I'm sure Stella doesn't mind." He glances toward her.

"Touch base with Nick when you go back. Your site is no charge. You can use our phone to call your wife."

"You're charitable, Stella. I hope the investigation won't take long. My publisher scheduled a signing at a bookstore in Montréal next week. Did I tell you my books are published in French, too?" He puts a finger to his lips. "I compile my own translations. Our little secret, okay?"

"Before you leave, Bryce, will you describe your colleagues for us—paint a picture of each one?"

"No problem. Edward and Frances are salt of the earth. You might be interested to discover Edward's work keeps food on the table. He's successful if you consider the challenges of selling books in this world. Greta is a fluff. Her editor does most of her writing. I don't know Mayko Doan, but a woman who likes dogs is fine with me. Elsbeth is a proper bitch. A bad mood for her is normal. The Whittletons are scrappers—as if they can't stand the sight of one another." He wedges his hat on. "Are we done here? I'll make my way to the park."

After he summons Moyer, and Bryce's boot thumps echo along the hall, Aiden turns to Stella. "Well, were you surprised? Lots of secrets for our victim to uncover."

"He had me fooled, for sure, but did he shove the kid?"

"Not enough information, yet. We can ask Mercedes and Matt Savioli to confirm his timeline and determine if he did, in fact, shop at Parlour Antiques. You check with Nick and Duke to discover if one of them noticed Bryce arrive or leave the park Saturday afternoon, and when."

Aiden continues to theorize. "The estimates fit. He might have returned to the venue to find Greta and the result was an altercation with Owen. When he went to his trailer, changed his clothes, and came back to town, he still found himself early, so decided to fill time at Parlour Antiques before arriving at the hotel."

"Does a man go shopping after he's killed a person, even if by accident?" Stella frowns.

"Bryce is a complicated character. He has a rich and eventful life he chooses to hide from the public with the creation of a persona related to his writing. He denies the existence of a spouse who sounds accomplished in her own right. He cats around with young women to play the part. God knows what else he does."

"Well, two completed and one more to go before noon."

"Mayko Doan is next on the list. Did you read her memoir?"

"Not yet. I have a lunch date at Yellow House and will pick up her book along with those of the others. Hard for me to imagine Mayko hurting anyone. I hope she's forthcoming."

"People are full of surprises. Never prejudge, Stella. You can't tell a book by its cover, as we have seen so far."

Did she hear a snicker? No. Aiden would never be so inappropriate.

CHAPTER 8

Rules Often Prove Insufficient

"What background information did you manage to find on Mayko? I understand she immigrated in 1975, before many of the boat people arrived. How old is she?"

"We uncovered very little," Aiden replies. "I guess her memoir represents her history. According to the investigator who skimmed through a few chapters, she was born in 1950 and left, as you said, in 1975. Her story suggests she obtained papers through the Americans but eventually chose Canada instead."

"In three years, she's written one manuscript. I gather she lectures at the university. Her work is successful now, but success takes time."

"I've often wondered how authors make a living in the first place. They need another source of income." Aiden stands as Moyer opens the door and Mayko sidles into the room, her airline bag clutched in her arms. Tanchau's little black nose pokes out the end where the zipper would close.

"I told Miss Doan pets aren't permitted, but she refused to enter without the dog, Sir."

"No problem, Sergeant." Aiden extends a hand to Mayko. "We can make an exception today. Please, Miss Doan, have a seat."

Mayko is wide-eyed. Her face is flushed, and her pupils burn black.

"Hi, Mayko. Welcome. I expect you've enjoyed a pleasant time as a guest of Hope Carlyle." Stella makes the statement to remind Mayko how people in the community have helped her. Hope has catered to the woman's every need.

"Yes. Hope is patient and kind, but I want to leave town now."

"Your home is in Fredericton, correct?"

She nods. "I've lived in New Brunswick for three years. The university published my book and then offered me an assistant professor position. I'm grateful." She turns to the bag placed on the chair beside her, removes Tanchau, and strokes her back.

Stella can hear Tanchau's contented murmurs.

Mayko relaxes. The dog is her pacifier, her magic elixir.

"Miss Doan, will you share your history with us? I understand you came to Canada three years ago. You escaped from Vietnam, correct?"

"Is our conversation confidential, Detective?"

"At the beginning stage of an investigation, any personal information you provide is held in confidence. If details turn out to be germane to the case, we will discuss consequences. Do you understand?"

"Yes. Thank you. I'm afraid I must inform you my real name is Mai Phan. I didn't escape from Vietnam. I went to the United States as the bride of a US soldier. My life was threatened in my marriage, and I fled to Canada in 1978," she exhales in a puff.

"You assumed another identity to hide from your American spouse?" Stella isn't surprised. Mayko has presented herself as skittish and reluctant since her arrival in town.

"Correct. He has a criminal record now and isn't allowed to enter your country."

"Rules often prove insufficient, Miss Doan." Aiden's tone holds a warning. "Not least of all, in cases such as yours."

Stella interrupts. "Mayko, is your memoir a work of fiction?"

Mayko strokes her dog for a moment. "No, the book isn't fiction, but neither is it a memoir. My dearest friend was Mayko Doan. She died when American Forces bombed Tanchau. I used her story, with the added fiction of her escape, to create the book. It was cathartic. I didn't anticipate such popularity."

Aiden shuffles a few notes. Stella seizes the opportunity to state the obvious, in the assumption the woman will elaborate. "You prefer your privacy because you hide your true identity behind a dead friend's name and a portion of her story."

Mayko does not meet Stella's gaze, but nods.

"My next question involves Owen Ellis-Thomas. Was he aware of your secret?"

Surprise clouds her face. "I would be shocked. Owen hated Tanchau. He told everyone at the retreat I was demented and needed a dog for comfort. He even suggested she might bite—if you can imagine." Her touch of the dog is reverential.

"You were incensed by Owen's attitude and behaviour," Aiden adds.

"Yes."

"Please tell us about your movements after the last session at the hall ended on Saturday?"

Mayko sits straighter in her chair. "I went directly back to Hope Carlyle's. Hester Painter walked with me as far as the café. I changed my clothes and took Tanchau for her walk. Hope often has customers in her weaving shop that time of day. We ate our supper at six, and I watched television with Hope. I believe we saw an episode of *Dallas.*"

"And what are your impressions of the other writers, Mayko?"

She hesitates. "I don't gossip, Stella, and everyone was good to me, especially poor Edward and Frances. Elsbeth Strauss is hard to assess. She's irritable, to the point of anger. Greta Walmsley never pays attention to people like me. The Whittleton couple are impatient with one another. Bryce Blanken is a nice man. He patted Tanchau."

"Greta Walmsley never paid attention to you?"

Mayko tilts her chin and meets Stella's gaze. "I am in no position to offer her an advantage." She pauses for a moment. "Greta sees potential only in those who can be of benefit to her." Sergeant Moyer escorts her to the exit.

****

On the short walk to Brigitte's for lunch, Stella reviews their interviews. Bryce, Greta, and Mayko each have a motive, based on their various interactions and observations of the victim. With the hall unlocked and Owen inside, each of them possessed opportunity in one form or another. It's possible Bryce appeared after the others left; Greta might have been the last person in the building with Owen; Mayko walked her dog and could well have returned to the venue. The kid annoyed each of the three in different ways, but did anyone have enough cause to commit murder? Which of the authors grabbed him by the throat and pushed him in anger? *Don't jump the gun. A crime may not have been committed.*

When she arrives at Yellow House, cars are parked near the front. Stella hopes they aren't customers. If Brigitte is busy, she'll need to discover a creative way to make conversation with her sullen sister.

Stella admires the traditional American Gothic farmhouse situated in the centre of town. The structure's origin dates to before 1880, when it was the primary dwelling of a fisherman who owned the land around what has become Shale Harbour. Main Street is transformed. Where once simple residences stood, businesses occupy the spaces. There are restaurants and a bank. The old carriage house is the café. Shale Harbour's history is written in the architecture.

She opens the front entrance to the sound of tinkling bells. A semblance of relief washes over her as she crosses the threshold. Overwhelming horror and grief no longer assault her. Stella recalls when she discovered the body of Paulina McAdams—slumped in her red velvet club chair in the library— with solemn sadness; not the physical onslaught of emotions she has taken many months to control. The door to the library remains locked with a small handwritten sign which states Employees Only.

Brigitte rushes out of the front room into the foyer. She whispers, "Hi, Aunt Stella. I have customers right now. Go ahead to the kitchen. Mom is making lunch. Mia is with her." She turns on her heel and returns to her work.

After a quick nod to a man, a woman, and two children, she makes her way through the parlour, the former dining room, and into the extension at the back of the house. The space is protected from public access by another sign which says Private.

Grandmother and granddaughter are seated at the oversized pine table. Mia, soon to be four years old, perches on a chair piled with two cushions to give her the height she needs to help her grandmother dish out strawberries into dessert bowls.

"Hi, guys." She stands in front of the now closed door, reluctant to disturb the scene.

Mia starts to wriggle off her wobbly seat. Trixie reaches out her hand to keep the child steady. "Stella, come sit, so Mia doesn't fall. Mia, sit still."

Both Mia and Stella do as they're told.

"Can I help with lunch? Brigitte might be awhile."

Trixie focuses on Mia while she talks. "Spinach salads are on plates in the fridge. French bread is cut and covered on the counter. We need to set the table, right Missy?" She pats Mia's pudgy hand and turns toward Stella. "Mia and I were doling out the berries."

She sees no light in her sister's eyes. Her enviable blond curls are pulled back and held with a rubber band. Her jeans are baggy, and it would seem today isn't the first day she's worn this grey sweater.

"Okay. Shall I start to pull salads out?"

"Sure." She returns her attention to Mia. "You and your busy life. The books you wanted are by the fridge."

Once Brigitte divests herself of her customers, she appears breathless through the connecting door and flops into the platform rocker near the window. "I thought they planned to stay the afternoon."

"I hope they bought a book." Trixie has little reason to be annoyed, but she sounds put out, anyway.

"Three books, as a matter of fact, Mom. Don't sound so miserable." Brigitte focuses on Stella. "I see you found the ones I left for you." She points to the pile near Stella. "Let's eat. Hard to predict how long I have before the bells rattle again."

Lunch proves to be a confused affair. Brigitte and Stella talk. Trixie contributes little. Mia chatters. Brigitte replies to Stella's query. Yellow House will support her. "The place hums every day. I manage to cover the expenses, keep money for myself, and send a cheque to Jane Braddon once a month. She appreciates the fact that Paulina's little business continues to do well. I've increased stock, too."

"Are there many adult customers?"

"Yes. One of the modifications relates to the library focus. I have organized the parlour to cater to children under sixteen. You'll find the other inventory is in the old dining room and each book is for sale. Paulina loaned books to adults. As a result, nobody bought."

"What do locals think of the change?"

"People were put off at first, but since I closed the adult library at the front of the house, everyone has assumed my reasons. I say there's a space issue—I have square footage for stock to sell but not to lend. I special order, too. From what I can surmise, Paulina didn't. She catered to the tourists and not the locals."

"Tell her your latest idea," Trixie grumbles, as she butters a piece of bread for Mia.

"Oh, Mom, don't make a big deal," Brigitte admonishes, before she turns back to Stella. "I think I'll stay open year-round—maybe with shorter hours and closed Monday through Wednesday; maybe close for January and February, and regular hours again in March." She lifts her eyes to the ceiling. "I haven't decided, but I want to pay more attention to Shale Harbour residents. They've supported me despite the business' new focus."

"You are becoming a savvy businesswoman. My vote, if you're canvassing for opinions, is for shorter hours year-round. Take a week or two for a trip south if you can. You guys would have a ball."

Trixie glares.

"I hear the bell. Gotta run, Aunt Stella. Keep the books for as long as you need them. Put my dessert in the fridge for later, Mom. Be a good girl for Grandma, Mia. Back in a minute."

Mia brushes a wisp of blond hair away from her little face and waves goodbye to her mother.

"Don't plant any bright ideas about trips to Florida," Trixie hisses.

"What? You love Florida. Listen, Trixie, climb out of your funk." She absently hands Mia a spoon while they talk. "You will unduly influence your small human charge with your black moods."

Trixie opens her mouth and closes it again.

"Come to the potluck on Saturday night."

"I'm not an owner anymore."

"Technically, you remain a partner until the end of December. Besides, you are my family. And what did you do with your sense of style? Before long you'll start to resemble me when you go out in public."

Her tease fails as Trixie drops her gaze to her baggy jeans. "I understand your motives, but I've never felt this empty."

"Care for your daughter and your granddaughter if you can't care for yourself. We'll care for you."

As she returns to the station, the six books in a cloth bag are a necessary burden. *Did I get through to my sister?*

****

Naomi Whittleton is their one o'clock. She could be a model in a safari travel magazine. The Whittleton book provided by Brigitte is titled *Camping in California.*

She takes a seat with trepidation, as if the upholstery might be hot or icy cold. Frail and willowy, she's attired in khaki Bermuda shorts with wide pressed cuffs, and a sleeveless white blouse cut in at the shoulders. The style accentuates her thinness. She places her wallet-sized leather shoulder bag on the table in front of her.

"Good afternoon, Mrs. Whittleton. I hope we haven't inconvenienced you and your husband too much with our request for you to remain in the vicinity for a couple more days."

She lifts her eyes in Stella's direction. "Shale Cliffs has been generous to let us camp at the park for no charge going forward." She turns to Aiden. "I'm given to understand, from Sergeant Moyer, we may need to stay. Has this become a murder investigation?"

"For a day or two." Aiden ignores her second question. "Our investigation is progressing as fast as possible. Let's begin, shall we? Please share your background with Miss Kirk and me."

Naomi crosses and uncrosses her legs. Stella senses her nervousness.

"I was raised in southern Ontario and met Gregory at university. We both liked to travel and decided to write books and take pictures. I'm more the photographer and he's the writer. We've experienced a measure of success over the years."

Stella estimates her to be in her mid-thirties.

"What time did you and your husband leave the hall on Saturday?"

Aiden's questions are blunt. She notices he never uses Gregory Whittleton's given name.

Naomi fixates on a spot on the wall over Aiden's right shoulder. "We finished our class shortly before four. The janitor appeared and told us to lock the door when we left because he was required at a family emergency. We departed before Greta and Frances' son, who was pacing in the foyer. I didn't acknowledge him, but he waited and watched as usual."

"You and your husband went home ahead of Miss Walmsley and the victim?"

"Correct, Detective."

"And where did you go afterward?"

"We returned to Shale Cliffs RV Park. We sat with Mildred Fox before supper and shared our meal with her."

"Fine. You were continually in the company of your husband?"

She pauses. "Yes."

"Naomi," Stella inserts, "tell us why you're nervous."

"Nervous? What makes you think I'm nervous?" She blinks and glances at the clock on the wall behind Aiden.

"Do you want to share information with the detective and me?"

"I am embarrassed."

"Because Mr. Reguly found you upset?"

"Oh. He told you."

Aiden nods. "Please explain your version of what happened."

"We argued. Gregory flirted with every young woman at the event and his behaviour humiliated me. We stopped packing to have words with each other. I thought we were alone. The janitor came to our classroom and said he needed to leave and if we were the last ones out, could we please lock the door." She shivers. "I was embarrassed and wanted to go home."

"Owen revealed your husband's flirtatious behaviour." Stella makes the statement. If she's correct in the assumption, Naomi will agree before she thinks her response through. If incorrect, she'll feel compelled to explain.

"Yes. He told me he saw Gregory with a girl in the janitor's cupboard. I'll admit I was furious, but more at Gregory, although Owen was hateful and enjoyed his moment of meanness."

"You confronted your husband. After the argument started, Mr. Reguly walked in."

"Yes," Naomi repeats, while she reaches for her bag.

"Did you and your husband resume your conversation in your truck?" Stella suspects she continues to lie.

"I don't bother anymore. I most often lose those discussions, so I shut up." She fiddles with the strap on her purse. "I'm afraid I can't be more help."

"Before you leave, will you provide us with your assessment of your fellow authors?"

"I keep to myself, Detective. Gregory embarrasses me at one point or another during these events. I know I've developed a habit of not getting too close to anyone, although both Edward and Frances have been considerate over the years. I would like to know Mayko Doan better. She's lovely. Will that be all?"

Aiden turns to Stella for confirmation before he stands. "Thank you for your cooperation and honesty. Will you wait in the front for your husband to finish?"

She stares at the floor. "No. I'll walk over to the café for tea."

"Good idea, Mrs. Whittleton. Let me escort you out." He glances at Stella before he opens the door for her.

Upon his return, he informs Stella that Gregory is in reception. "Naomi didn't say a word on her way past."

"The woman lied to us, Aiden."

"What makes you certain?"

"She watched the clock constantly. She fidgeted. Her eyes barely blinked. She must still be angry at Gregory. She referred to him by name but never called him her husband. I smell a rat." She snickers despite herself. "My mother used the phrase when Trixie or I tried to put one over on her."

"For sure, she lied. The investigator who did their background checks uncovered anomalies."

"Will you share?"

"Not yet. As with Bryce Blanken, I prefer you analyze the interviews without any prior influence. Trust me."

Stella doesn't appreciate her current position outside the loop, but Owen's death is Aiden's investigation. She's the sidekick; the consultant. "This is your party, Aiden. Time for Gregory?"

"In a minute. I think I'll let him stew."

❧

Chapter 9

No Need to Be Snide

Gregory Whittleton pushes ahead of Sergeant Moyer. "I've been out front, cooling my heels for fifteen minutes since Naomi left. My time is valuable, too, people."

Aiden doesn't acknowledge his presence, nods at Moyer, and turns to Stella. "We'll complete an analysis after each interview." He turns toward Gregory, stone-faced. "Thank you for consenting to a chat. Sorry for the wait."

Gregory Whittleton is fine-boned and wiry. Stella studies him while Aiden sorts through his papers.

He brushes a thick curl of wavy and dirty-blond hair off his forehead. "I must admit, I missed any clue you were a cop." A sheen of perspiration coats his upper lip.

Aiden straightens in his chair. "Stella consults for the department, Mr. Whittleton. Shall we begin?"

"We're forced to remain in Shale Harbour for another two days at least—your sergeant told me." His tenor indicates he's not pleased.

"Correct, and we appreciate your patience. We require additional time to complete our initial investigation."

"Okay, fair enough. Did someone push the little creep down the stairs?"

"Not determined, Mr. Whittleton. Please describe yourself, how you and your wife met, and how you became travel writers."

His response sounds rehearsed. Memorized salient points resemble a constructed list. For a writer, his story remains unconvincing.

"And Saturday afternoon. What happened after your workshops concluded?"

Gregory squirms in his khaki pants and readjusts the collar of his crisp white shirt. The sleeves are rolled up, and the neck is open. His revealed skin suggests a hairless body. *Might he shave his chest?* Stella focuses on his arms. Everybody has hair on their arms. *Does he shave his arms?* She crawls out of her revere to listen to his response.

"The class ended at quarter to four. Naomi was in a snit."

"Why was she upset?" Aiden's tone remains level.

"Did she spill the beans? Did she tell you the whole story?"

"She revealed your indiscretion to us, Mr. Whittleton. We're interested in your version."

"Edward and Frances' son reported he spied yours truly in the janitor's cupboard in the middle of a mutual cuddle with a cute and promising writer." He snickers at his recollection.

"What was the writer's name?"

He crosses one leg over the other and begins to relax. "No idea, but she had great," he meets Stella's gaze, "assets, if you get my drift."

"Does Naomi become upset easily when you flirt with young women, or was her anger because of the identity of this particular person?"

His arms wave in explanation. "She pouts. I'm used to her moods."

"Continue." Stella pushes.

"The caretaker barged in during one of our countless arguments. Naomi bleated and bawled as usual. After he left, she threw the rest of our paperwork into her bag and flew up the stairs and out. I followed. I found her at the truck."

Aiden poses the next question. "What time did you leave?"

"Five minutes after four. Wait a minute." He points an index finger across the table. "You two don't think Naomi or I were anywhere near the rat when he fell, do you? God! We write books and describe trips, fancy hotels, and how to pitch a tent. Do we look like killers?" His eyes dart from Stella to Aiden.

"Your marriage appears to be on shaky ground." She allows her statement to sit between them.

Gregory's eyes narrow. "We're fine. I'm a flirt. She tolerates me."

"A troubled marriage places your careers in jeopardy by default." She states the obvious.

He squirms in his chair and examines his hands.

Before he replies, Aiden turns to Stella, who nods and asks, "Who remained at the hall when Naomi left in a huff, and you followed?"

"The rat was in the foyer, and Greta Walmsley was still in her classroom."

"And the remainder of your evening?"

"We returned to the park, enjoyed a drink with the charming Mildred Fox, and barbecued—which we shared with her. I wish my mother were half as sweet as Mildred." He glances at the ceiling.

There must be another Mildred Fox, because he hasn't described with any similarity the woman she has come to know over the last few seasons.

"Please provide us with assessments of your fellow writers, Gregory." Stella isn't convinced he's paid attention. His interests are elsewhere.

"Not friends with any of them, except Frances and Edward. Naomi and I travel much of the time and when we take part in events, she acts as our front person. I stay in the background."

"Or in the janitor's cupboard, Mr. Whittleton?"

"No need to be snide, Detective. If you don't approve of my behaviour, you're welcome to be honest. Greta Walmsley is flaky, Elsbeth Strauss swears like a sailor, Mayko Doan is a total mystery, and Bryce Blanken is a blow hard. Satisfied?" He sneers at them from his position across the table.

"I think we're done for now, Mr. Whittleton. I expect we'll follow up in a day or two. We thank you for your cooperation."

"Oh, Gregory. Naomi said she was off to the café for tea."

He turns back to Stella and nods.

When Aiden and Gregory leave, Stella ponders the couple's stories. They both lied. She senses deception hidden behind their well-rehearsed history.

"Can you tell me what you unearthed about the two of them, now?" Curiosity has overshadowed her annoyance with Aiden because he didn't level with her prior to the Whittleton interviews.

"They are brother and sister."

"What? Are you sure? I thought they were divorced, or should be divorced, and maintain an act because of book sales."

"You were close. They maintain an act because of business and hide the fact they're siblings because their entire professional persona is based on the idea of the adventurous couple who travels."

"They resemble each other. One of my thoughts was how people are often attracted to others with similar characteristics. So much for that concept. We need to confront the situation."

"In good time, but I wanted to afford them the opportunity to explain."

"Owen might have discovered their secret. Motives don't come any stronger than a threat to one's livelihood."

"I agree. The primary detail to be determined is who left the hall first. Greta claims she did, and the Whittletons both say they were gone before Greta."

"With Yellow House across the street, there's the possibility either Trixie or Brigitte was nearby at four o'clock on Saturday and noticed departures. Oh, and Parlour Antiques is next door. Maybe they caught a glimpse of one of the authors. We must consider Bryce Blanken's timeline, as well."

****

Elsbeth Strauss has aged with grace and dignity. Stella imagines the woman's beauty in her younger years. She remains attractive. Stella estimates her age to be in the neighbourhood of seventy. Elsbeth's cultured air changes the minute she opens her mouth.

"Why the hell do you need to talk with me? I demand to go back to Halifax." She slams into the chair offered by Aiden and drops bracelet covered wrists on to the tabletop. Her thick white hair flies around her face. "What do you two want with me, and why the hell are you here, Stella?"

"Stella is with me because she's a consultant with the department." Aiden opens the file with a calmness Stella sees as forced. "You are here because of Owen Ellis-Thomas' death, which we suspect occurred late Saturday afternoon or early evening."

"I've known him since birth. I didn't kill the wretched kid, although it baffles me how Edward and Frances managed the aggravation for twenty years. Someone, no doubt, pushed him but your murderer damned well isn't me—although the storyline could have potential. Parents hire crusty old friend to knock off their obnoxious son." She titters. "Good one," she congratulates herself.

Aiden continues. "Are you able to account for your whereabouts after the workshops were over, Miss Strauss?"

Elsbeth straightens both her posture and her red cashmere pullover. She fingers the pearls around her neck for a fraction of a second before she begins. "I left with the hordes and walked straight back to the hotel."

84

"You didn't stay behind to sort your papers?" Stella knows the authors often carried materials with them to the sessions. Both Greta and the Whittletons noted the time required for the task.

"God, you two. I'm a fixture at writing events all over the country—for more years than I care to remember. I don't need props. I enter the classroom, sit behind a desk, and talk. Most of the students are fans of my mysteries, and they want me to sign copies and answer questions. On Saturday, I focused on the necessary horror of editors—both the pain and the pleasure. When workshops end, I take off. I endeavour to arrive ahead of schedule to talk with attendees. Am I free to go now?"

"Not yet, Miss Strauss. What happened after your last workshop?"

"As I said, I left. I anticipated a quiet evening. Did Frances tell you I played taxi driver to the idiot, Greta Walmsley? Only as a favour to Frances. Anyway, she had a date with Bryce Blanken. He used to write Harlequins under the name Penny Luckett." She guffaws with abandon. The movement causes her wavy hair to fall into her face. "He thinks nobody knows, but dammit, I'm old. I remember back in the day. I've seen him with his wife, too."

"Tell us the reason Greta bothers you, Elsbeth."

"Greta doesn't know a paragraph from a predicate." She leans across the table as if she's on the verge of divulging a conspiracy. "You've both met her. Have you read her two books?"

"Yes," Stella admits.

"Here's my question." Elsbeth continues to conspire. "Could a fluff piece with Greta's skills possess the wherewithal to compose a manuscript with even a vague resemblance to either of those titles?" She holds her hand to mimic a stop sign. "I expect not. Her editor wrote them. I've worked with Victoria Barlow at Sailboat Publishing. As a matter of fact, I'm certain I'm acquainted with everybody who is anybody in the business after half a century." She leans back and takes a breath. "Greta's books are best sellers and make the publisher, not to mention Greta, a bucket of money," she huffs. "But believe me...Greta Walmsley did not write them. Listen to her talk. The girl has no education."

"You were pleased she had a date with Bryce?" Aiden attempts to rein in control of the interview.

"Ecstatic. I went back to my room, freshened up, took a stroll around the shops, and gobbled a scrumptious lobster dinner, mercifully alone, at the hotel. The evening was great—the morning when Farley Tompkins called—decidedly worse."

"When did you stroll and where did you stop, Miss Strauss?"

She clears her throat and gives her hair a dramatic shake. "Let me think. I left my room around four-thirty. I stopped at Hope Carlyle's and bought a runner for my kitchen table. I wandered into Parlour Antiques and discovered a vase I couldn't live without. You can check with them, or with Blanken. He was there, absorbing space and hogging all their attention. I almost didn't buy anything, but the yummy Italian offered me a deal."

"Thanks. We'll follow up. When were you in the shops? Do you remember?"

The mystery author frowns. "I was fifteen minutes at the weaver's because there were multiple choices, and I was over at the antique store before five."

"Did you notice any other authors in the vicinity?"

"Bryce popped into the hall before he came to the antique shop where I saw him again. There's a piece of useful information." She widens her eyes for effect. "And Mayko was at the other end of the street when I walked from Mrs. Carlyle's shop to Parlour Antiques."

"Anyone else?"

"No, Detective, and I didn't care. I prefer my quiet time after workshop events."

"You returned to the hotel. Did you encounter any authors once you arrived?"

"Not a soul. I enjoyed a half-hour of solitude and went to the dining room where the lovely Pepper served me my lobster platter—and before you ask, I made my way back to my room, took a hot bath, and worked on an idea for my next mystery." She raises her hand for the second time. "And before you ask again, my recent scribbles don't involve a fall or stairs. The focus is poisons." She wiggles her white eyebrows for effect.

"Elsbeth, will you describe your colleagues to us?"

"Sure. Bryce and Greta have been discussed. Edward and Frances are generous and kind. I knew them when they dated. Owen became their burden. Edward's the writer. Poor Frances isn't, but his publisher manages her work."

"Are you a friend of the Whittletons?"

"Different genres. Different circles. They don't act married." Her eyes turn wistful. "I tied the knot once. When people become two halves of their same universe...." She searches the faces of both Aiden and Stella. "Perhaps you comprehend? Stella, you, and Nick are a pair. And you, Detective?"

"Understood, Miss Strauss, or am I mistaken, and you prefer Mrs.?

"Miss is fine, Detective North." Her eyes glisten.

****

"We need a plan." Aiden's teeth clench between words. "I expected the investigation to be finished by now."

"Owen's death still isn't a bona fide case." Stella maintains a level tone. There's more on Aiden's mind. He sounds frazzled. "We're early stages, and with a handful of suspects, we might as well settle in. Answers will take time. What's left to do? Shall we split the alibi checks?"

"I want us to remain together as much as possible. Two sets of ears are better." His eyes cloud. "Mary Jo asked me to go and visit Rosemary next week."

Stella scrounges a pen and paper from her purse. Circumstances with Aiden's wife must be changing. He'll reveal details when he's ready. "Okay. You do what's best for Rosemary. I want to talk with Hester. I seem to remember she said she sat by the window at Cocoa and Café while she waited for Owen."

"Good idea. We need to double-check Bryce and Elsbeth's alibis with Parlour Antiques and have a word with Hope Carlyle to help verify Mayko Doan's story. We're still to call her Mayko, correct?"

She shrugs. "I guess. There are as many secrets in this group as there are authors. The retreat served as the perfect opportunity for poor Owen. We can visit Marnie Firth at the Purple Tulip in Port Ephron and find out the time Bryce and Greta ate dinner. We need to interview Pepper at the hotel. She'll be full of information—who appeared where and when."

"Pepper can't possibly catch every detail. She doesn't work the dining room and the front desk simultaneously."

"Her fingers are into all areas of the business. She has help, but if anybody knows the lay of the land, Pepper will."

"And the books?" Aiden focuses on the satchel Stella used to carry them from Brigitte's.

"I hope I kept those well hidden."

Aiden retrieves the bundle from beneath the table. He pulls out the volume on top. "Mayko Doan's book is called *Tanchau Burning*. I'll skim through hers tonight."

"Sure. Elsbeth's title says volumes: *Blood on the Knife*. Sounds gruesome. I'll ask Nick to do a review. This is Bryce's latest—*Cowgirls Love Horses*. I must say, I'm curious."

"This one of the Whittletons' is titled *Camping in California*. I'll take their book, as well."

Stella sorts the pile. "Frances' newest is called *He Said Yes* and Edward's most recent one, although the title is three years old now, is *At the End of the Cave*."

"I've heard of the book. Sci-fi readers in the office raved about *At the End of the Cave*."

"Good. You can skim Edward's example. I'll take Frances'. I hate sci-fi. Never did make any sense. I've read Greta's two books: *Creating a New Self* and *Improving on Self* but I'll dust them off at home."

"Greta tried to crawl under your skin during her interview." Aiden peers at her when he makes the statement.

Her cheeks flush and she holds her breath for a moment. "She tried. Everyone said she can't write, and she's a fluff-brain. I liked her books when I read them. Trixie and Cavelle did, too. Not sure how I feel, now. Isn't there an old saying—don't meet your heroes?"

"Point taken. We still need to talk with Greta's publisher and examine the box full of scribbles and newspaper articles the team collected from Owen's bedroom."

Stella reorganizes the stack of books and replaces the ones she will lug home back into the satchel. "You're right. Lots of tasks yet."

"Before you go, tell me your assessment to this point."

"Everyone but Elsbeth has a clear motive. They each had opportunity." She stops while she puzzles over the list of authors. "Between the Whittletons and Greta Walmsley, someone has lied. They both say they left the hall first. Bryce's motive is obvious, and he admits he went to the venue. I'm not sure Elsbeth or Mayko are in contention, even though they were on the street at what we assume is the time of an altercation. Elsbeth doesn't care and Mayko is unlikely to tangle with anybody. Hester sat at the café. Owen's parents were back at the park. The caretaker went to his brother's house. If a person or persons unknown fought with Owen and pushed him, a confession will be our only bet."

"I want to interview everyone again day after tomorrow. Let them all stew and then dig a little deeper. Are you game?"

"Absolutely. Thursday," she muses. "Still two days before our potluck. Let's spend tonight and the morning with books. We can do alibi checks in the afternoon. I'll come into the station. A visit with Mildred Fox is in order before lunch."

"Mildred Fox?"

"Yes. The Whittletons spent much of their off time with her. Despite her lemonade, she might produce a useful observation or two." Her smile is wistful. "Remember after Lorraine Young disappeared? Mildred is more insightful than people give her credit." She scribbles on her list. "I'll call Hester in the morning, as well. Brigitte and Trixie will be at the park on Saturday night, so no need to bother them beforehand. And you? Game for the potluck?"

"Maybe."

He has too much on his mind. She doesn't push. "Okay. Sounds good. See you after lunch tomorrow."

She returns home to be greeted by Nick, a cold beer, salad, barbecued chicken, and ice-cream. They spend the cool September evening wrapped in blankets on the veranda, their laps covered in books. Stella snuggles into his side. If anyone were to drive in the yard, they would never suspect the couple to be deep into research of potential murderers.

❦

CHAPTER 10

I Have Skills

Nick and Stella huddle, bleary-eyed, around the full coffee carafe at the kitchen table as Duke struts in, Kiki wedged in his armpit. Both are decked out in bright green turtleneck sweaters. Kiki's fur sprays above the fabric and turns her tiny face into the centrepiece of a puppy bouquet. "Good mornin', you two. What were you folks doin' overnight?" He leers in typical Duke fashion. "Wear yourselves out?"

Stella manages a feeble reply. "We read until three in the morning—don't be crude," she rebukes.

"What were you readin'?" Duke expresses a surprising interest in the written word. He sits down and helps himself to coffee and a piece of brown bread toast.

"We thought it might enlighten the investigation if we reviewed examples of writing from each of the authors."

"Yeah. Elsbeth Strauss was in town." He rocks back and forth while he chews. "She's a great writer. I've read every book Strauss has written."

A stunned silence ensues. Duke's eyes dart from one of them to the other. "Don't look at me like that. I read books. Mysteries are my favourite. Elsbeth Strauss makes the murderer the least expected antagonist. Often, the villain isn't even a main character, or a person with an obvious motive. She's considered the queen of the twist." He pats Kiki and feeds her a morsel of his toast.

Nick and Stella exchange glances. Duke suddenly sounds educated.

"I sure wish I'd stayed for your party." His remark has a ring of sadness. "My date wasn't worth the sacrifice."

"What a shame, Duke." Stella's curiosity piques when he shares his disappointment. "What else do you know about Elsbeth Strauss?"

"Oh, not much as a person. Her mysteries are translated into a dozen languages. Everybody knows she'll write a twist, but we never have any idea when or where." He sips his coffee, watches his audience of two, and puffs his chest in the role of mystery writer expert. "The twist is unpredictable. How she manages to shock readers every time is beyond me."

"I skimmed her latest book, *Blood on the Knife,* last night. I didn't read the story from cover to cover, but the antagonist doesn't have a major role in the plot," Nick adds.

Duke bounces on the oak chair. "Can I borrow it? I haven't read *Blood on the Knife* yet."

"Why don't you buy it from Brigitte after we finish with the investigation?"

"Okay. I saw a review of *Blood on the Knife* in the paper.*"* He reaches for another piece of toast. "Great!"

Nick glances over at Stella. "I'll cut more bread."

"What else did you guys read, since you were awake half the night?"

"I flipped through Greta Walmsley's two self-help books again, and I'm now convinced the other authors are correct. Greta didn't write them. After her interview, I find it hard to believe she could compose a grocery list."

"Harsh," Duke admonishes. "I admire writers. I sure couldn't put a book together."

"Neither can she," Stella adds, before she continues. "Her books instruct the reader on how to re-purpose a life; re-invent themselves. She's twenty-six. No way Greta's the writer." She pauses before expanding her thoughts. "Bryce's novel seemed odd to me. I think the overall theme relates to people who assume the obvious. *Cowgirls Love Horses* refers to girls who aren't fond of horses."

"I've never read any of Blanken's stuff. Not into the romance. He used to write as Penny Luckett. Bet you didn't know that." He sips his coffee. "He makes a better cowboy. Edward Thomas' books are good," he continues to muse.

"You think?" Now, Nick sits dumbfounded.

"He writes lots of science fiction." Duke stops for a moment and runs his fingers through Kiki's fur. "Poor guy, havin' his son die. I can't imagine."

"Aiden took Edward's latest novel, *At the End of the Cave.* Even the title gave me the creeps."

"Tell Brigitte not to sell Edward's either. I'll take his book off her hands.

92

I expect another long winter."

With sudden realization, Stella understands how Duke spends his time stuck in a motel efficiency suite from mid-October until mid-May each year. With no family since his mother died, and a romantic flirtation which appears to be on the skids, books must be his escape. Well, good for him. "No problem. The other one I skimmed was Frances' latest called *He Said Yes.*"

"Another romance writer." Duke screws up his face, as if the cream in his coffee has soured.

For a guy who's been married three times, Stella's surprised he doesn't enjoy the genre. "Other authors suggested her books are published because Edward's publisher handles her work as a favour—to keep Edward around."

Nick offers coffee to each of them in turn but focuses on Stella. "What did you think?"

"I'm not a romance reader. The story was awful. The theme, again, was the unconventional. The title illustrates the complete plot. A woman proposes to a man, and he says yes—self-evident. It took forever to get to yes and a woman proposing to a man is perfectly acceptable."

"No news there. Completely predictable," Duke mutters, as he sips his brew. He's taken a break after two pieces of toast lathered in strawberry jam.

"What? Duke, you could be one of those reviewers we read in the newspaper."

"I wrote reviews in school." He continues to focus on Kiki, before he lifts his eyes to Stella and Nick. "I have skills."

"You do, Duke. Now, Mayko Doan or the Whittleton couple? Are you familiar with their work? Aiden planned to review their most recent books, plus *At the End of the Cave.*"

"Haven't read Miss Doan's memoir. Naomi and Gregory are scrappers. Never interested in their genre 'cause I don't go nowheres, but every time I cruise past their trailer, I hear an argument. They get along when they're sittin' by the fire with Mildred. The old lady enjoys them." He chuckles. "They give her booze and food."

"Duke, be nice." Stella admonishes but doesn't reveal the fact the Whittletons are siblings. She glances at Nick for long enough to clarify the information isn't shareable. "Now, if everyone's through demolishing Nick's fresh brown bread, I will clean the table, pour another cup of coffee, and call Hester."

"Kiki and me, we're off for a spin around the park. Any check-outs today, Nick?"

"Nope. Everybody who's still here plans to be at the potluck on Saturday. By next weekend, they'll have moved out. And you?"

"Here for the shindig. Afterward, I'll stay and help until you shut off the water and power. Makes me feel better if the place is buttoned up before I move back to the motel. If you two want to do more renovations, call. Kiki and me, we'll come runnin'.""

"Thanks, Duke." Nick glances at Stella before he continues. "The septic work is scheduled to start after we close. Maybe you can help when I need an extra pair of hands?"

The security guard's face lights. "Geez, sounds great. And Stella will doggy sit, the same as last year."

****

"My friendship with you is appreciated, Stella, but you are aware I hate the telephone. Please visit the farm. Jewel will make you a tasty cup of coffee. I do not understand the mind of a coffee drinker, but I respect your right to consume the bitter concoction."

Between clenched teeth, Stella tries to wrestle control of the conversation. When she called, Jewel expected Hester to refuse a telephone discussion. From what Stella ascertained via the open mouthpiece, it took considerable persuasive efforts to encourage Hester to accept the receiver.

"Hester, you possess a perfect memory, and you're a valuable witness. Detective North has given his consent for me to ask you preliminary questions. Can you try to have patience?"

"I will spare no effort to be patient, although I avoid particular devices and one of them is the telephone. You are my friend. I am sad Owen died and want to cooperate."

"Okay. I'll be quick. If I recall our initial conversation, you said you sat at the table in front of the window at Cocoa and Café. The spot affords an excellent view of the street, correct?"

"Correct. Cocoa and Café sits ten feet back from the curb, whereas other businesses are further from the sidewalk. As a result, if one positions oneself in the front window area, there is a clear visual past the vacant repair shop next door, the entrance to Parlour Antiques, across Birch Street, past the hall to Elm Street, and beyond. On the opposite side, my unobstructed view consisted of Yellow House and various other locations, across Birch again, and toward the hotel."

"Will you describe to me who you observed and when, while you sat and waited?"

"I did not spy. I watched for Owen."

"No one has accused you of bad behaviour."

"Fine."

Stella hears a definite huff in her voice.

"I arrived at the café by three fifty-five and chose my seat. Others pertinent to your inquiry left the venue at the same time as me. Mayko Doan walked beside me. We exchanged pleasantries. She continued to Mrs. Carlyle's. She said she wanted to walk Tanchau and asked me to come along, but I planned to meet Owen. Elsbeth Strauss turned at the door and raced to the hotel. I overheard her rudely ask an older woman to move aside."

"Typical Elsbeth. Go on."

"Owen's parents took off with everybody else. Mr. Reguly left the hall soon after the crowd. As I sat, Mr. Reguly's truck pulled out of Birch Street, crossed Main, and drove along Birch on the other side."

"You're sure the person was Valentin?"

"Yes. His truck is somewhat old and red—a 1974 Chevrolet C-10 Custom. I am familiar with makes and models of vehicles, Stella."

She steels her patience. "To be sure. Shall we go on?"

"I prefer you drive to the farm for a cup of Jewel's coffee."

"Me, too, but I have other people to meet. I'll come visit you next week."

"Perfect. I will try to harness my annoyance." She continues. "By four-fifteen, the Whittletons pulled their truck away from the curb where they were parked near the café. Naomi arrived at their vehicle first and Gregory lagged by two or three minutes. She appeared angry, but of course, her emotions are an assumption on my part, determined by body language alone."

"Did you observe Greta Walmsley leave?"

"For a moment. She exited the hall at four-forty-five and walked on Birch Street. I assumed she wanted to stroll the side streets before her return to her lodgings."

"You're positive the time was four-forty-five?"

"Certain. Two minutes later, Mr. Blanken parked across the street and tore into the hall. He stepped inside for no more than a minute. He exited and sauntered into Parlour Antiques where he lingered. After he returned to his truck, he moved to park nearer the hotel. He carried a package from the antique shop, and it was ten past five."

"Anybody else?"

"Yes. Mayko Doan walked Tanchau past the café. She plodded around town. I caught sight of her three times. Miss Strauss strutted past the window, too. I couldn't tell where she went from my vantage point, but she came along again with a bag from the weaver's. She then visited Parlour Antiques. Before you ask, I checked the time—five to five. Her books must garner her excess funds, as she carried another parcel when she left the shop and returned to the hotel."

"Are you finished?"

"No."

Stella takes a breath. "What else, Hester?"

"Greta Walmsley appeared from Elm Street and crossed Main. She went to Harbour Hotel."

"What time?"

"Well, she missed Mr. Blanken. He possibly saw her when he moved his truck closer to the hotel. I caught a glimpse of her at ten past five, near the same time when Mr. Blanken parked his truck."

Despite her absolute trust in Hester's accuracy, Stella feels confused and can't isolate the reason.

"Are you still on the line?"

"I'm here, Hester. I guess my imagination has failed to picture everyone on the street."

"I should make you an activity map."

"What?"

"Jacob will fetch me a small roll of brown paper from Mr. Gorman's shop. I can use Kenny's little cars and draw a map of Shale Harbour. My time will be well spent. When can you come and look?"

A map with the times incorporated could help. Who knows? "Let's plan for Tuesday next week. We need to conduct final interviews before the authors return home, and Detective North wants to go to Ontario to visit his wife. I have the park potluck to host, too. I'll call."

"Fine, Stella. I should have suggested a map in the first place and then I would not have been forced to endure this electronic conversation." Hester, in her usual fashion, hangs up.

****

At last, and not a minute too soon, Stella grabs yet another cup of coffee, this time in her travel mug, and sets out to take a walk around the park. Her main goal is a discussion with Mildred. There's the possibility she can shed a light on the Whittletons. In addition, she wants to check in with a few of her seasonals to determine if Owen bothered anyone. Several attendees mentioned he helped himself to items which belonged to other people. Hester missed her mechanical pencil, later discovered with Owen's effects.

The sun proves to be warmer than she expected, and she's thankful for the shade provided by Curtis and Elroy's awning. "Good morning. I'm pleased you both plan to attend the potluck before you start for home."

The two men glance at one another. "We're glad we can stay," Elroy begins. "Has anyone in the park discussed the young man who died on the weekend?"

"I wondered if he met any residents. He wandered around much of the time."

"He lurked and crept, and stole, if the truth be known." Elroy pats Curtis' hand.

"Did Owen take any items of yours?"

"Yes, Stella. I hate to speak ill of the dead, but the kid was a klepto. He took a heart-shaped rock out of our garden. I painted it for Elroy the first year we were here." Curtis' eyes well as Elroy continues to console him.

"We'll find another rock, Curtis."

"Are you positive the person was Owen?"

"As we were enjoying our lunch, he walked over, scooped the heart into his pocket, and waved at us." Curtis' nostrils flare and his eyes bulge. "I ran out on the deck and asked him to return our property. He laughed. Stella, he laughed in my face, hollered 'prove it' over his shoulder, and meandered off."

"You never told me. When did the incident happen?"

"Saturday morning. Once we heard of his death, it didn't seem right to mention a rock," Elroy says with an apologetic air.

She hears the same story from Rob and Sally Black, Buddy McGarvey, and Ted Metcalfe. Each one of them identified Owen as involved in a theft.

Ted avoided a confrontation. The others tried and failed. Rob Black suggested the group talk to his parents at the cottage on Sunday. By then, it was too late.

After her short visit with Rob and Sally, Stella wanders across the lot to Mildred's spot. She's flopped in her basket chair on her new deck, enjoying the morning sunshine and what Stella hopes is coffee.

"Well, here comes the boss, in the flesh. What brings you down here from on high? Thought you'd be busy with cute Detective North...or did you decide the rotten kid fell?"

"Hi, Mildred. What do you mean by rotten?"

"He was a thief and a liar. I think he stole stuff from most of the residents, whether they were seasonals or short-term. He tried to nick barbecue tools from Bryce, next door to Naomi and Greg, but Bryce caught him and gave him hell."

"Did he steal from you?"

She cackles. "What's he gonna take of mine—one of my new second-hand nighties? Come on." She points an arthritic finger in the general direction of Stella's face. "I think he steals his stories, too. That gruesome piece he read on Friday sounded familiar. I bet he copied the idea from another writer." She takes a sip before she scolds. "Don't be shocked. I do read, although not here in the park. I'm a people watcher in the summer." She smooths her caftan. "You haven't been around much, or I probably woulda mentioned Owen. Us regulars talked and decided we'd wait until Sunday to rat the kid out. We were too late."

"Sorry. Yes, I've been busy, first with the retreat, and now with the investigation."

"Was he murdered?"

"Honest answer, Mildred, we aren't sure. Lots of people possessed motive. Many had opportunity, but we don't know. I've come by because I understand you've spent time with your neighbours."

Mildred nods. "Two real nice kids. They enjoy a good rum and coke, and he cooks a mean steak. Best neighbours I've ever had." She hoists her grimy cup in a salute. "I'll be sad when they go."

"Anything else?"

"Not much." She glances around and lowers her voice.

Stella leans over to better catch Mildred's words above the flap of her awning in the morning breeze.

"They try to act married, but they fight all the time. I think they stay together because of their travel books. A divorced couple can't write stories about stayin' in fancy hotels and goin' on safaris. They don't act married."

Almost afraid to hear the old woman's response, Stella asks, "How do married people act, Mildred?"

"On Friday night, when you and Nick hosted the party?"

"Go on."

"Nick leaned against you or touched your shoulder before he took off to the kitchen. You rested your hand on his knee while Hester read. He covered your hand with his."

The comfort of a shared truth guides her response. "You're observant, Miss Fox, but Nick and I aren't married."

"I can remember love. Don't be surprised. You and Nick are in love, and it shows. Naomi and Gregory ain't. I wonder if they're even in like."

$$\maltese$$

Chapter 11

You Can Pick Out the Lies

"I hope you discovered more than me."

Stella sits across from Aiden, who frowns while he passes books back to her. "Tell me your thoughts after your review of the Whittletons' latest coffee-table creation."

"Since I'm aware they're siblings, the prose feels forced. I sensed no joy in the vacations they described. The pictures contain no images of either of them. If people are enthusiastic about the topics and locations, their status wouldn't matter, so why the secrecy and sham?" He leans toward her and places both elbows on his desk. "Edward's book is a horse of a different colour. *At the End of the Cave* was a page-turner. I stayed awake half the night to finish."

"Did the story or style reveal any secrets related to Edward?"

"Depends on whether you accept symbolism, I guess. Not to ruin the final scene, but at the end of the cave, you find yourself in another cave. I was left with the impression Edward tried to portray the idea of an endless struggle. The work may reflect how Owen impacted his life."

"And Mayko?"

"In the simplest of terms, once you understand the truth, you can pick out the lies. The whole account could be a dream sequence instead of a memoir. How did you do?"

"The first piece of information I want to share is that Duke revealed he's an avid reader and mysteries are his favourite. Nick skimmed *Blood on the Knife*. He described the story, and although Duke hadn't come upon this title, he's read every other book written by Elsbeth. They discussed her skill with twists. Her antagonist is the person least expected," she scoffs. "We can take a lesson from Elsbeth and search for the twist."

"What about the other authors?"

"First off, Greta didn't write her two books. Since I've met her and talked to her retreat colleagues, I'm positive her publisher or an editor did the work. Maybe Owen heard the details from his parents?" She rearranges the pile in front of her. "Bryce's *Cowgirls Love Horses* points out how circumstances aren't obvious. I guess the theme addresses his own lifestyle. Frances' romance lacks maturity. When I described the story to Duke, he used the word 'predictable', and I agree."

"I admit I enjoy a good book. Biographies are my favourite," Aiden mutters, "but our exercise accomplished little."

"Don't be discouraged. I learned a great deal from Hester and did a run around the park to uncover impressions of Owen from a handful of my guests."

"Okay. Let me find us coffee and you can tell me what you discovered before we start on alibis."

While he's gone, Stella pulls out the notes she jotted after her conversation with Hester. She stares at the times, sure there's a clue here, but no revelation springs off the page.

"Here you go. I gather your exchange with Miss Painter demanded note-taking." He nods toward the sheet of paper she has on her lap and grins.

"The timeline is certain to be correct, although Hester has decided to create an activity map to illustrate the movements she noticed from the window of the café."

He furrows his brow in response.

"Hester caught a glimpse of each author at one time or another in the two hours she waited for Owen. I think most of her observations match what they revealed in their initial interviews, but we still have vague areas."

Aiden moves to the edge of his seat. "Who exited the hall first, the Whittletons or Greta Walmsley?"

Stella scans her sheet. "Hester, and I trust her memory, reports Gregory and Naomi left at four-fifteen. She describes their departure the same way the two of them did. She couldn't hear but said their body language indicated a fight."

"And Greta?"

"Four-forty-five."

Aiden's eyebrows lift.

"Greta's movements were weird. Hester says she came through the door and scurried along Birch Street away from Main. Hester spied her again when she emerged from Elm and crossed to the hotel at five-ten."

"Where was Blanken?"

Stella peers at her scribbles. "He parked his truck and raced into the hall, Hester said, two minutes after Greta left. The time was four forty-seven. He ran out after a minute, walked back to Parlour Antiques, left there, and moved his truck nearer the hotel at five-ten. Hester wondered if he spotted Greta when she crossed Main and entered the hotel, or if she made her way inside before he noticed."

"She had a date for dinner with Blanken, right?"

"Correct. Maybe she saw his vehicle and decided on the scenic route to avoid him. It seems, if Hester is accurate, she took her own sweet time before she returned to her room."

"Bryce still possessed sufficient opportunity, along with motive. Somebody lied somewhere. Alibi checks might help."

"Yes, I have the times people passed the café, entered, or exited the hotel, and moved vehicles. We have no witness who observed actions on Main Street after Jacob collected Hester at six o'clock—our one loose end. Do you think there's a chance he left the hall and returned after six to fall or be pushed down the stairs?"

"The medical examiner didn't rule out the slim possibility he died later in the evening or in the wee hours of Sunday. Condition of the body indicated death occurred between four and ten PM." Aiden nods to himself. "I'll ask two of the detectives from Port Ephron to interview the property owners and merchants along Main for their observations regarding Owen. What's the story in the park? What did your guests have to say?"

"Well, the long and short of the issue appears to be Owen stole, or tried to steal, possessions of one stripe or another from many campers. Elroy and Curtis confronted him when he removed a hand-painted rock from their flower garden, right under their noses. Apparently, he hollered for them to find proof, guffawed, and left. A group of seasonals planned to tell Edward and Frances on Sunday morning, and then he was dead. Bryce wrestled his barbecue tools away from the guy, but the others were intimidated."

"Another talk with his parents is necessary, and we'll take a look in his room again."

"Finally, Mildred, in our conversation, quickly pointed out how she finds Naomi and Gregory's relationship abnormal. She enjoys their company but listens to them fight whenever they aren't with her. She told me they don't act married. She said for sure they don't love one another, and they may not even like each other. Mildred hypothesized they stay together because of their career." She reacts to the tension on his face. "No, I did not tell her the truth."

****

"Hi. Hope? Stella here. How are you today?"

"Fine, Stella. And you?"

"I'm fine, thanks. Detective North and I want to double-check the whereabouts of the authors Saturday afternoon and evening."

"Oh, certainly. Mayko came home just before four, changed and walked Tanchau. They didn't return until six. We had supper and watched television."

"Yes, Mayko said she watched television with you."

"She is a lovely young woman. I've invited her to stay with me any time."

"Thank you, Hope. I appreciate your corroboration of Mayko. I imagine you're busy. Take care, now. Bye."

Stella turns to Aiden while she pushes his phone back across the desk. "Hope reports the same story as Mayko told us. She returned to the house, changed her clothes, and walked her dog. She stayed out for almost two hours. They ate supper together and watched television. Hester observed Mayko with Tanchau as she wandered along or crossed streets, at least three times. Mayko didn't re-enter the venue."

Aiden dials the Purple Tulip while Stella listens to his side of the conversation.

"May I have a word with Marnie Webb?" He closes his eyes for a second.

"Hi, Miss Webb. Detective Aiden North. I hope you're well."

"Yes. No, my wife is in hospital."

"Appreciated. Everyone struggles to make her better. I've called to confirm the whereabouts of two authors who say they ate at your establishment on Saturday night past. The couple's names were Bryce Blanken and Greta Walmsley."

He laughs quietly and glances over toward Stella. "Yes, a cowboy and the writer of the self-help books. I gather they graced the Purple Tulip. Can you give me the times?"

"Thanks a lot. I hope we're able to enjoy another dinner at the Purple Tulip—without the addition of broken dishes. I appreciate your patience. Bye for now."

Stella waits and hopes she's succeeded in rendering her face expressionless. The last time Aiden and Rosemary visited the Purple Tulip was for Valentine's Day. The restaurant happened to be an element in their investigation into Lucy Painter's death. Rosemary was in the middle of the paranoid phase of her condition and because Aiden was acquainted with Marnie Webb and called her by name, Rosemary flew into a rage and threw dishes. Damages were extensive enough for him to be required to make significant reparations.

"First off, I never intend to take my wife back to the Purple Tulip regardless of the medications her doctors choose to give her. I've been humiliated by her in the past, as you are aware—need I remind you of her diner/sock hop dinner party—but Valentines Day last year was by far the worst."

"Now I understand why we phoned Marnie instead of a personal interview in Port Ephron." She smirks. Her tease is understood but unappreciated.

His voice softens. "Never mind. She confirmed Blanken and Walmsley were at the restaurant from six on Saturday evening until eight. At least their stories match. Let's pay a visit to the hotel and Parlour Antiques before the afternoon's over. Will you assist with interviews tomorrow? We'll have no choice but to let them leave town after their second go-round with us."

"You're right. Are you off to Hawkesbury soon? How unpleasant is Rosemary's report?"

"To answer your first question, yes, her sisters have insisted I come for a case conference with her doctors; scheduled for Saturday. I'll make the drive on Friday and return on Sunday," he replies with a sad smile. "It'll give you a couple of days to focus on Nick and your business. I'll close our trailer once I get back."

"No problem, Aiden. My concern is for Rosemary."

"Mine, too, but circumstances now force me to depend on your help. Here you are with a season-end party and a park to button down while I run off to a psychiatric hospital to endure an interview with my wife's shrinks." He tilts his head in that way he does, and his snow-white hair falls across his forehead. "I appreciate your support." He twists his wedding ring.

She nods. "Nick understands the work we do. We'll be fine. And Rosemary?" she persists.

"If Mary Jo and Toni are to be believed, she screams like a banshee most of the time. When she isn't yelling her face off, she's curled in a corner quivering and whimpering. I can't imagine the turmoil inside poor Rosie's mind."

"Sad. I *am* sorry." There's little else she can say.

"Stella, years ago Rosie and I lived an almost normal life. There were periodic ups and downs, but her condition worsened when we were told, in no uncertain terms, we couldn't have kids." He clenches his hands into fists on the desk. "She has never been on an even keel since. I'm unable to manage her alone anymore, which is why I accepted Port Ephron as my final post before retirement. I hoped for improvement because Mary Jo and Toni are here."

"You've been devoted to her for the life of your marriage, Aiden. Her sisters, for their entire lives. There are occasions when people don't recover."

She's sure his sigh is audible outside in the hall. "Understood. Believe me. The doctors think she should be admitted on a quasi-permanent basis—the reason I've been summoned to a case conference."

"What do they mean?"

"I gather they keep her in their facility for a cool three thousand a month and I am cordially invited to visit for a couple of days every few weeks, the same for her sisters. Mary Jo warned me."

"And what do you want?"

"My wife back, but Mary Jo points out I was never married to a sane person. I found segments of sane mixed into a salad of crazy."

"Once you see her, you'll sense what to do, Aiden."

"Hopefully, you're right." The curtain falls once again to shield his personal demons. "Let's go over to the hotel."

****

The leaves show a faded promise of fall, as the crisp air continues to retain residual warmth. Their walk from the police detachment to the Harbour Hotel consumes five minutes. Business must be good. The turquoise shingles sport a fresh coat of paint and the yellow trim shines deeper and richer than Stella recalls. Although she considers the place a 1940s reject, a movie prop for a Somerset Maugham mystery, she appreciates the owner's effort. The wide veranda sounds hollow underfoot. Scattered Adirondack chairs, in a variety of colours, sit empty. The afternoon sun has accumulated into a muggy haze inside the glassed porch. Bells over the interior door jangle when they cross the threshold.

"I hope she isn't busy with supper preparations yet."

"She's probably alone. The summer help has returned to school." Stella approaches the desk. "Hi, Pepper. I thought you might be gone. My staff has flown the coop."

Pepper Ferguson's perfect teeth flash, and her blond ponytail flutters. "Hi, Stella. Detective North. Full-time and permanent now. This will be my second winter. No more college for me. Dinner isn't served until five-thirty, but I'm happy to find you coffee and a scone." She fingers the menus stacked near the phone.

"No, Pepper. Information is our request today. We need your help with the movements of a few of the authors last Saturday afternoon."

"I'll do what I can. Let's go sit in the breakfast room." She leads them to a small dining area off the entry, equipped with a trestle table and sideboard where a buffet breakfast is served to guests.

Aiden begins. "Pepper, I expect the hotel was busy after four o'clock on Saturday, but are you able to tell me who you noticed in the way of authors over the next couple of hours? Your observations may be helpful."

The girl's deep blue eyes shift toward Stella. "Did one of the attendees at the retreat murder Frances and Edward's son? Are you serious? He was an odd duck, for sure, but lots of people are odd. In the hotel business, you meet all kinds."

"Elsbeth Strauss, Pepper. What do you recall?" Stella isn't convinced the desk clerk / waitress will be able to provide details comparable to Hester's.

"She's easy to remember, with her crazy white hair and her," Pepper bends closer to them, "obnoxious attitude. She flew in here right after four, barking for guests to move out of her way. She breezed out around four-thirty to explore the shops. She first stopped to ask what was available for supper and if she could pre-order. I gave her the menu, and she chose a lobster platter for six o'clock."

"When did she return to the hotel?" Aiden moves to the edge of his seat.

"I have no idea. I served her meal on time in the small room at the back. You two have eaten in the space before."

"Are you able to recall Greta Walmsley and her movements?"

The girl frowns. "No, not until a gentleman named Bryce rang the bell on my desk and asked me to call her room."

"When?" Aiden hops on her response, impatient to hear the answer.

"Oh, five-twenty. I remember because she said she wasn't ready yet, and the Bryce-person grumbled. He muttered they were done at four and wondered out loud what took her so long. He stomped out to the veranda, and I returned to finish setting tables because reservations begin at five-thirty." She pauses. "My boss doesn't spend many hours here at the hotel. She has high expectations of me and says I'll be the manager soon."

"Who has the position now?" Stella thinks Pepper does most of the work.

"Well, the owner, Eugenie Charlebois, I guess. Do you need answers to other questions? I'll soon need to prepare for supper service."

"You've been a great help. I hope you're given the manager title. You deserve the recognition." Stella touches the girl's shoulder once she stands to leave. Aiden nods his appreciation.

As they wander along Main Street to Parlour Antiques, Stella can't resist a comment. "I think the owner takes advantage of Pepper. If I'm correct, she's quit university to work at the hotel. She told Meredith Tompkins she didn't want to learn the real estate business because she hopes to be promoted soon. She supervises the staff in the summer and now covers the whole place except the kitchen in the winter. She amazes me."

Preoccupied, Aiden responds, "Her reports coincide with what Hester and others told us about the whereabouts of Strauss, Blanken, and Walmsley. Here we are." He gazes at the Open sign in the window of Parlour Antiques.

They shuffle into the main showroom of the little antique store. "Come in. Come in." A couple, plus another woman, are intent in their examinations of the stock. Matt hustles them past credenzas and Victorian lamps, through to the private sitting room at the back. "I assume you're not here to shop for Victorian sconces. Mercedes will serve our customers. Sit, sit." He bubbles with enthusiasm.

"We suspect two of the authors were in your store on Saturday and wonder if you recall and can give us an estimate of the times."

Matt Savioli leans toward them from his perch on a slipper chair with a seat far too close to the floor. The position renders him bent in half as he asks, "Do you think the young man was murdered? Do people need alibis? Bad for business, Stella. Our little town will develop a reputation. Three murders back-to-back, and possibly another?" He pauses, panting. The heat of his anxiety warms her face.

"We want to cover our bases, Matt." Stella's eyes meet Aiden's for a moment before she continues. "Were any of the authors in the shop on Saturday afternoon? If the answer is yes, please tell us who and when." She wants to refocus him away from commerce. He has been preoccupied with the village's reputation ever since Paulina McAdams' assassination across the street in May.

"I covered the premises alone then. Mercedes left to complete a few errands. The cowboy author—what's his name?"

"Bryce Blanken?" Stella attempts to help.

"Yes, he's the one. He strolled in. He spied a piece of Ridgway pottery he claimed on the spot and started to bluster. His wife collects and tries to add to the pieces bequeathed to her by her grandmother."

Stella wonders if Aiden noticed how Bryce dropped his single-cowboy persona in the presence of Matt and Ridgway pottery.

"When did Bryce arrive?" Aiden pulls his notebook out of an inside pocket in his suit jacket.

"Ten to five—perhaps two or three minutes later. We engaged in one of those typical boring exchanges where the antique dealer is forced to feign interest and listen to a description of the precious pieces someone else owns, when the older woman with the white hair arrived at five to five. I remember I noticed the clock because I expected Mercedes back any minute."

"Elsbeth Strauss," Stella contributes.

He pauses for a second and peers at each of them in turn. "I don't gossip, but she is one cranky lady. She decided to buy a mid-twentieth-century vase—not old or collectible, but the item attracted her, and I was happy the ghastly piece would leave the premises—a poor purchase dating from years ago." He stops for breath. "I gave her a generous discount. Mr. Blanken entered first, and I made a huge mistake when I suggested she wait while Mr. Blanken paid for his pottery. Miss Strauss became unreasonable and agitated. She told Mr. Blanken to stand back and not interrupt." Matt pushes dark hair away from his brow. "I must tell you, the atmosphere was uncomfortable for a moment. Mr. Blanken took the time to enjoy another few minutes in front of the Ridgway shelf while I finished with Miss Strauss."

"And the times they left?"

"Let me think. She left by five past five, praise be. Mr. Blanken was kind. He went out five minutes later."

On the return walk to the station, they decide Hester's descriptors of the various movements around town are accurate and dependable. Bryce entered the hall after Greta took off, which gave him ample opportunity, but within a short period. Greta's timelines don't match Hester's observations. If Owen died between four o'clock in the afternoon and ten in the evening, there were many chances—and a lengthy list of motives attributable to every player. Still work to be done.

"We'll interview each of the authors again tomorrow. Can't ask them to stay any longer. See you at nine, Stella." He pats the hood of the Jeep as she settles behind the wheel.

CHAPTER 12

Second Nature

"It's been four days since Aiden called after they found Owen's body." Nick splashes milk into their mugs and pours hazelnut coffee on top. "Feels like weeks. Here. You'll need the fortification for the interviews later."

When she tilts her face toward his, he blushes, and she enjoys the effect she has on him. "Right now, I'd appreciate my life back." She spoons jam on her toast. "Too busy, but at least we've reached a pause of sorts. Aiden's off to Hawkesbury tomorrow and won't return until Sunday night."

"Does he plan to drive Rosemary home?"

"I expect not. The doctors proposed she stay in the facility indefinitely and he's not thrilled with the idea. I suspect Mary Jo and Toni will come back with her in tow sooner rather than later, though."

"He wants a normal life. I feel for the guy."

Stella nods. "Exactly what he said. But Rosemary's sisters are right—she has never been stable. He has to face facts."

"Not to change the subject, and you know I love talking about Aiden and Rosemary," he teases, "but we'll be well prepared for the party Saturday night. I'll put together a grocery list for you tomorrow." He watches her as he sips coffee. "Since you'll grace me with your presence for the next three days, I hope I can make the investigative lull worth your while."

His eyes remain visible above the rim of a pottery mug. His eyebrows wiggle. She giggles, then blushes.

****

Her drive into Shale Harbour is quiet. Tourists are gone. Roads are empty. Crisp and cool air hovers over water tinged with indigo. The hue reminds

111

Stella of the cold days to come. The ocean reflects turquoise when the weather's warm, darker blues as fall approaches, and grey in the winter—her sky in many ways.

The Whittletons checked out and drove past her house before she left. Their truck and trailer are parked further along the street. Aiden is in conversation with Moyer when she arrives. "Are they here?" She's breathless when she interrupts.

"Nope. They probably stopped to buy coffee before their interview. They're not due for five minutes, yet. Come on. Let's go. Thanks, Sergeant."

Moyer nods to Stella before they wander along the hall to the conference room. "I want to confront them right off the bat, Stella. Make them uncomfortable and watch where their truth lands. Agreed?"

"Nothing to lose. They're siblings. To be frank, they behave like brother and sister—ones who don't appreciate each another much. We might as well observe their reactions. As for Owen, we confirmed the Whittletons left for the day, before Greta, and spent the evening with Mildred. They didn't go back to the hall during the main window of opportunity."

"Right. I'm convinced they're not involved, but I want them to squirm because they lied to us."

Sergeant Moyer escorts Naomi and Gregory into the interview. Without a word, they take their seats across from Aiden and Stella. Both are dressed as if they've readied themselves for a cliché safari on a movie set, in khaki pants and white shirts, their uniform of sorts. In unison, they remove their brimmed hats and place them on the empty chairs beside them.

"Good morning." Aiden doesn't avert his eyes from the file when he addresses them.

Stella nods.

Gregory communicates first, after a short and silent consultation with Naomi. "We told you every detail, Detective North, Stella." The tremor in his tone illustrates his nervousness. "We fought and left the venue shortly after four. We returned to Shale Cliffs RV Park and spent a lovely evening with Mildred Fox. What else can we tell you? Was the little worm killed?"

"This remains an investigation." Aiden stares at them for the first time. "Mr. Whittleton, Miss Whittleton, we spoke to a witness."

Naomi's eyes widen at the salutation used by Aiden.

"Well, good. Whoever witnessed us knows we left. We parked our truck in front of the café." Gregory crosses his arms and juts his chin. He did not note the greeting extended to his sister.

"You departed the curb at four-fifteen, to be precise. Your description of the circumstances matches our witness, and Miss Fox has provided corroboration regarding the remainder of your day."

When Gregory makes a move to stand, Naomi places her long fingers across his wrist. Her eyes remained locked with Aiden's. "I think the detective is interested in another topic, Gregory."

"What?" He yanks his arm away from her touch.

"You're astute, Miss Whittleton."

A flash of understanding crosses Gregory's face.

"The two of you are brother and sister. You lied to the police—a serious offence."

Naomi takes the lead. "I told you we should tell them the facts. If the press doesn't sniff out our story, what difference does the truth make?" She turns her attention from accusations aimed at her brother, toward Aiden and Stella. "You're correct. Our status has been an outright lie for years and has become second nature. I'm sorry. We apologize, right, Gregory?" She slaps him on the arm.

"Second nature," he grumbles.

"Did Owen suggest he'd reveal Gregory's behaviour, Naomi, or was he aware you two are brother and sister? Did he threaten to tell people the truth?"

"Oh, I don't suspect, for a minute, he considered us siblings. He tossed the news of Gregory's supposed infidelities in my face. Owen's attempted coercion didn't upset me. Gregory risking our reputation dictated the reason for my anger." She turns to her brother. "Gregory's behaviour requires discretion, if we are to carry on with our travel books."

Gregory pouts. "Yes, the resulting circumstance was certainly my fault." He shrugs his shoulders. "In any event, Edward and Frances are ignorant of the truth. None of the authors who came to the retreat are aware. Owen activated his mean streak. He assumed we were married, and I was cheating. He searched for a way to use the information to his advantage. He frequently took pleasure in the discomfort of others."

"Do we face consequences, Detective North?"

"No. You may go now. You're no longer suspects in the death of Owen Ellis-Thomas, but we reserve the right to call you back if necessary. Please provide updated contact details to Sergeant Moyer before you depart." He rises.

Stella stands.

"Thank you for your hospitality, Stella. We will mention your business in our next newsletter. Goodbye." Naomi grabs her hat, points at Gregory's reminding him to retrieve his, and they leave. Aiden accompanies them.

****

She's certain the Whittletons were not involved in Owen's tragic demise. They were aware of Greta's continued presence in the hall, and they didn't return to town once they arrived at the park. Stella leans back in the chair and closes her eyes for a moment. The interview with Greta will round out their morning. Nick stuffed a sandwich and a cookie into her purse before she left the house. The end of today can't come soon enough. Perhaps they're on a wild goose chase, and Owen fell. Conversely, the initial incident report said Lucy Painter toppled into the basement and died, but her death turned out to be caused by poison. The flutter of heels gives her reason to abandon her reverie.

"Miss Walmsley was ready and waiting for us in reception, Stella." He motions to a chair. "Miss Walmsley."

"Detective, I told you to call me Greta. Everyone does," she simpers.

Today called for frills. Greta has chosen to wear a long pale blue skirt with tiered ruffles. Her blouse cascades in layers of fabric around the bodice and sleeves. Her denim bag is gathered at the clasp. She straightens her flounces as she sits.

"Greta." Aiden meets her gaze and squints. "We uncovered anomalies in the timelines related to when you departed the community hall and returned to the hotel on Saturday." He shuffles loose papers in a file on the table in front of him. "You reported you left the venue before Naomi and Gregory Whittleton, correct?"

What appears to be mock horror crosses Greta's face.

"Yes. Did I speak incorrectly? Oh, Detective, I am terribly sorry if I made a mistake. What can I do to resolve the problem?"

What can she do to resolve the problem? Tell the truth, for once.

"Our witness, Greta, says you left the hall at four-forty-five, not five past four as you reported. In addition, the same witness observed you travel on

Birch Street and emerge on Elm, where you crossed to the hotel at five-ten. Please clarify your whereabouts on the Saturday afternoon of September 26."

The ruffles tremble. The writer swallows. "Okay, you've found me out," she titters as she avoids Stella's stare and focuses on Aiden. "I didn't want to tell you I left the retreat venue last, except for Owen. I take time to jot notes after my workshops. It helps me improve from one session to the next." She sits straighter in her chair. "Review and reflection are hints in my books." She wags her index finger at them. "But I possess pertinent information which I will share. I was scared before, but not anymore."

"Did you talk to Owen before you left the hall?" Aiden has refused to allow curiosity to cross his face.

"Briefly. He was Frances and Edward's son. I complimented him as I recall. I told him the story he read the night before at your place, Stella, was exceptional. I asked him where he found his ideas. He expected to meet another party and wondered if anyone still remained in a classroom, and I assured him no." Her words come out in a rehearsed flood. "I reminded him the janitor requested the last person out to lock the door."

"Why didn't you tell us these details the first time, Greta?" Stella's suspicions and annoyance bleed into her tone.

"Because you would believe I might have been the last person to see him alive."

"And you use the word 'might' because?" Stella has a vague notion they're getting played.

Greta leans across the table, much more relaxed now. She acts as if she's prepared to take them into her confidence before she spreads the latest gossip. "As you are both aware, I was invited to dinner in Port Ephron on Saturday night with Bryce. Well," she puffs, before she continues. "When I left, he was parking his truck. I ran along Birch and took my time to walk around the block to avoid him." She stops and makes eye contact with them both. "He entered the hall behind me. Did he report this?"

Aiden ignores her question. "You spent twenty-five minutes on your stroll. You emerged from Elm and went into the hotel. Did you spot Bryce as he parked his truck?"

Her eyes narrow and she stares over Aiden's shoulder at the wall. "I didn't observe Bryce again until I came downstairs to meet him to go to Port Ephron." She pauses. "He was agitated. I assumed, at the time, his attitude was because I wasn't ready, although I wasn't late." Her tone has developed an out-of-character thoughtfulness. "If he pushed Owen down the stairs, he had an obvious reason to appear agitated, correct?"

Once again, Aiden avoids a direct response to her question. "We want to thank you for your time today, Greta. The authors from the retreat are permitted to leave for home after their second interview."

She reaches for her bag, which she settled on the chair beside her when she first came in. She fusses with the frilly decoration. "I must wait for mean and cranky Elsbeth. I anticipate a long drive back to Halifax."

"I'll show you out." Aiden stands.

Aiden returns to the doorway. "Did you bring lunch with you?"

"As a matter of fact, I did."

"Good. Let me grab mine and we can talk in private before Bryce arrives."

Settled with lunches and tea, Stella wants to debrief. "Greta tried to pin whatever happened to Owen on Bryce, and she assumed the kid was pushed."

"Did she lie?"

"She lied to us in the first interview. Today, she needed a story to make her delayed departure sound plausible. I wonder if Bryce spied Greta when she left the hall or went into the hotel before him. Why did she avoid him?"

"Bryce's interaction with his readers—the way he finds it necessary to live a false persona in order to sell books—makes me suspicious."

"Everyone has a secret in one form or another, even us."

"Yes." He meets her gaze for a fraction of a second, then returns to the discussion at hand. "But which ones did Owen uncover? Not the Whittletons'. Maybe Bryce; maybe Greta. Mayko's identity remains unknown except for those involved before she immigrated to Canada. The queen of the twist, Miss Strauss, seems to leave her life wide open. My money is still on Bryce or Greta."

****

"Mr. Blanken, Detective." Sergeant Moyer steps aside to enable Bryce to enter the interview room.

Stella understands she hasn't hidden her surprise. Bryce sports a ball cap which advertises a country radio station in Ontario. He has chosen to wear a white T-shirt and olive cotton slacks, along with sneakers instead of his standard-issue cowboy boots. She remembers a television interview which featured a famous country and western singer. He didn't wear his signature Stetson and Stella found it difficult to recognize him. She has the same unsettled response when she greets Bryce.

"Once I abandon the act, I'm not the same person. Don't be shocked." He drops into the chair opposite them and tosses his cap onto the seat to his right. "All loaded and ready to drive. Won't make the long trip home tonight but will push to Paradis de la Petite Montague in northern New Brunswick before sunset. Hate to hook up the trailer in the dark."

"Good afternoon, Mr. Blanken. We'll try to be brief. A witness has reported your movements in town on Saturday after the workshops."

She studies his reaction—not even a twitch.

"Great. Did your witness validate me?" He asks the question with obvious confidence.

"Yes, although a window remains, providing time for you to engage in an altercation with the victim."

"Didn't happen. I hollered for Greta and when I heard no answer, I left and walked to Parlour Antiques."

"We've confirmed your whereabouts." Aiden doesn't want to let him off the hook. "Our questions today revolve around the movements of Miss Walmsley."

"I never saw Greta until she came out on the veranda at the hotel." He leans forward. "The pretty girl with the ponytail called her room and Greta reported she was behind, but she'd be with me in a minute. She wasn't late. I was early." Bryce relaxes back in his chair. "I must have been excited to wrap my hands around an end-of-the-day beer at the Purple Tulip."

"Bryce, you didn't bump into Greta when she left the hall or entered the hotel?" Stella has trouble with the idea and mistakenly permits her feelings to show. Aiden glares.

"No. I wanted to visit the antique store. Then I had a difficult job finding a spot to park close to the hotel when I moved the truck. I fiddled to manoeuvre in near the curb, in a place better suited for a sedan." He stops for a moment. "Greta was nearby?"

"Not necessarily. We need to confirm our information and obtain corroboration as we go. We may contact you again, Mr. Blanken."

Surprise darkens his eyes. "Your sergeant took my details." In a more conspiratorial tone, he adds, "Did one of the authors shove the kid?"

Aiden glances at Stella before he continues. "Sir, you hide behind a secret which Owen could use against you. We are given to understand the victim tried to steal from you and an altercation followed. The hall was accessible."

"Am I a suspect?" Bryce's face has turned bright red. "I killed the little thief because he wanted my barbecue tools?"

"Everyone is a suspect, Mr. Blanken, but you may return home now. We have no obvious reason to detain you."

The cowboy author stands, bends to retrieve his ball cap, and rests his hand on the back of the chair. "Owen was an idiot and a burden to Edward and Frances. He stole, lied, and blackmailed. I couldn't stand him. I imagine there are a dozen people who harbour the same assessment, including his poor parents. Don't hesitate to call if I can be of further assistance."

As he reaches for the door handle, Aiden rises to accompany him to the front of the building.

He's told them the truth. But...if her feeling is wrong, and he pushed Owen, she's doubtful there's a clear path to proof.

Elsbeth Strauss slams into the conference room, tosses her purse on a chair, and hauls thick strands of white hair off her face. "I am in no mood for you people. I want to put the trip back to Halifax behind me as soon as possible. You realize I'm stuck in a car with Greta Walmsley for the next two hours? What can I tell you?"

"Good afternoon, Miss Strauss."

Stella knows Aiden well enough to recognize the smirk he's trying desperately to conceal.

"Hi, Elsbeth. A witness has attested to your whereabouts as you visited the shops on Saturday afternoon. Were you in a position to scrutinize any other authors on your journey?"

"You two should take better notes. Did I fail to mention I ran into Bryce Blanken at the antique shop? I watched the cowboy race into the hall as I made my way to the weaver's." She grabs her purse and holds the satchel in her lap. "I want to leave. Mayko Doan is out in the foyer. She wants to go home, too. She has a much longer trip." Elsbeth squints for a second. "She walked her dog on Saturday. Didn't I provide information on her earlier?"

"Yes, Miss Strauss, and our thanks. You did not run into Miss Walmsley in your travels?"

"No, I did not. Damn it, people, I must leave." She stands.

Stella will be as happy as Elsbeth when the woman exits the premises. She watches Aiden.

"Thank you for your cooperation, Miss Strauss. If we need more information, we'll be in touch."

The mystery writer races out the door, and her heels click along the hall before Aiden rises from his chair. He jogs after her since Moyer hasn't had time to return to the interview room and escort her out.

Elsbeth can be obnoxious. She and Greta will make a great pair on their trip back to Halifax, but she didn't lie. Stella stands when Aiden escorts Mayko into the room. Tanchau cuddles inside her airline bag. No one has objected to the little dog this time. "Hello, Mayko. We won't keep you too late. The drive to Fredericton is long."

"No hurry. Hope has offered to host me for another night. I can begin my journey after breakfast tomorrow."

"Good idea, Miss Doan. A witness observed your whereabouts on Saturday. Today, we need to know if you spotted any of the other authors in the neighbourhood."

"The cowboy jumped out of his truck and ran into the hall when I turned on to Birch Street. As I walked, I remained behind Greta Walmsley—two houses back because I didn't want to overtake her."

"Why not?" Stella leans forward. She already knows Mayko considers Greta to be indifferent toward her.

"She doesn't like me. I don't know the reason. She meandered slowly, as if she wanted to waste time. When she paused to inspect a flower bed on someone's lawn, I stopped, too. She often glanced around. If she noticed me, she never acknowledged my presence. I followed her back to the hotel and then I returned along Main Street until I reached Mrs. Carlyle's."

"Did she see you?"

"Oh, yes, I'm sure. I didn't hide, I talked to my dog, and I maintained a respectful distance. As is normal for Greta Walmsley, she ignored me. Hester Painter must be your witness. She sat at a table in the café window."

They clear Mayko to leave the interview.

"Quick assessment before we clock out for the day?"

They haven't learned much. "We confirmed Bryce's movements and decided he had opportunity. Greta's behaviour comes across as odd on several counts. She lied to us the first time we asked her when she left the venue. She revealed her conversation with Owen after we told her we talked with a witness. At the speed Greta walked, Mayko had a chance to enter the hall, push Owen because he tried to blackmail her about her identity, and then catch up to Greta soon after."

"Miss Walmsley omitted any mention she saw Mayko, but watched Bryce go into the venue. Details still seem out of whack." He frowns. "And Hester didn't report seeing Mayko slip inside, either. I leave for Hawkesbury in the morning. Detectives are assigned to complete merchant interviews and forensics will gather Owen's compositions and research. Once I'm back, we'll visit the parents and discuss any new issues."

As she stands and gathers her belongings, she forces a smile. "I hope your trip to see Rosemary and her doctors works out. Safe travels." She touches his arm as she moves past him toward the door, hoping he takes time to reflect on his wife.

"Until Monday."

❀

CHAPTER 13

A Match Made in Heaven

The clock says ten and Duke still hasn't shown to drink her coffee, eat a pile of brown bread toast, and then make his rounds. Granted, by early October, seasonals are her only guests, but the minimal expectations of her security person have not been met today. "I hope he's not sick," she mutters to Nick, who's on his way out the kitchen door.

"I hear him now. He can help me rearrange furniture before he does a spin around the grounds, okay?" Nick pauses and frowns. "He has someone with him."

"Who?"

"A woman. They've come from the direction of his trailer. Good morning, Duke. We wondered what happened to you."

Stella reaches the living room as Duke and his companion enter her house. "Hi, Stella. Sorry I'm late. Me and Cloris lost track of the time." He flashes a leer in Nick's general vicinity. "You two can relate, eh?" He sets Kiki on the floor. Tiny nails click on the hardwood when she runs to check the front office for Alice. With disappointment wrapped around her like her tight neon yellow park T-shirt, she returns and sits by Stella's feet.

Cloris blushes and studies the carpet until Duke remembers his manners. "Cloris, Honey, I want you to meet my bosses, Stella Kirk and Nick Cochran. Stella. Nick. This here's Cloris Kincaid."

Nick stretches out his hand in Cloris' direction. "Welcome, Cloris. Any friend of Duke's...," he says as he glances toward Stella for an instant.

"Hi, Cloris. Come on in. I've made fresh coffee. Care for a cup?"

The woman nods with enthusiasm while she pats her floral cotton dress in a gesture of matronly nervousness Stella tries to assuage. "Follow me to

121

the kitchen. I know Nick wants to discuss Duke's morning rounds. Did you manage to unlock the gate, Duke?"

"Oh, my jeez, I didn't. Sorry, you guys. I'll run out right now."

She hears Nick tell Duke to go inside and find the coffee. He'll make the trip himself.

"Man, Stella, I'm sorry," he repeats. His ears turn red. His sheepish manner accentuates his apology. "Cloris and me, we lost track of the time," he reemphasizes.

"I gather." She tries to appear magnanimous. "You don't often arrive late, my friend. How do you take your coffee, Cloris?"

"Black is perfect, Stella. I appreciate your hospitality." Her eyes remain focused on the table as she unties her triangular scarf, wrapped around her head, and knotted under her chin. The act exposes her pageboy hairdo.

Duke snuggles into the space beside Stella at the counter and reaches for the loaf of brown bread. "How's about some toast, Stella? Me and Cloris worked up an appetite."

"No need to be crude, John. Don't impose on Stella. We can find a bite at your unit."

"Not a chance. I eat breakfast here at the house. Nick makes the best coffee. We have an understanding. Right?" His eyes seek Stella's for agreement.

She nods. "Duke and Kiki join us at the kitchen table most mornings. Will you ride with him when he does his rounds?"

"Yes. I have a trailer over at Port Ephron RV, but Duke has encouraged me to consider a seasonal site rental from you. He's promised to take me on a tour."

"We're happy to accommodate you. Nick and I plan to have sewer connections installed later in the fall...more modern conveniences."

They discuss costs and the best time to move a rig between parks. Stella notices Duke as he watches Cloris. Satisfaction stretches from one of his ears to the other.

"Tell me how you two met."

Cloris giggles, and Duke jumps in. "At the dances over in Port Ephron. Cloris, here's, a helluva dancer."

"You don't say." Stella's imagination can't conjure an image of her older guest on the dance floor with Duke. "Lotsa fun."

"John and I love to dance. Despite my age, we have much in common."

"Listen, Cloris. I told you, seven years is nothin'. Stella and Nick are nine years apart, and he's younger, too. Right, Stella?"

"Did I hear my name? Are you three discussing me when my back's turned?"

Stella stares at Nick with an exaggerated guise of normalcy glued to her face. "Duke and Cloris were telling me how she's seven years older, and how much they enjoy dances."

"And we both read mysteries, too."

Nick pours himself a cup of coffee. "A match made in heaven. Do you two plan to attend the party tomorrow night?"

Duke pats Cloris on the hand. "We do. I want to introduce my lady to the folks here at Shale Cliffs, so she'll feel welcome next season."

"While you're here, Duke, will you help me rearrange furniture in the living room and carry the kitchen table out on the veranda for drinks? Stella and I can manage the rest of the work."

"No problem." He rises from his chair, hitches his pants as if he plans to expend considerable effort on the job, and follows Nick.

"Thank you for your kindness, Stella. I'll make certain John opens the gate when he's supposed to and does his rounds tomorrow."

"Duke's excited you're back together."

"You have me confused with my sister. John and Ruth were involved for two years, on and off. She happens to be fifty-eight—his age." Avoiding eye contact, she ties her scarf around her hair. "I'm interested in moving my trailer over here because Ruth is not enamoured with the fact I have, in her estimation, stolen her boyfriend. She dropped him for another guy, to tell the truth, and I was waiting patiently in the wings. Ruth has been reluctant to support me in any interests of my own." She bends to grab Kiki and wedges the little dog into her armpit. Kiki squirms her annoyance with the clutch-purse treatment.

****

Curtains flutter as cool morning air drifts across her exposed shoulder. Sunrise will be hampered today by overhanging clouds. She closes her eyes again. Calloused fingertips caress her cheek and push tangled wisps of grey-streaked hair off her brow. Without words, she snuggles closer. The down comforter cradles their warmth.

"The season's soon over," he whispers into her ear. "A dark and snowy winter can't come fast enough."

"Why, for heaven's sake?" She leans back to check to see if he's serious. "Aren't you anticipating, with unbridled relish, plumbers, septic systems, and construction?"

"Yes, but once the seasonals are gone, we'll find more quiet mornings." Despite the looming work involved to prepare for the evening's potluck, they take advantage of an uninterrupted start to their day.

An hour later, Nick traces the soft skin in the bend of her elbow with his thumb. "I don't know if I've ever said this straight out, but you and Shale Cliffs have given me the security and sense of purpose I needed."

Despite an effort, her breath catches in her throat. Circumstances forced an estrangement from his parents after he fled the States during the Vietnam War. Although reconciled and pardoned, the intervening years took their toll. "Oh my, aren't you suddenly serious?"

His eyes are black with emotion. He snuggles his nose against her cheek. "A man in love, Stella."

She cups his face with both her hands. "You are my rock, Nick. When I came back home to help Dad, I expected to be alone forever." She plants a warm kiss on his lips. "You and I are a team, now. You, Mr. Cochran, have managed to make an old girl fancy herself fabulous, and I don't intend to abandon one sliver of whatever we've found."

Silence speaks volumes.

"Mildred Fox even commented."

Nick furrows his brows in a mock frown.

"The other day when I visited, her remarks surprised me. She compared us to the argumentative Whittletons. She said she watched how we communicate without words; how we act our love for one another."

"I haven't given old Mildred enough credit for her observation skills."

"She'll be here tonight. Be nice."

"I'm nice. Didn't I help build her a new deck?"

"You did, indeed. Time to face the day." She glances at the clock. Eight o'clock and the sky reads cloudy. "I hope the weather doesn't turn to rain. We need to keep as many people on the veranda as we can. I expect the place will be packed."

"I'll throw on pants and run out to open the gate. Duke mentioned he might be late again." Nick banters as he pulls on shorts and a T-shirt. "The old boy still has life left in him, I gather."

"Well, Cloris appears happy enough. Wise to check, I guess, but Cloris told me she'd remind Duke of his responsibilities. I'll make coffee."

While he takes the golf cart out to the gate, she permits herself a moment to appreciate how far they've come. By the end of 1981, Nick will be her partner in both business and life. Imagine, forty-six years old and besotted. She crawls into a pair of blue jeans and a Mount Allison University sweatshirt before she races into the kitchen to make the coffee she promised. She wonders if Duke and Cloris plan to appear for breakfast, or did the woman take matters into her own hands and stock Duke—John's—cupboards?

****

Brigitte, Mia, and Trixie are first to arrive. They clamour inside. Mia wanders toward Stella with a bouquet from the garden at Yellow House. The little one approaches her great-aunt, but instead veers and offers her gift to Nick. Everyone bursts into laughter. Trixie, as usual, has arrived laden with a bucket of crushed ice which, today, contains shrimp for the barbecue. Brigitte steadies a bean salad in one hand and two monstrous bags of potato chips in the other.

Nick sits on his heels and touches Mia's fine blond hair. "Thanks for the flowers, little lady."

"You do most of the work, Nick. More logical she gave them to you anyway," Trixie huffs. "Stella, help me."

Stella jumps to her sister's command. She shares the handle on the bucket, and they struggle into the kitchen.

"I can carry the shrimp, you two," Nick offers, but they disappear around the corner.

"Here, Nick." Brigitte hands him the bowl she's balanced against her hip since she came in the door.

As their contributions are safely landed on the counter-top, Stella assesses her family. Brigitte did not include Carter Stephens as her plus one. Although a park party, Carter would be welcome. Trixie has begun to act closer to normal, despite her lower-key attire today. She's in skin-tight jeans and a baggy sweater to guard against the chill. Three heavy and gaudy necklaces dangle down the front, but Stella sees no bracelets whatsoever. Her strawberry blond curls are held back from her face with a tortoiseshell clip. Her leather satchel could comfortably house two Kiki-dogs.

Before she has an opportunity to pass comment on the fact Brigitte has attended without her new boyfriend, she hears a shout at the veranda door. She races into the living room to be met by Cloris and Duke. They have chosen to colour-coordinate in roses and greens. Kiki snuggles into a matching turtleneck sweater. For a moment, her eyes hurt. "The party can start anytime now, Stella." He holds out his contribution of a large glass casserole covered in tinfoil. "Cloris here's a fine cook." His yellowed teeth flash despite their neglected condition.

Cloris blushes while she fusses with her long skirt. "I made cabbage rolls. He'll say he helped but...," she grimaces and gives her head a wee shake. "You understand. Men."

"Not around here. The domestic credits are Nick's. Right, Duke? Come on out to the kitchen. I'll pop your dish into the oven to keep warm and introduce you to my family."

While Cloris meets Trixie, Brigitte, and Mia, Nick handles the onslaught. Stella can hear him usher people to the chairs on the veranda and place contributions beside the bean salad on the dining table in the living room.

By the time they leave the kitchen, the house throbs with activity. Rob and Sally Black have managed to drag Mildred away from her deck and fire. Stella sees her stretched out in one of the leather chairs near the darkened fireplace. Elroy and Curtis have cracked beers, for those interested, out on the veranda. Ted Metcalfe and his new flame, Lily, who has stuck by him throughout the summer, cuddle on the rattan sofa. Kiki jumps onto Mildred's lap. She's lucky Nick hasn't served her a drink, yet. People are packed in everywhere. Dishes of food cover the table, and Sally has toddled off with her pot of chili to set on the stove.

Nick lights the barbecue after they visit with their guests. He plans to cook burgers, chicken, and Trixie's shrimp. The gang should be happy. Stella roots out more napkins and pours herself a beer before she sits on the arm of Mildred's chair to relax. "Are you taken care of?"

"Yup. Nick found me a drink. I'm comfy. I'll eat whatever's goin' and you can fix me a plate when the time comes." Her varicose-veined legs are crossed at the ankles as she leans back. She balances her glass on her extended tummy. She taps Stella on the leg. "Duke's new girlfriend—she's kinda long in the tooth, ain't she?"

"She has a few years on Duke." She bends to whisper in Mildred's ear, "Which doesn't make her a bad person, old girl."

"Okay, you're right, I guess. Did you ever meet Duke's mother?"

"Loretta? No, why?"

"Years ago, they camped out here together. Never knew of any father in the picture." Mildred stares at the ceiling, playing back a movie in her mind. She waves a hand, as if to bat away the experience. "Cloris is her name? She's the image of Loretta. They used to come to Shale Cliffs when your parents ran the place."

"People say men are attracted to women who resemble their mothers. Or perhaps the other way around."

Mildred slaps her leg and cackles. "You and your man bucked the trend for sure."

Stella stands. "Let me find you some food."

As she loads a plate for Mildred, she overhears the old woman discuss Owen's reading with Duke and Cloris. When Stella returns with Mildred's supper, they include her in the conversation.

"Duke and Cloris both remember Owen's story, too. They recall a news report, Stella. Right, Duke?"

Cloris interrupts. "Those murders were ten or more years ago."

Owen's bedroom was full of newspaper clippings. Stella doesn't find it unusual to think a writer could transpose an actual event into fiction.

"Yes. A guy from out west somewhere killed his girlfriend's family."

"And the girlfriend? Owen made a girl the main character."

"The news never mentioned anyone else took part, but I remember the rest."

"You guys have piqued my interest. Enjoy your supper." She nods to each of them in turn. "Must make my rounds."

"How are you managing, Nick?" She slides her arm beneath his elbow. "Ready to take a break?"

He turns from the grill. "In a minute. Everyone's having a good time. Did you eat?"

"I'll grab a plate and another beer for each of us when you give the tongs a rest. I want to have a quick word with Trixie and Brigitte, first."

Her sister, niece, and great-niece are curled together in a corner of the living room on a blanket. Mia and Kiki have become fast friends. Mia offers little bits of bun to the dog. "Hey. You guys okay?"

"We're fine, Aunt Stella. Kinda wish I'd invited Carter, but Mom," she nudges her mother, "didn't want to break out her new man, so we decided to both come alone."

Stella peers at Trixie. "New man? And who might he be?"

"Tell her, Mom." Brigitte nudges her mother for the second time. "She'll find out soon enough."

Trixie mumbles her displeasure. "I've been out two or three times with Val. The death at the hall adds complications, okay?"

"Okay." Stella remains noncommittal despite her surprise. "How did you meet Valentin Reguly? He's the Val, right?"

"Yes. I visit his sister at least once a week. Mallory doesn't have much time left. I've known them for years, Stella. Almost by accident, Val asked me for coffee at the café. And the rest, as they say, is history."

"How long?"

"Am I under investigation? Don't be nosy." She pats Kiki. "Three weeks."

"You weren't with him the night of the murder?"

"No!" She sounds shocked.

"Trixie, I'm happy for you. You're right. The circumstances could be complicated, but not from what you've said. While we're on the subject, were either of you out front on Saturday? Did you see any of the comings and goings at the hall?"

"We were busy, Aunt Stella. Mom kept Mia out on the deck while I handled customers. She and Mia were in the kitchen to prepare supper later. We don't often sit near the street, not with such a nice back yard."

"Cavelle worked Saturday afternoon." Trixie's thoughtful. "Grey Cottage Realty is on Birch Street, and if anybody walked by the office, Cavelle would have seen them."

"Thanks. I'll call her next week. Maybe the three of us can meet for lunch."

By eight-thirty, everyone has left. Stella finds a sweater for protection from the fall chill.

"Turned out pretty fair." Nick wraps an arm around her shoulders while she stacks dishes on the counter. "Let me help. I can wash. You dry."

She leans her body against him and attempts to absorb his energy. She could sleep at the kitchen table. "Works for me. The party was fun. I tried to speak with everyone. I don't think I skipped anybody."

"No harm done if you did. We packed the place. Cloris will fit in fine."

"Yeah. I saw her huddle with Trixie and Mia for a while. I hope Trixie attends again, even after she's sold her shares. She suggested, on her way to the van, how tonight might be her last end-of-the-season potluck."

"I missed Norbert."

"When Trixie called to talk to him, he told her he didn't want to come. She spoke with the nursing assistant on his floor who said they were scheduled to enjoy an ice-cream social. He wanted to stay but wouldn't tell Trixie the reason."

"We can invite him to the house once the park closes—a family affair— the six of us." He wraps his arm around her again, and the soap from his hands bleeds through her shirt.

Don't Be Hasty

"Was the party a success?"

"Yes, and I uncovered possible useful information, but you go first. Has Rosemary improved? When do you expect her back?"

Aiden's groan drifts through the phone line. He sounds tired. Her watch indicates past nine in the evening, and his call is a surprise.

"Mary Jo and Toni will drive her home. Living arrangements are the biggest news. Mary Jo and Rosie are both to move into Toni's house." He pauses. "She's not good."

Stella doesn't interrupt.

"They told me to expect to be on my own for at least six months. Mary Jo plans to rent her duplex."

"Is Rosemary not managed on medication?"

"Not sure. Mary Jo, typically, says the doctors messed with Rosemary's treatment plan. The primary goal is to bring her home."

"And Toni's opinion?" Stella sees Toni as the practical one, whereas Mary Jo, despite her gruff exterior, is the pushover.

"Toni considers Rosemary beyond repair. She maintains she and Mary Jo are obliged to be caretakers because I am, in her words, 'deeply involved' in my job."

"They think you should quit work?"

"Rosemary expected me to retire when we moved back to our original neck of the woods." He clears his throat. "Anyway, enough of my problems. We've been given two weeks by my bosses to figure out what happened to Owen."

She takes a breath. "Okay. Here's what I heard last night. First, Trixie and

131

Brigitte were nowhere near the front of Yellow House. They can't help. Second, Trixie told me Cavelle worked in the real estate office Saturday afternoon. Both Greta and Mayko walked straight past her window if they've been truthful. Cavelle should be able to confirm their information. Plus, Mildred said the story Owen read sounded familiar, but she couldn't recall why."

"An old lady's scattered recollections."

"Well, don't be hasty. She described the sordid piece to Cloris Kincaid and Duke." She stops for a brief clarification. "Cloris is Duke's latest love interest. In any event, Cloris remembered a murder out west which resembles the story, although no girl was involved."

"We need to go through Owen's papers. We're scheduled to meet with his folks again tomorrow. They might recall where he found the idea for that particular piece."

"Will we interview Frances and Edward in the morning?"

"At ten. Granted, the reading was gruesome, but I'm convinced his death relates to his habit of stealing."

"Your theory?"

"He stole from Bryce, Mayko, or Greta. One of them argued with him and in the scuffle, they pushed him, and he fell. The guy was anti-social. He took what he wanted. He may well have plagiarized the work of other writers and helped himself to items right out from under their noses. We've discovered his bad habits. His parents' opinions might help."

By the time she hangs up the phone, Nick has tidied the kitchen. Blackcurrant tea steeps in the brown ceramic pot. She approaches him, admires his grounded steadfastness, and wraps her arms around his waist.

"After a busy day of final check-outs, you didn't need Aiden North to call."

"No, but Rosemary's a mess, the sisters plan to move her in with them, and he seems worn out." She unwinds her hug and drops into a kitchen chair. "The tea smells heavenly. You read my mind."

"When does he expect them home?"

"Soon, I guess. Aiden's sure Owen stole from one of the authors who confronted him. This resulted in an altercation with both accidental and tragic consequences. I'll meet him in Port Ephron at the Ellis-Thomas' house at ten, tomorrow. More conclusive evidence he was pushed might be revealed if we discover missing property."

Nick pours their tea. "I gather you two aren't on the same wavelength."

He never asks questions, which avoids issues she can't discuss. He waits. She appreciates his understanding. "Owen's story is connected. The pieces don't fit together yet, but an incident out west more than a decade ago vaguely resembles his reading. I plan to read every newspaper article I can find in the box forensics collected, to try to discover his inspiration."

"Are you done for the night? Come on. Let's turn on the news and enjoy our tea. Those Irish hunger strikers finally quit."

****

Aiden waits in front of Frances and Edward's bungalow. She pulls into the space behind him. Stella observes Owen's mother at the picture window. Her hair is braided in her signature halo crown. She might have been in the garden if one considers her baggy denim pants and loose shirt.

"Hi, Aiden." She waves her hand without lifting her arm, aware of Frances' watchful eyes.

"Good morning. No telling where this interview leads us, Stella. How much do they know of Owen's thievery? I'll ask if we can snoop for stolen items. His papers are in a box back in the evidence room."

"I want to hear their opinions and observations related to his thefts of other people's ideas; and what they have to say regarding the influence of various newspaper articles." Frances remains at the window. "Let's go inside."

As they approach, Aiden adds, "And the backgrounds of the other authors? Did Owen possess incriminating information?" He leans closer to her ear. "Should be a morning of enlightenment."

"Frances, hello. Sorry for the delay. Aiden waited for me to arrive from Shale Cliffs."

She pushes the aluminum door open. "Welcome to you both. Edward and I are anxious to hear an update on your investigation."

As they shuffle around the corner from the tiny vestibule, they discover Edward swallowed into a vaguely familiar brown corduroy recliner. "Good morning." He rises from the nest of folds to shake their hands.

The chair used to be in the basement, in Owen's room.

They seat themselves on the flowered sofa and Frances delivers coffee cups on a wooden tray.

Aiden clears his throat. "We want to speak with you today regarding the other authors at the retreat and your personal awareness of their backgrounds. Although difficult for you, it's also necessary to discuss Owen's habit of helping himself to items which did not belong to him."

"We're anxious to hear what you might know of Owen's story inspirations," Stella adds.

Edward gasps and meets Frances' eyes. "He said he stopped, Frances." He turns toward Aiden. "Detective, was my son stealing again?"

"There are reports of a few incidents, Mr. Thomas. I understand my forensics team packed his papers, research, and manuscripts for analysis, but Stella and I need to check for items reported stolen by various people while he spent time in Shale Harbour and at Stella's park."

Frances jumps from her chair. "Certainly. His room sits as your staff left it—except for the chair."

"We returned the recliner to the living room and tidied, though. There was a cardboard box at the cabin. We brought it home and left it in his room. Your people didn't seem interested when they were here. I'm not sure what's in it. We didn't touch any of Owen's belongings." Edward pats the arm. "Just the chair. Owen demanded my Christmas present from Frances last year be his to use downstairs."

Imagine your son insisting he be given your gift.

Aiden raises his hand to Frances. "We want to discuss additional topics. Let's drink our coffee and examine your son's space afterward. Our investigation has revealed Owen collected the secrets of others. As his parents, are you able to tell us any details?"

Frances opens her mouth, but Edward cuts her off. "Be honest with them, Frances. They're the police, for God's sake." He turns to Aiden. "Blackmailing the devil, if given an opportunity, was not out of the realm of possibility for Owen. He could be positively gleeful when he discovered a way to play with people's emotions. If he considered you vulnerable, he exploited the fact. We lost many friends, and in the last few years, any matters of consequence were never discussed around him." He shudders. "Owen was my son, but he possessed no moral compass. He hurt people for sport. Remember his fourth-grade teacher, Frances?"

Continuing to sit on the edge of her seat, poised to escort them downstairs, Frances takes a deep breath. "We heard a rumour that Owen's grade four teacher had relations with a grade twelve student. We discussed the possible affair in front of Owen over dinner—a horrible mistake. Owen confronted the woman and said he expected straight As in exchange for his silence. We were mortified. He was ten.”

“We often wondered to each other if Owen possessed a blackmail gene.” Edward crosses his arms. He no longer resembles a father stricken by grief.

Stella decides to start from the top. “Do you have knowledge of any secrets Mayko Doan might be hiding, and if so, was Owen aware?”

They both shake their heads in unison.

“Elsbeth Strauss?”

“The woman is a crank with a dirty mouth, but her personality is no secret,” Frances huffs.

“Greta Walmsley?”

“We don’t know Greta well, do we Edward?”

He murmurs a negative response.

“We invited her because her publisher knows ours.” Frances leans forward. “I’ve wondered if she wrote those two books herself. She’s not smart enough.”

Edward’s frame moves back and forth in a steady rhythm of full body agreement. Aiden continues to take notes.

“Did you mention your thoughts in front of Owen?”

“My dear, I hope not. Did I Edward? Possibly. Oh, no. I’m sure I didn’t.”

“Were the Whittletons discussed?”

“Not by us, but Owen couldn’t wait to tell me about catching Gregory in the broom closet with a young female attendee. I was horrified and determined to talk with Gregory. He should attempt discretion, at least.”

“You’re aware of no other secrets of the Whittletons’ except for the behaviour he tries to conceal from Naomi?”

“He doesn’t hide them. She knows each move Gregory makes. I don’t understand why she stays with him.”

“Then there’s Bryce. He says you’ve known him for years.”

“Yes. Edward and I both honour his request to maintain his cowboy facade in public.”

“Did Owen consider the information a secret he could exploit?”

“Jeez, I’m doubtful. As much as Owen was perverse, a tangle with Bryce Blanken sounds out of character for him.” Edward sniffs. “Only minor gains for Owen because Bryce wouldn’t care. He’s well known and popular. Any rumour started by the likes of Owen would be disbelieved or ignored.”

"Detective North, are you digging for a motive for one of the retreat authors to kill our son?" Frances' voice trembles.

"We search to uncover the whys and wherefores. We may never discover the truth of what happened, but we're working hard to find out."

"Before we go downstairs, Frances, can I ask you about Owen's influences. Do you know where he found the idea for the work-in-progress he presented last Friday at my house?" Stella hopes Owen's parents at least read his work.

"Goodness, me. He never shared his research, but he watched crime fiction like *Kojak* and *Columbo* on the television. He consumed detective stories and newspaper articles about murder." She pats her braid. "I have to be honest. He made me nervous every now and then. That's all I can tell you."

"Thank you, Frances. Shall we examine his room?"

"Follow me." She jumps out of her chair. Edward remains in his.

Their basement has a damp and musty aroma. "Sorry for the smell. Owen used a small heater in the fall before Edward started the furnace. I never turn the contraption on...don't want to leave an appliance unattended." She reaches inside the door and flicks the switch. White, fluorescent light fills the space. "We'll be upstairs if you need us." She turns on her heel and mounts the steps.

Frances never glanced in the actual direction of the room.

The single mattress now sits on a frame and the bed is made, covered in a hockey quilt with each of the NHL teams listed. The bookshelf is organized. Stella pulls forward a cardboard box tucked away beside the bookcase. When she opens the flaps, she calls Aiden, who has been busy with dresser drawers. "I found his stash."

Packed inside, she discovers the heart-shaped rock, two metal toy cars small boys play with in the sand, a Beatles T-shirt, a journal full of poetry with the name Connie in the front and dated 1978, and a host of other souvenirs of his thievery.

Aiden rifles through the contents. "I'll take this back to the station. I hope we find a connection."

"Or maybe we've found a collection of random personal property Owen stole to presume himself powerful."

As they climb the basement stairs, Aiden carries the box and Stella decides to ask Frances and Edward an opinion question. "Your son took people's possessions. Did he want to hold power over them or was the behaviour a compulsion he couldn't control?"

136

"Neither," Edward replied. "He stole because he could. Stealing was fun for him."

****

"Cloris should be here anytime. We're takin' her truck to go back to Port Ephron RV to load her barbecue and outdoor furniture." He sips coffee and feeds bites of toast to Kiki, whose waistline shows his indulgence.

"Kiki looks as if she's puffy, Duke. Two pounds amounts to one-quarter of her body weight. Be careful."

Duke regards his little dog with a frown. "Are you gettin' portly, honey? You need to spend more time runnin' around in Stella's big house."

"Can't babysit today, my friend. Want to try to organize a lunch with Trixie and Cavelle, and I'm off to the Painter farm with Aiden afterward."

"Okay. No harm done. She can stay at my trailer. Cloris is not too keen on havin' Kiki in the truck. Says she makes the cab smell doggy. And my old '68 Beetle ain't gonna carry a barbecue."

"Knock, knock."

Nick, already in reception because two seasonals will leave in a matter of minutes, dashes for the veranda door. "On my way."

"Good morning, everyone."

Stella peeks out from the kitchen and lifts the coffee pot in Cloris' general direction.

"I'm pleased to tell you I availed myself of breakfast before I drove over here," she says, as she shakes her head. "John and I decided to move my outdoor paraphernalia before I haul my rig out of Port Ephron RV Park. The temporary site you've provided will be perfect for the winter—sheltered near the house and out of the way of your contractors. Once I pull it over, we'll load my extra gear inside."

"Works for me, Cloris. I wrote the contract yesterday. Let's go through the details while you're here and you can settle in when it's convenient."

"Shall I pay you now for next season?"

"No need," Nick adds, while he pours another coffee. "Fees are due in May, right Stella?"

She nods agreement. "A good faith deposit is sufficient, Cloris. We don't stand on too much formality around here."

"These guys are way nicer than the folks at Port Ephron, eh Cloris?" Duke continues to munch and ignores Kiki, who stamps her little feet. "They want your seasonal money at the end of the old year, not the start of the new—and they charge storage if you leave your rig for the winter. What a rip-off," he mutters, mouth full.

Cloris is indulgent. She directs her attention toward Stella. "John is protective. Shall we do our paperwork and then John and I will let you get on with your day?"

Nick sits at the table with Duke while Stella and Cloris make their way to reception. "Here you go. Straightforward. I'm not fond of complicated legal documents."

Duke's new flame digs for her cheque book and perches on the bench near the window to review the seasonal conditions. "I appreciate the permanent lot you've assigned for me in the spring, Stella. The spot has a passable view and isn't too close to John."

"You asked for a site on the other side of the park, and I tried to accommodate, Cloris."

"What I wanted." She signs the document with a flourish and completes her payment. "If John and I don't work out, I need to be able to come here and not run into him every five minutes."

"Not to change the subject, but did you happen to give more thought to the story our victim wrote?"

"I admit, Mildred's words bothered me. The tale rings true, although she mentioned ghoulish details related to the young daughter of the family. In the news item I remember, the boyfriend never implicated a girl, and he went to jail for the crime." She glances from her purse where she's stowed her cheque book. "I guess the writer's prerogative is to take an existing circumstance and change the particulars to suit their imagination. I must say, Mildred was incensed by the reading, and she doesn't strike me as a woman put off by much."

After they leave, Nick and Stella tidy the kitchen before they begin their daily duties. Stella plans to manage the office for the morning while Nick checks pumps and completes maintenance on one of the mowers. She wants to call Cavelle to see if she'll take a break for lunch. Since the tourist season has slowed, she hopes Trixie can join them. And she must confirm with Hester. She and Jewel are no doubt busy with preserves. A confirmation will be required.

****

"Meet you at the café? Business or pleasure?"

"Both," Stella answers Cavelle's upbeat voice in her ear. "I want to ask you what you observed on the sidewalk while you manned the office a week ago Saturday. Trixie told me you worked in the afternoon. Besides, I haven't seen you since the day the retreat began."

"Will Trixie be there, too?"

"If I can talk her into coming."

"Perfect. We speak on the phone, but she's been unavailable most days because of babysitting Mia."

"Right. Significant effort was required on my part to convince her to come to the year-end potluck, but I'll try today. The tourists are mostly gone. She should be able to break away for a bite to eat. By the way, are Hester and Jewel busy with canning?"

"Oh yes," she grumbles. "Be aware. The place smells like pickles. They said you might be over this afternoon. Make a list of what you want. Besides the time Hester set aside for the writers retreat, she and Jewel have run an assembly line in the kitchen."

"See you at noon, Cavelle."

On to the next call.

"Jewel, Stella here. Does Hester still expect Detective North and myself today?"

"Yes, she does. And I don't mind sayin', I'll be happy to get the dining room back. Bottles are piled on every counter and table, and folks comin' to the door in a steady stream to buy jam and pickles, not to mention herbs—Hester's department."

Stella remains silent. *Is Jewel becoming chatty?*

She continues. "When the men come in for lunch, I give them their food and send them off to the front porch because Hester has a map laid out on the big table and no place for them to sit." She pauses for a breath. "When will you be here?"

"We decided on two o'clock, if the time works for you, Jewel."

"Great. Don't mind me. I'll tell Hester you called. Can I put anythin' aside for you?"

"Yes—a dozen bottles of jam, six strawberry and six raspberry, and four jars of bread and butter pickles. They're Nick's favourite. Did Hester create those variety packs of herbs she does every fall?"

"She did and tells me they sell out."

"Okay, three of those as well. Thanks Jewel. We'll be there at two."

❀

Chapter 15

Her Involvement is Off-putting

"You and Valentin Reguly?" Stella hears Cavelle tease Trixie as she approaches the bistro table at the rear of Cocoa and Café. Persuasion was in order but, with Brigitte's help, she convinced her sister a lunch with Cavelle would do her good. The scene she faces proves her theory. The younger women, with heads together and elbows on the tiny glass top, are deep into their conversation.

"Make room for me." She slides into the third chair.

"Trixie is giving me all her new flame details."

"The two of you have no mercy." Trixie fluffs her curls and pats her shimmery blouse with the open neckline. "Val and I have been out a few times." She titters. "Funny, though. Brigitte and I need to trade off evenings because one of us stays with Mia." She leans forward and whispers, "My beautiful daughter and Carter Stephens are rather serious."

Cavelle's shoulders heave. "You and she are quite the pair." She taps Stella on the wrist. "Your life is wrapped in a big bow, too." She makes her bright red lips pout. "I, on the flip side, spend my nights in the company of family... you both know how much fun my siblings can be."

Although Cavelle's chatter is light-hearted, Stella senses the realtor yearns to meet someone. As a result, she avoids any remarks related to Nick, even in jest. No need to flaunt one's happiness. "What's the special today, Tiffany?" she asks the co-owner, busy checking receipts behind the counter. As is usual for October, the café is almost empty. Her staff, and Stella's, returned to school weeks ago. Andrew and Tiffany Blair will manage their restaurant themselves until university year ends next May.

"Corn chowder and ham croissants with Swiss cheese. Sound good?"

They nod in unison.

"Specials for everyone, and I'll grab the coffee pot. Stella, tea instead?"

"The coffee's fine, Tiffany."

Once they're settled, with their orders placed, Stella decides she might as well ask her questions. "Cavelle, Trixie told me you covered the office on the Saturday afternoon when we assume Owen died. Did you notice any authors in your vicinity?"

"Lunchtime inquisition?" She pats Stella's hand and smiles. "To answer your question, not until later in the day. The woman who writes the self-help books, Greta Walmsley, wandered past around ten to five. I thought she might be on her way in to discuss a retreat issue with Farley, but she examined the flower beds near the sidewalk and meandered along. The author with the little white pup...."

"Mayko Doan," Stella contributes.

"Yes, Mayko. I didn't remember her name. She's the writer Hester admires. Anyway, she wandered past the front window a few minutes later. She murmured to her dog and stopped to let the creature sniff. They dawdled."

"Notice any unusual behaviour?"

"No, except one might expect two authors from the same event to walk along together, but Mayko maintained a respectful distance for whatever her reasons. I don't recall anyone else, Stella. I worked a long day, happy to make my way out to the farm at five."

"And Farley?"

"I covered on the Saturday of the workshops because of his involvement with the retreat. Once the afternoon classes were over, he left the hall and returned to the office. He stayed on after I left."

Their food arrives and for a few quiet moments they enjoy Tiffany's offerings.

"You and Aiden North are scheduled to be out at the farm after we're finished here, right?" Cavelle asks between mouthfuls.

"Yes. When I called to confirm, Jewel sounded stressed and wants Hester to move her map from the dining room table."

"I've learned Jewel does not survive well when disrupted. She's an excellent organizer, an advantage since she runs both her house and ours. Hester's chaos is organized in Hester's mind alone, which becomes her challenge. You'll understand later today. I believe she has everyone and every vehicle she scrutinized last Saturday laid out on her brown paper map of Shale Harbour. She made little paper clocks. The hands move. She adjusted them as she developed the scene." She dabs her lips with a napkin. Both the napkin and her coffee cup are streaked with candy-apple red. She glances at her gold bracelet watch. "Gotta go, girls. Hope I helped, Stella. Bye."

"Trixie, before you leave, let's plan a supper out at the house with you and Valentin."

Her frown is unexpected. "Might be too soon. I don't want to spook him with family."

"He's met Brigitte and Mia. I assume he's run into Carter on occasion. Nick and I both know the guy." Mildly affronted, she asks, "What's the problem?"

"Give us more time. Once your investigation winds down and you aren't preoccupied with murders, we can work out a supper together—maybe at the Purple Tulip—neutral ground."

Suspicion clouds her response. "Truth, Trixie."

"Right now, he considers you an investigator. You were with Aiden when he was questioned. He doesn't trust cops." She stands and straightens her skirt. "Give me more time," she repeats when she leans over closer to Stella's ear. "He's still skittish in the basement of the hall. He sees Owen in a heap at the bottom of the stairs. I don't blame him. You're the person used to dead bodies; not the rest of us."

As she pays her bill and flounces out the door and across the street to Yellow House, Stella continues to sit. Throughout her work on three previous cases with Aiden—three successfully resolved cases, she hastens to add to herself—no one closest to her ever suggested her involvement was off-putting.

****

Hester sits in the sun porch. Stella senses she's there, although she can't see her. Aiden pulls in beside the Jeep. The profile of the Painter farm has changed with the tidy bungalow settled into a permanent spot next door. Sheets billow on the line in the back, and a sign, nailed to the gate, informs customers to ring the bell for service.

"Are you ready? Jewel and Cavelle say she has her detailed map laid out on the dining room table for us."

Before Aiden responds, Hester materializes on the front step. "I'm happy you are here. I waited patiently, although Jewel will tell you I am bereft of patience."

"We're right on time and excited to have a gander at what you've put together."

"Good afternoon, Hester. Nice to see you."

"You, too, Detective North." Her withered manner strays toward the irritated. "I am prepared to assist with your investigations once again. You need a larger staff, Detective."

Aiden acquiesces. "I happen to enjoy my work with the two of you. You contributed to the resolution of Paulina McAdams' death. This time, you're a pivotal witness in Owen's case. Your observations are critical."

His compliments are ignored. The gloom of the primary hallway assaults them before they traipse through the formal living room into the dining room at the back.

The table has been enlarged with two leaves while six chairs are pushed against the walls. A roll of brown paper has been unfurled and laid from one end to the other, held from curling by various knick-knacks, which are housed in the enormous china cabinet under normal circumstances. Stella peers at the map of Shale Harbour while she drags off her jacket and drops the garment, along with her purse and keys, on a chair near the bow window.

Hester stands at the far side of the table, arms crossed over the blue cardigan she has matched with a green plaid skirt. The combination jars but mysteriously works. Hester might be ignoring Jewel's suggestions of late. Stella knows she balks when her independence seems threatened.

Aiden steps closer. He hasn't removed his coat.

"Shall I explain? You may find my map complicated and therefore require an explanation." Hester doesn't move.

"A tour sounds fabulous. You even drew little clocks by each person and vehicle." Stella glances toward Aiden. Hester's display incorporates their various interviews.

Without pulling his eyes away from the table, Aiden nods.

"As you can note, my map comprises the six primary streets in Shale Harbour. The large cross in the centre represents Main Street intersected by Birch. Maple is parallel to Main to the west and Chestnut is parallel to Main in the east. The border streets are the highway and ocean to the south and Elm to the north. The result becomes a black cross with a black frame to represent the six principal streets." She pauses for breath.

"Go on, Hester." Aiden's eyes remain fixated on the map.

"I will start again after we offer refreshments."

Jewel has appeared at the door which leads to the kitchen. "Tea or coffee, Stella? Detective North?"

"Tea sounds lovely, Jewel." Stella knows the young woman is stressed as she waits for the house to resume some semblance of normalcy.

"Tea for me as well, Mrs. Winslow. Describe the clocks, Hester."

"Okay. Let me simplify first. The bank sits here on the north side of the highway. The building faces the dock and the water. Mrs. Carlyle's weaving shop is on Main." She points to the house with a small stick. "As we travel north from the weaver's, I drew Cocoa and Café and Parlour Antiques before we reach Birch. On the corner, across Birch, I've marked the community hall. You continue north on Main to where the street meets Elm and I've drawn the hotel, which sits on the opposite side of the street and faces west." She uses her pointer to touch each structure. "As we traverse back along Main, in the south, or opposite direction now, we cross Birch again, and Yellow House is the first spot I've drawn on your left, across from Parlour Antiques." She taps the map again. "If you recall, we relished the sun on Paulina's wide, eastern-exposed deck. Grey Cottage Realty is halfway along Birch, as we travel west to Maple." She flips greasy hair over her shoulders. "Does my presentation make sense? If you are oriented to the map, we can proceed."

Hester has taken on the persona of a fractious professor.

"I'm with you now." Aiden removes his coat and takes a sip of the tea placed on a side table by Jewel. "You've created a bird's-eye view of downtown."

"Precisely. Now for times. I added two clocks at the café. The first shows three fifty-five, when I entered the restaurant to wait for Owen. The second depicts six o'clock when Jacob came for me. The other clocks indicate the times I surveyed various vehicles and authors. One clock, with Owen's name printed across the top, says four and is at the hall, where we assume he waited for me." Her eyes reveal the sadness brought about by the presumed misunderstanding of where they would meet. "After I sat in the café, Mr. Reguly's old red truck pulled out of Birch Street, crossed Main and continued along Birch toward Chestnut. The clock says four-oh-seven." She moves the little truck along the streets mentioned and removes the toy from the table. "The Whittletons drove away. The clock for them says four-fifteen." She reaches over to retrieve the green plastic truck and the clock.

Stella glances at Aiden, who remains intent on Hester's lecture. The information matches what Hester described earlier. Her report corroborates much of the individual evidence they've collected.

Their primary witness continues. "If there are no questions, I'll keep on. Elsbeth Strauss and Owen's parents left the hall when I did. His parents drove away, and Miss Strauss rushed off to the hotel. No need to add clocks for them, but Miss Strauss has been assigned one later. Mayko walked her dog around town. I witnessed her three times. She strolled Birch Street, I presume along Maple, and she reappeared on Elm across from the hotel. I'll return to her in a moment."

Aiden and Stella make eye contact but remain silent.

"This clock says four-forty-five, when Greta Walmsley...." She stops and squints at Stella. "I don't think she wrote those books, by the way. When Greta Walmsley left the hall. A minute or two later, Mayko turned on to Birch." She pauses again. "I have no personal knowledge whether the two met at any time. Greta emerged on Elm and entered the hotel at five-ten. Mayko appeared once again one or two minutes later and walked back south on Main."

"Does this represent Bryce Blanken's truck?" Stella touches a blue plastic Volkswagen.

"Please attempt to use your imagination. Mr. Blanken arrived and parked near Yellow House at four-fifty. He ran into the hall and back out right away. He proceeded to Parlour Antiques. He came out with a parcel, climbed in his truck, and moved closer to the hotel. He struggled to park in such a small space. The clock said five-fifteen." She lifts her eyes from the map. "I'm curious why people will consume five minutes to wedge an oversized pickup into an inappropriate spot when they can use a side street. Shale Harbour isn't large." Her long hair moves from side to side, as she scrapes strands behind her ears again. "Mr. Blanken and Greta left the hotel and drove south past the café and toward the highway at five-thirty." She gathers the clocks assigned to Bryce, Greta, and Mayko.

"You missed Elsbeth, Hester."

"She's not important. She never returned to the hall after she left. She visited the antique shop at the same time as Mr. Blanken and came out before him. I think she shopped at Mrs. Carlyle's because when she strutted past the café, she carried a bag with Mrs. Carlyle's logo."

"Your map has been helpful, Hester. You aren't aware, but the information matches most of the other tidbits we've collected from interviews. Will you share your insights if you developed any?"

"I certainly developed insights, Stella."

She borders on huffy and Stella worries she offended her friend.

"We're interested," Aiden adds. "You invested many hours immersed in your project and the result illustrates your efforts."

Hester outwardly ignores a compliment for the second time. "Mayko Doan is not a violent person. Greta Walmsley was the last one in the hall, except when Mr. Blanken ran inside. I'm not sure he had adequate time to argue with Owen and push him if you believe the scenario to be correct. I found him indifferent to Owen. I think he searched for Greta Walmsley. I bet he yelled for her from the foyer, although I didn't hear. Also, if Greta had turned toward Main instead of Birch when she left, she would have seen Mr. Blanken park his truck." She pauses, which creates a dramatic effect. "Or she did see him and skirted the other way to avoid him."

"Are you suspicious of Greta?"

"Yes. As the only person with real opportunity, the problem becomes motive. One scenario suggests Owen simply tumbled down the stairs with nobody to help him." She tilts her chin forward. "Or he fell, and Greta Walmsley denied him assistance."

Her comment hangs in the air between them.

"I'll fold the map for you after I tape the clocks back in place. I regret you cannot take the cars."

****

"I want to speak with Greta Walmsley's publisher." Stella sips her coffee and watches Nick cut bread for toast.

"If Aiden can't uncover information, why do you expect her publisher— what's their name—to shed light?"

"Sailboat Publishing in Halifax. The actual contact person is Victoria Barlow. I called the office earlier and asked. I left my number but told the receptionist I'd call back later."

"Seriously, Stella. If Greta was placed into foster care at thirteen as she claims, I'm doubtful her publisher has any knowledge of the details."

"Thanks." She reaches for the plate of toast before she continues to peel her orange. "No harm in asking the questions."

"What does Aiden say?"

"Much the same as you—a dead end. Greta Walmsley isn't who she appears to be."

"None of the authors are."

"Greta's the only individual we're certain was in the hall for at least a half-hour while Owen remained. If someone else was present, she had every opportunity in the world to report them...although she tried to implicate the Whittletons at first. Hester put a halt to her theory. They left one right after the other by four-fifteen." She gazes out the kitchen window at the sunny but cool morning. "Not to take a drastic change in subject, but have you planned for today, since I'm around for once to cover reception and check-outs?"

"I'll start my day with a tour—inspect the vacated lots." He reaches across the table to pat her hand. "You know the drill."

She squeezes his fingers. "You'll be my full-fledged business partner in another couple of months. Might as well begin with rounds, although where's Duke?"

"He told me he'd be late." Nick wiggles his eyebrows at her. "I ran out to open the gate when you were in the shower. I think he's happy, Stella."

"Agreed, but Kiki is a different story. Poor pooch isn't enamoured with Cloris. You do your inspections." She glances at the clock on the kitchen wall "Off to the office. I'll call Halifax at nine."

****

"Sailboat Publishing. How may I help you?"

"May I please speak to Victoria Barlow? My name is Stella Kirk."

"And your call is in reference to...?"

"You may tell her I consult with the police and want to discuss the author, Miss Greta Walmsley."

"One moment, please. I'll check if she's in and available."

"Good morning. Victoria Barlow here. How may I help you?"

"Miss Barlow. Thank you for your time. My colleague, Detective Aiden North, and myself are investigating a suspicious death which occurred September 27 in Shale Harbour. The incident happened during the Shale Harbour Writers Retreat, and Greta Walmsley attended as a presenter and workshop leader."

"Yes, I'm aware."

"There's little historical information on Greta, and we hoped you might be able to fill in the blanks."

"Did you ask her?"

"Greta claims she was dumped into the foster care system at the age of thirteen. She revealed her parents were both killed in a car crash, and she says she has no real recollection of her life before the tragedy happened. We thought you could add perspective."

"Well, you're wrong." The tone of Victoria's voice has travelled from formal to haughty in a matter of seconds. "I edit and publish Greta Walmsley's work. We aren't close."

She makes her next question sound more like a statement. "You write the books for her."

"Miss Kirk, correct? No need to take such an aggressive attitude with me. I think our conversation is finished. I wish you goodbye."

The receiver thuds in her ear. Miss Barlow became upset with little provocation, and Stella frowns. The woman didn't query the investigation or even repeat Greta's story.

Before she invades reception to review the final check-outs and make sure each of her guests will be gone by Thanksgiving Monday at the latest, she places a quick call to Aiden. "Want to come out to the park for lunch on Saturday? We're busy since the stragglers leave this weekend. I can't take off unless there's an emergency."

"My unit needs to be winterized and Saturday works as well as Sunday."

"I talked to Victoria Barlow of Sailboat Publishing."

"No luck, I bet."

"Aren't you smart? She didn't shed any light on Greta's story. She sounded miffed to be asked, though, and now I'm curious. We might benefit from a short road trip to interview her in person."

❧

CHAPTER 16

Stella Has Her Doubts

Unsettled—the best way to describe her current state of mind. Stella watches Aiden's Citation cruise past the office toward his trailer. He's in the park to blow out the lines and pour anti-freeze into the drains to prepare his unit for winter. She expects her lingering seasonals to check out over the next three days, with most gone by tomorrow. Nick is busy with the schedule to determine who needs his services to winterize—jobs he performs each fall for anyone who doesn't have the knowledge or tools to complete the necessary tasks by themselves. He collects and tags keys and will spend most of what remains of October focused on the care of trailers or motorhomes left behind. In the spring, the process reverses, and he readies the units for occupation.

Ted Metcalfe parks his 1960 Oldsmobile 88 and hops into the office. He's spry for his eighty plus years. "Here's my keys for Nick. Lily and me are ready to end another season, Stella."

"Thanks, Ted. You two enjoyed the summer?"

"Couldn't ask for better." He turns to catch a glimpse of the white-haired woman who sits in the passenger bucket seat of the Olds and stares straight ahead. "We're on the right side of the grass," he grins.

Stella accepts his keys and deposit cheque for 1982.

"I added extra money to pay Nick. Easier to let the young fella do the grunt work, if ya git my drift?"

"You and lots of others, Ted. Your job is to enjoy your unit. Until next year."

"But you'll call me if you discover a problem?"

He asks the same question each fall. "Nick and I walk the park every day. Never fear. We'll get in touch if necessary."

151

"Okay, I'm off." He tips his felt fedora and skips the two steps to the driveway.

Buddy McGarvey and Bell arrive soon after. She hoped to make a pot of coffee but didn't find her way to the kitchen. "Prepared for the winter, Stella. Been a great season."

"You and Bell settled into your fancy digs, I gather."

"Yup. Hate to go home to the duplex, but summer's over." He drops his deposit, in cash, on the counter, lifts a finger to his ball cap, and turns to leave. The elderly bulldog waddles behind.

A steady stream of seasonals drop in. She exchanges pleasantries and wishes everyone a happy winter.

Despite the distractions, her mind returns to the case at hand. She prepares lunch and ponders. If Owen fell, they've wasted two weeks delving into an accident. What does she need to do to push through their impasse? Specific issues niggle her brain. Greta Walmsley's publisher is less than cooperative, and what kinds of information might be uncovered from Owen's research? Egg salad sandwiches, coleslaw, and lemonade are the offerings today. Chocolate chip cookies, made by Alice and Paul's mom, hidden at the bottom of the freezer, round out her preparations. When Aiden arrives, she plans to ask him if she can have the box of materials still languishing with the forensics department.

Duke appears first on the veranda. He and Kiki are decked out in creamy fisherman knit sweaters. Stella wonders if both fit more snugly than last year. "Cloris told me to tell you she'll move her rig over on Monday. I said her timing's good because, as far as I can figure, everyone will be out except Mildred, and the old lady knows I'll help early Monday afternoon." He ogles the cookies. "Did you make 'em?"

Stella steps aside as he sashays across the kitchen straight toward the green glass plate. He takes two, sits at the head of her table, and munches while he shares tiny morsels with Kiki, who begs at his feet. "Tell Cloris her schedule is fine. You'll help her, or should Nick be available?"

"She don't need nobody to park for her or nuthin'. She drives better than most. I'll be here after I take Mildred. No problem."

"Anybody home?" Aiden stands in reception.

"Come on through to the kitchen."

"Walked from my lot. Close to done. How are you folks?" He glances at

Duke before his eyes rest on Stella.

"Kiki and me, we're fine. Hate to say goodbye to the old place for the winter."

Stella counters Aiden's question with one of her own. "Not long before Rosemary's home, eh?"

"Yeah. Nine days." His appearance betrays him.

She has little time to address his obvious anxiety before Nick materializes. "I'll run upstairs to wash my mitts. Be right back." He eyes the stack of sandwiches in the centre of the table. "My favourite."

The four of them settle for their lunch. "Need any help with your rig, Aiden?"

"You taught me well, Nick. No need. Left my deposit cheque on the counter."

"We're happy you decided not to sell. I'm sure, by next summer, life will be back to normal for Rosemary." Despite what she says, Stella has her doubts.

"How's the missus doin', anyway?"

Aiden turns to Duke. "Sadly, not good. I expect her sisters to arrive in Port Ephron with her October 19. They plan to live at Toni's for now. Mary Jo has rented her house out." His shoulders stoop. "I can't predict how long their arrangement holds. Nothing will change unless she improves, or I retire."

"We'll do whatever we can, right Stella?"

Despite occasional negative experiences with Rosemary in the past, Nick remains supportive in any way possible—one of the many reasons she loves him.

"Anything you need, Aiden."

In between bites of another cookie, Duke adds, "My Cloris helps people with mental problems, Aiden. She sits with folks when family go to town to do errands and stuff. She took care of a woman's mother who had dementia. I'll talk to her."

Aiden lifts his brows. "Possibly, after we square Owen's case away, Rosemary can come home, with Cloris to stay with her when I'm at work." He frowns. "If we ever figure out what happened."

"Let's have a visit in my office after lunch. I have thoughts I want to run past you." She adds, "Might mean an errand this weekend."

"Now I'm curious."

****

His trips aren't necessary this late in the season, but Duke and Kiki wander off to ride the golf cart around the park, nevertheless. Nick and Stella walk the property regularly, but the assistance helps because the days are shorter, and he'll scope out any damages, loose garbage, or any fire pits in disarray. She appreciates his efforts. Nick leaves to mow because the weather's good. She doesn't anticipate many more times when 'cut the grass' is on his list.

"Before we discuss business, have you met Duke's new lady-friend?"

"Yes. She's nice; seven years Duke's senior. Comes across as capable. Drives her own truck and pulls the trailer."

"I could hire Cloris as a help for Mary Jo and Toni after we wrap the case. Then Rosemary can move home."

The statement sounds thoughtful, not conversational. "No doubt you'll need help, Aiden. There'll be another case around the corner."

"I'll check with Duke and meet her." He shifts gears. "Okay, on to Owen."

"His box of research and writings—did forensics notice any documentation related to our suspects?"

"No. A waste of time, in my opinion."

"May I dig through them?"

"You want me to go home to Port Ephron, retrieve Owen's belongings from evidence, and leave the carton at the Shale Harbour detachment for you to collect?"

She attempts contrition. "If not too much trouble."

"Sure, but you won't find answers."

"I think we've narrowed a huge suspect pool to three contenders."

"Talk to me."

"Here's my hypothesis—let's say we discover a newspaper clipping in the box which relates to Bryce, Mayko, or Greta—a plagiarized story he's written where he used the work of one of them. I'm convinced there's a clue or a trigger missing."

"Again, for any of your theory to make sense, someone possessed what they believed to be good reason to give Owen a shove—not necessarily with intent to kill the guy, but the consequences are undeniable. I gather you've ruled out every attendee at the retreat, the other authors, and anybody he maligned or from whom he stole?"

She ignores the possibility of a dozen or more suspects. "Listen...Owen collected secrets. Mayko and Bryce both have those. I'm convinced Greta's editor-publisher, Victoria Barlow, knows more. Owen may have discovered Greta's books are ghost written."

The bell above the door to reception jangles.

"Shouldn't be a minute." She rushes off to find Rob and Sally Black filling her front office. "Hi, you two. Still plan to leave tomorrow?"

Rob is draped in the palm fronds of his favourite Hawaiian shirt despite the recent dip in temperatures. Stella has never laid eyes on the man in long pants. He holds a cheque aloft for her to grab. "Here's your deposit. We're off by nine in the morning. Decided we'd take a walk and say goodbye today." He hands her the money.

"Thanks, you two. Good summer, eh?"

"Yup. We dropped over to Detective North's. His car is parked at the trailer, but there's no sign of him. I hear Rosemary hasn't been well."

"No, she's with her sisters for now. Aiden came out to winterize his rig and popped in for lunch."

"Ah." Rob's leer-soaked wink assaults her like a bad smell. "Nick's out on a mower." No one inserts a sexual innuendo into every conversation like Rob Black.

Sally pats his hand. "We won't keep you, Stella. I imagine you have lots of meetings, what with investigating that horrible boy's death." Her eyes remain focused on Stella. "He was a thief...and rude."

Keeping her own counsel, she refrains from a direct response to Sally's remark. "We're set. Thanks for the deposit. Have a safe trip home."

Once the screen door clicks shut, she returns to her office. "I don't expect anybody else today." She puffs her annoyance. "Rob Black is such a sleaze-bag."

"Give me your honest impression." Aiden guffaws. "What's the lecher done now?"

"He insinuated you and I were here alone, up to no good while Nick cuts the grass."

"Everybody but poor Nick assumes there's a spark between us."

She lets the sentence sit for seconds, considers a retort, and pushes on. "When can I have the box?"

"Monday's a holiday, but I'll make sure to leave word at the front desk, okay?"

"Perfect. Gives me the day to weed through the contents. Should we try to contact Greta's publisher again?"

"If you insist. Come into town on Tuesday, return the evidence, and we'll call Victoria Barlow together." Aiden doesn't sound enthusiastic. "Maybe if the police, meaning me, talk to her, she'll be more cooperative."

"Great. I might even buy you coffee." She pauses to gather her thoughts. "I understand we can't drag the investigation out much longer, but I hate the idea of 'death by misadventure' written on the certificate if there's more to what happened."

"Agreed. I'll make requests to both the Fredericton and Québec City police investigative divisions later today and ask them to re-interview Mayko Doan and Bryce Blanken. We'll confirm their movements, but I want to find out additional details related to their secrets and focus on what they believe Owen discovered. I'll schedule an appointment with Greta Walmsley to meet her in Halifax."

"We could speak to both Victoria and Greta on the same road trip."

"Yes, Stella, but if we don't uncover any other leads, the next step will be to stand down. Tell me, honest assessment, was he pushed?"

Stella stops for a moment to organize her thoughts. "Owen was not a nice young man. Sally used the word horrible a minute ago. He used information he gathered to his advantage, or even against individuals for sport. Hester made herself crystal clear. Mayko, Bryce, and Greta were the three people, out of the attendees and authors, with obvious access to the hall and Owen after four o'clock. Whatever happened, one of them knows the truth."

"I've wondered if his fall was an accident; if Greta was still in the building and she stepped over him as she left. She walked along Birch to Maple to avoid attracting attention, because she feared Bryce might already be back to town from the park."

"Why didn't she call for help? A phone sits on the desk in an open office."

"Correct, but I've uncovered examples of nasty people in my day, Stella— many who would never risk their own hides to assist another soul. They don't want to be involved."

She drums her fingers on her blotter. "Better to find out someone pushed the guy, than consider he fell and Greta, or anybody, stepped over him, climbed the stairs, and went on their merry way." She meets his gaze. "Doesn't speak well of human nature."

"One more topic to discuss before I go back to finish my trailer—the interviews the detectives did with the merchants on Main Street. We heard corroborative feedback." He digs in his pants pocket and retrieves a list scribbled on a piece of paper torn out of a coiled notebook. "I copied a few notes to share with you. Curious?"

"Enlighten me." Stella places both elbows on her desk and her chin in her hands.

"First, he spent an inordinate number of hours in the café, to the point where Tiffany told him to purchase more than one coffee in a two-hour period or go sit someplace else. She reported he sat at the window and took notes as folks walked along the street or visited the shops."

"Sounds like Hester, although she never has to document her observations."

"Owen searched for people in compromising situations, whereas Hester reports whatever she's seen when asked. Big difference."

"Go on."

"Each merchant noted how he wandered Main Street repeatedly. Mercedes Savioli said his posture and attitude resembled an inspector. Pepper Ferguson, and her boss, Eugenie Charlebois, told investigators Owen quickly became a nuisance."

"In what way?" His behaviour is no surprise, but the details may prove significant.

"He often turned up at the hotel and sat in an Adirondack chair on the veranda. He made comments, unwanted from the reports collected earlier from attendees, and was asked to leave on two occasions. He used foul language in response."

"And the other shopkeepers?"

"Every business said he entered their establishment at one point or another. From their accounts, significant shoplifting occurs during the high season— apparently the cost of the tourism trade. Everyone mentioned consumer traffic has started to slow, there were fewer customers inside their shops, and they were sure Owen pilfered stock. The articles he stole are in the carton his parents lugged back from the park and you found in his room. They'll be returned to their owners once we've put the investigation to rest." He stands. "Now, a walk back to the trailer to load my car. Thanks for lunch."

"Don't forget the box."

He glares at the ceiling. "Stella, I won't forget."

"I'm happy Hester didn't have an opportunity to become friends with Owen."

"Hester would have been hurt."

"Yes." She sees him out and returns to the kitchen. She soaps the dishes and imagines the type of individual able to come upon a person collapsed at the foot of the stairs, and step over them while ignoring the victim's condition. Warm arms, with the faint smell of motor oil, wrap around her waist.

"Duke?" She giggles, unable to deliver the joke.

"Hi." His soft voice purrs against her neck. "Aiden finally take off?"

"Yes. He wants to finish. And you?"

"Lawns are done. I might close Ted Metcalfe's trailer before the day's over. What's the story on Mildred?"

"She won't go until Monday. Duke plans to move her home. I'll want to have a talk with her before she leaves, too."

"You're preoccupied."

"I am. Aiden theorized Owen fell in the community hall while Greta lingered in her classroom. She walked out, stepped over him, and left. He expects she wandered from Birch to Maple, to avoid a chance meeting with any other authors or attendees, especially Bryce, if he happened to return to town early." She wipes her hands and turns to face him. "Could such behaviour even be possible?"

"People are strange. Aiden's supposition has merit. Death by misadventure and victim ignored by a nearby individual who refused to help."

"Murder through neglect. Let's have tea out on the veranda before you winterize Ted's trailer. I'll put a sign on reception to say they can come around to the back."

"Did you ask Aiden if you're able to dig through the box?"

"Yup. He'll deliver it to the station tomorrow for me to pick up Monday."

"Which means we have Sunday to ourselves," his voice rumbles.

"Well, except for the check-outs, yes." She sounds pragmatic, but she didn't miss his intent.

"I'll cook us a chicken."

When the phone jangles during their quiet time on the veranda, Nick runs the considerable distance from the back door to answer. She can hear bursts of surprise, laughter, and murmurs of agreement. Ten minutes later, he returns to his spot.

"Company for dinner tomorrow. I guess my chicken idea will work."

She attempts casual curiosity. "And our guest is...."

"An old high school buddy—Wilson Shobbrook. My parents told Wilson about Shale Harbour."

"Does he want to stay at the cottage? We could vacuum and dust; use extra linens from the house."

"*She* booked into the Harbour Hotel."

"Wilson is a woman?"

"Oh yeah." Nick's grin stretches from ear to ear. "She joined up and became a military nurse. Saw the world, I guess." He bounces on the rattan chair. "You'll like her."

❦

CHAPTER 17

Not What She Expected

Wilson Shobbrook impairs her normal ability to laser-focus on the investigation. Familiar anxieties and inadequacies scramble to become priorities as she drives to Shale Harbour to retrieve Owen's box of research and clippings—a trip usually appreciated no matter how many times she travels past the twinkling ocean waters and into the village.

She squints through the streaked windshield of her Jeep and tries to harness what she understands to be irrational fears. Wilson, a school friend of Nick's, appeared yesterday afternoon. Stella was instantly reminded of Hot Lips Houlihan from the *Mash* series on TV. With tumbling blond curls and a fitted creamy linen jumpsuit, Wilson Shobbrook hurled her skinny person into Nick's arms as if she were a long-lost lover. *Damn it.* She stood back in the shadows of the living room and took stock of the miracle of unwrinkled linen and the crimson cotton shrug which emphasized Wilson's narrow waist not yet subjected to the ravages of aging, the thick shoulder-length hair, and the makeup done to perfection. Wrapped in familiar envy, she felt dowdy, the typical country bumpkin. She wanted to hide away upstairs and pretend she wasn't home.

Nick turned to introduce her, and Wilson bubbled her hellos. The two decided on a stroll around the park before tea, and Stella rushed to call Trixie—her faint hope to elicit reinforcements for supper.

"Stop, Stella. Don't act threatened. You know Nick loves you."

"She's beautiful, Trixie—a military nurse and good friends with Nick's parents." She knew she sounded whiny. "Can't you come out tonight? Nick's cooking dinner."

"Sorry, kiddo. Brigitte and I invited Carter and Val over. The house is open and busy today—weekends until Christmas, and then we'll close for two or three months." She hastened to add her details before she suggested, "but if she stays over for another night, I'll come tomorrow and lug out shrimp. The weather's still warm enough to barbecue on your veranda."

"Thanks," she moaned. "I hope your help won't be necessary." But in the end, Trixie's assistance was required, and Wilson will honour them with her presence once again tonight.

Nick acted star-struck and over-compensated last evening. She didn't understand his reasons. After their walk, he poured wine. He insisted he complete the meal preparations alone, leaving her stuck in strained conversation with Hot Lips.

"You're a military nurse." She makes the statement in the hope Wilson will talk about herself.

"Yes. Nick and I joined at the same time but went off in different directions." Her eyes drifted toward the door. "He tore up here to avoid the war. I studied for my nurses' degree and have never been happier." She ran a finger along the still perfect seam of her trouser leg. "Nick was a fool. He could be an engineer or a pilot—any number of professions—by now." She gazes over the railing. "Instead, he's a handyman. Sad."

And not dead in Vietnam. "He will own fifty percent of the business the end of the year, Wilson." *The woman pities him.*

Her eyes narrow when she addresses Stella. "Half of your little RV park won't propel him anywhere in the world today. Nick missed major opportunities."

Stella wondered, at the time, if Wilson expressed her opinions to Nick while they were on their tour. When he materialized at the kitchen door, Stella felt the relief of rescue.

"Are you able to come sit with us, Nick?" Wilson issued the invitation before Stella found the opportunity to organize her thoughts.

"Need help?" Stella inserted her question as Nick began to answer Wilson.

His face swivelled between both women. Stella imagined he appeared nervous or tense. She might have projected her own issues.

"Dinner will be in ten minutes. I'll refill your wine and you two sit until we're ready. Stella, do we have a treat squirrelled away in the freezer for dessert?" He tittered when he turned to Wilson. "Didn't have time to make you a cake."

"We have butter tarts." Stella jumped and ran for the pantry, not convinced she liked this version of Nick. She uncovered the pastry, made last August, and buried for safe-keeping—full of calories and yummy. When she returned to the veranda, Nick and Wilson were on their feet.

Wilson met Stella's eyes and winked. "No dessert for me." She pointed to her tiny waist below her short jacket. "Still try to watch my figure, for as long as nature cooperates."

Stella's analysis continues while she makes her way toward the RCMP detachment. To be honest, the visit wasn't catastrophic. Although Nick catered to Wilson's every need, she didn't feel neglected. Dinner was great. She ate three butter tarts as she reached the conclusion she couldn't compete with Wilson even if they were the same age and both enjoyed glorious hair. To reach the end of the evening with Nick still by her side became her goal.

Nick acted uncomfortable when Wilson decided to stay another day. Their guest appeared not to notice. She hopes Trixie's attendance at supper might act as her buffer. She giggles at the absurdity. The sister, in whose presence she has deemed herself to be less than adequate, has become her safety net.

Bedtime was odd, too. Under normal circumstances, their routine dictates a pot of tea and perhaps a visit in their upstairs suite with the balcony doors open to let the ocean breeze tease the curtains. Nick, more often the communicator, remained silent. As a result, his behaviour left her unbalanced, but she didn't push. She mentioned she invited Trixie for supper the next day and she promised to bring shrimp. He nodded agreement and said he felt tired. They retreated to bed, and he began to rumble softly in no time. She, on the other hand, stared at the ceiling and questioned every move she made.

As expected, the station isn't busy on Thanksgiving Monday. The fellow assigned to staff the front desk makes a call and another unfamiliar face arrives with a file box. He requires she show identification and sign an evidence form before he assists and places the container on the back seat of her Jeep. Aiden did not fail her.

On the way home, she formulates a plan. She wants to sort through the contents and scan for any manuscripts or news stories related to Greta, Bryce, or Mayko. If she's correct, a reference buried in his research could blow the lid off one of the suspects' secrets. She has the afternoon. She expects Cloris to move her rig today and park near the house. Duke is available to assist if necessary. Nick will entertain Wilson when she arrives later. She won't be needed.

****

Stella sets the file box on her desk, then hollers for Nick while she peels off her jacket. After she wanders into the kitchen to make a fresh pot of coffee, she returns to don latex gloves supplied by the detachment and to stare at the carton in front of her. She snips the tape with scissors, removes the lid, and leans it against the wall behind her chair. Stacks of plastic bags, each sealed and numbered, confront her. She picks the top one—a newspaper report from 1978, which tells the story of a group of Vietnamese boat people. Owen's interest in the circumstances of the population who fled war-torn Vietnam becomes obvious. She searches through the packages and retrieves ten related items and a page of notes, which appear to represent a crude outline of a plot which involves American soldiers who sold children—not what she expected.

She finds newspaper stories of murders which have taken place in every part of the world. She squints and wonders where he obtained the clippings, many over thirty years old.

"Are you here?" Nick's kind-hearted tone holds curiosity as he makes his way from the veranda, across the living room, and toward her office.

"Yeah, sifting evidence."

"Aha! Caught you in the act. I knew you wanted to jump right in once you dragged the box home."

"No one needs me this minute. I thought I'd take advantage of the time. When will Wilson be back?"

"Not until four. I expect her to return to her hotel early, too. She leaves in the morning."

Stella stares at the plastic bags. "I'm glad Trixie said she'd come. I need reinforcements."

"From Wilson?" He grunts. "She suggested I wasn't the best of men because I deserted the red, white, and blue. Sounded like Dad."

Aghast, Stella touches his arm. "Why the hell did you invite her back?"

"Time for lunch?"

She stacks the bags of evidence, and they meander into the kitchen. They scrounge a tin of tuna, crackers, cheese, and pickles. Nick turns on the radio to local easy-listening music and waltzes her around the table. He kisses her forehead. "Wilson doesn't worry you, does she?"

"No," she murmurs into his chest. "Hot Lips Houlihan is no concern to me." She leans back to meet his eyes and knows he knows she's lied.

After she cleans the kitchen, she returns to the task at hand. She decides to search for a story which could have inspired the grisly tale Owen told to the retreat group when he read aloud in her living room. She discovers reports of parents who killed their children; one where a child starved to death in the basement; another where little ones were abandoned in the woods. After the examination of criminal behaviour at its worst, she finds an excerpt from a Winnipeg paper where the older boyfriend of a thirteen-year-old girl murdered both her parents and her younger brother. He was incarcerated for the crime, and judging by the dates, remains behind bars. Owen's reading described a similar murder, but from the point of view of the daughter who he characterized as a participant in the carnage.

Stella checks her watch—almost two. She'll make a cup of tea and wander down to talk with Mildred before Duke moves her home to her apartment. When she hears the rumble of a vehicle, she watches out the window as Cloris, with the agility of a teamster, parks her trailer near the house. If Mildred gets lucky, Cloris will be the one to help her move instead of Duke.

"Anybody around?"

"Hi, Cloris." Stella struts toward reception. "You're parked, I see. What can I do for you?"

"May I leave my truck here for a few minutes while I try to find my boyfriend?"

"No problem. Duke's at Mildred's helping her pack. I wanted to have a quick word with the old girl, anyway. I'll walk with you."

As they make their way along the main road through the park, Stella remembers Cloris also told her Owen's story sounded familiar. "Cloris, do you recall when Mildred mentioned the reading by our victim, Owen? You said it reminded you of a news item?"

"To be sure. Did you uncover the connection?"

"Sort of." She describes the newspaper article to Cloris.

"It's the story I remember. I felt sorry for the poor girl but wondered, at the time, if she put her boyfriend up to homicide. When I saw him on the TV, he didn't strike me as the sharpest knife in the drawer, if you know what I mean?"

"Thanks, Cloris."

"Did Owen take a tragedy in Winnipeg from thirteen years ago and rewrite the details to make the events worse? The exaggeration of a family's murder can't be worth a person's life, though."

Stella lifts her brows in response.

Mildred Fox, still resplendent in a caftan of questionable condition, waves both flabby arms as the women approach. "We'll be done soon, Stella. Have you arrived to give me the boot?"

"Not a chance, old girl. I wanted a quick visit, and Cloris came to help. Can we go sit on Aiden's deck for a minute and have a word?"

****

The elderly woman, and long-time seasonal resident, drops her abundant rump on to the flat wooden surface. Her flip-flop endowed feet float above the grass. Before Stella joins her, she removes the newspaper clipping, which tells the story of the murdered family in Winnipeg thirteen years ago, from her back pocket. "Here, Mildred. Tell me if this article reminds you of the one Owen read when he was here."

Mildred eyes the plastic.

"Sorry I can't take the paper out of the bag. With your cataract surgery behind you, you're better able to scan the papers than me, now," she teases.

Squinting in the afternoon sun, she turns her back to Stella and holds the protected sheet in the shade. Stella watches Duke and Cloris load Mildred's meagre possessions into his Beetle. She can't hear them but clearly interprets their body language. Cloris wants them to use her truck. Duke shakes his head, stamps his foot, but acquiesces.

"I remember this story." Mildred touches Stella's arm. "God, those killings happened thirteen years ago. Time goes fast and slow at once."

"You're right. Has to do with aging, I imagine. It appears Cloris took off to retrieve her pickup."

"Good. The move takes three trips with Duke, although I appreciate his help. The other feller charged me a hundred bucks and I couldn't pay no more." She wiggles off the deck. "Did the dead kid copy stories from the newspaper and change them around to suit his creepiness?"

"It appears he did, my friend." Cloris' truck emerges at the top of the rise. "I'll make my way back to the house. You are well in hand. Have a safe winter. See you Victoria Day weekend."

Mildred's open embrace cannot be avoided.

Following her walk, she steals a few minutes to call Hester. "May I read you an article from a Winnipeg newspaper dated in 1968?"

"Why?"

"Hester, I need to know if the report I've discovered reminds you of the story you recognized when Owen read out loud."

"Okay, Stella, but I am busy with preserves. You understand, my days are hectic right now."

"I do, and I appreciate any scrap of help you can provide. Here goes." She reads the newspaper article.

"The report is the incident I recall, Stella. If you remember, Owen's rendition was much grislier. The young daughter in his story committed the murders and took no end of satisfaction in her mother's death. Correct?"

Stella shivers as her mind races back to the Painter family history. "Yes. I found a copy of his writing in the evidence box as well. I didn't read the piece."

"A wise choice. Did he use the Winnipeg slaughter and embellish the facts? The concept is macabre, but not illegal."

"I'm not sure yet, Hester. My biggest goal for now was to confirm you, Cloris, and Mildred each remembered the same story."

"And did we?"

"Indeed."

Trixie arrived early for their holiday Monday dinner. Nick sprinted out to her Microbus and fetched a bucket of shrimp, nestled in ice.

"I still have pull at the plant, even though I barely work a day a week." She struts across the hardwood floor in platform heels, skin-tight blue jeans, and a short angora pullover. She is every bit the sister Stella expects Trixie to be.

"Will you meet Valentin later tonight?"

"*Val* and I have plans, yes. I wouldn't waste my outfit on you, Stella, no matter how worried you sound." She pats the sweater and leans closer to Stella's ear. "But I need to check out Nick's war hero friend. Still threatened?" She squeezes her pink lips into a perfect bow.

Stella continues to assemble salads to accompany the shrimp. "She's not a war hero, to my knowledge," Stella mumbles.

Nick remains on the veranda while he prepares for the barbecue by immersing each shrimp in his signature marinade.

"He isn't as smitten as when she first came over yesterday. They spent hours together, but he acted relieved when she left. I'll see how this evening goes."

"Are you worried?" Trixie's tone has moved from teasing to serious.

"I don't know. I've been up to my elbows in an evidence box filled with Owen's writings, musings, and newspaper stories, which helped distract me." She meets her sister's gaze. "Nick assures me her visit will be short-lived. I suspect she has a hidden agenda—to take him back to Florida."

"What? Did I hear a car?" She mimics panic. "Quick, hand me a glass. I'll pour a drink and be the welcoming party." She sloshes wine and scampers out to the veranda.

Stella continues to find unnecessary tasks in the kitchen until Nick comes in search of the wine and glasses. "Will you join us?"

"Yup. Trying to tidy. Are you okay?"

He frowns. "Trixie's lathering on the charm. I don't expect Wilson to stay much after supper. She has an early day tomorrow."

Good. "You said. Are you to chauffeur?" *Was I too snide?*

"No. She arranged transportation. I never offered."

"You're still troubled."

"We'll talk, Stella," he says as he chews his lip and wraps an arm around her shoulder. "I need time to work out what almost happened here." He studies her. "We both have busy days on the horizon. Let's find a quiet time tomorrow and lock the door. I'll tell you why I'm so infuriated right now, I could throw her out on her ass."

"You're much too polite to turf a guest." The elixir of relief spreads through every blood vessel in her body.

CHAPTER 18

Tell Me Your Thoughts

Both Trixie and Wilson departed before ten o'clock. Disappointment washed over her when Nick said he wanted to go to bed. He promised to handle meal preparation for their date the next evening. He plans to winterize trailers all day. She lay awake after his gentle rumbles began beside her. The glow of the clock radio shimmered two before she drifted off.

"Hi, Tiffany. I'm to meet Detective North. A cup of your hazelnut coffee when you have a minute." Aiden wasn't at the detachment when she dropped off the evidence box. She expects him anytime.

"Welcome, Stella. Pick a spot. I'll be over in a sec." Stella drifts between the tables accompanied by music from the easy-listening Port Ephron radio station and chooses the most private option.

They plan to discuss her discoveries, such as they are, and set further goals. Although Wilson has left, or will leave in short order, her mind remains preoccupied with the woman's presence and Nick's peculiar reaction. He acted enthusiastic to renew his friendship with her, but reticence appeared after they spent time alone. Trixie asked if she felt threatened. She frowns. *No, not now.* Her thoughts tumble. Nick readied himself for his workday, spoke little, and flew outside before she found a chance to raise the subject of Wilson. Ten weeks until the formalization of their partnership. Stella huffs in silence. *Calm down.*

The bells jangle as a gust of cool October air rushes inside when Aiden plows through the door. "Good morning, Stella. Hi, Tiffany. Coffee, please, in the biggest mug you can find." He rattles the chair as he sits. "Sour mood? I expect you found a big fat goose egg in those piles of Owen's notes." He divests himself of his topcoat.

"I'm fine," she mutters. "To be honest, there wasn't much to learn. Spent most of yesterday on various roads to speculation. How are you?"

"Good." Tiffany places a mug on the table, and he nods his thanks. "Dragged myself away from a busy office in Port Ephron to try to find peace and quiet over here." He holds one hand in stop sign fashion. "Nobody's dead. Other annoyances. Tell me your thoughts."

"Owen's box is full of newspaper stories related to murders across Canada and the States—even a few overseas. He was obsessed. I discovered his reference to the reading he performed at my author gathering September 25. Owen, from what I can surmise, took the legitimate report and added embellishments to include the daughter who wasn't involved."

Aiden's eyes narrow. "Did you replace the contents?"

"No need to worry. Yesterday, I checked my hunch out with Mildred, Hester, and Cloris. They each mentioned Owen's story sounded familiar and when I shared the article and, although the murders were reported thirteen years ago, in Winnipeg, each remembered the event."

"Okay. When did the incident happen again?"

"In 1968."

"We need to call Winnipeg police, ask for a copy of the file, and try to find out whatever happened to the girl. The boyfriend might be out on parole. I'll be interested to discover how many, if any, of the details Owen used in his story match information Winnipeg never revealed to the public." He nods when he sees Tiffany lift the coffee pot in the air. She trots over to provide refills for them both.

"What's the special today?" Stella has decided she might as well eat here instead of home. Nick will be busy, and he doesn't expect her.

"Andrew made lobster coquettes. I have a tossed salad as a side."

"Sounds perfect. Early lunch, Aiden?"

"The same, Tiffany." Once the owner bustles to the kitchen with their orders, Aiden continues. "I called police detachments in Québec City and Fredericton before I came over to the café."

"Good. Will they re-interview Bryce and Mayko?"

"If necessary. I asked them to review our interviews, find any holes, and determine if we missed information. I expect to hear back by week's end. I requested detailed local background checks."

"Bryce doesn't care if his truth becomes common knowledge. I think he could easily drop the cowboy act, given the opportunity."

"Correct, and I have made myself clear that Mayko is not to be harassed in relation to her identity and how she came to be here. She carries enough guilt and fear. We don't need a domestic assault added to the mix."

"Agreed. Will you request Halifax police arrange an interview with Greta?"

"First, do you still want to talk with her publisher again? We can go to my office and call after lunch."

"Yes. The problem for me is Greta. She lied to us from the start. She took the long way back to the hotel and didn't acknowledge Mayko. Her behaviour makes little sense, and she can't explain herself."

"We should invite her to Port Ephron for an in-depth discussion after we speak with her publisher."

"She doesn't drive. A trip to Halifax to meet with her might be in order."

"Are you game?"

"She's my biggest loose end with her vague history. We've missed a connection. When you talk to Winnipeg police, ask if they'll research information on the thirteen-year-old daughter of the murdered family."

"You're suspicious the girl could be Greta Walmsley?"

"The dates roughly match. She revealed her age to be twenty-six. Maybe she spoke to Owen because he wrote her personal tragedy as an original story. She argued with him, and he fell—the one logical scenario."

Tiffany delivers their lunches, and they eat in companionable silence for a few minutes. "Far-fetched, Stella. If Greta has tried to make a new life for herself and put the death of her family and her teenage years in foster care behind her, she did not reveal her truths to Owen. She wouldn't give him the satisfaction."

Stella nods. "You're no doubt right. As a successful writer who has managed to rise above such a terrible ordeal—why risk exposure because of a kid?" She pats her lips with her napkin. "Convince her publisher to clarify the murky picture of Greta Walmsley." She grins across at him. "Easy-peasy."

****

They stroll back to the detachment. Although not sure he'll want to redirect their focus away from the investigation, she's compelled to ask, "Plans are still in place for Rosemary to come home on Monday?"

He shoves his hands into the pockets of his coat. "Yes. Talked to Toni last night. They'll leave Monday morning. If Rosemary becomes too difficult, they plan to stop overnight and not push straight through."

She knows he sees the worry on her face.

"Rosemary isn't good." He repeats the now familiar refrain. "Toni is convinced she needs long-term treatment in an institution, but Mary Jo refuses to accept the idea. I told them Cloris Kincaid agreed to help, and Toni says she can be their back-up but doesn't expect my wife to move home anytime soon."

She touches his arm for a moment before they enter the station. "I'm sorry, Aiden."

"Yeah. Me, too. I hoped the treatment might work. Reality, I guess." He shrugs his shoulders; to Stella's eyes, a faint attempt to push his worry aside.

"You go along to my office. I'll check in at the desk. We can contact Winnipeg first and talk to Victoria Barlow afterward."

While she waits for Aiden, Stella telephones the park. Maybe Nick is in the house. He answers right away. "Hi. Are you okay?"

"I'm good. Climbed out of my funk, I guess. On your way home?"

"Soon. Aiden and I have two calls to make. I have a theory, but the puzzle pieces don't fit, yet."

The sound of his voice warms her ear. "I've planned a romantic supper for us tonight—a pot roast with fresh veggies."

"Wow! I might keep you around." Her voice softens. "Better day, Nick?"

"Difficult times, but I'll explain."

They say their goodbyes when Aiden materializes in the doorway. "I called Nick to tell him when to expect me." She hesitates before continuing. "We've experienced a rough patch."

"Serious?"

"Not sure. A high school friend—they began in the military at the same time—turned up. She's an army nurse, now. At first, Nick was excited. I became the third wheel." She shrugs. "In any event, the visit didn't go as planned. She left today. Nick has arranged a special supper tonight to tell me the details."

"Are you concerned?"

"Oh, no. Not anymore. I was a wreck day before yesterday. Back to work. Winnipeg, first?" She can push personal issues out of the way, too.

"Yeah. The front desk found me the number."

Aiden introduces himself to Detective Bishop of the Winnipeg Police Major Crimes Division. "I have you on speaker phone, Detective. I'm here with my partner, Stella Kirk. She's our community liaison. We're interested in the Gordon family murders, which took place in 1968."

"I remember the case well. I wasn't the lead. He's retired, but I held the second-in-command position. What information do you need?"

"Can you send us a copy of the file? A jury found the daughter's boyfriend guilty on three counts, correct?"

"Yes. Gosh, he must be thirty-five by now. He was twenty-two when he killed the parents and the younger brother. The daughter was thirteen, and the prosecutor contended her folks didn't want her to go out with an older guy, and he murdered them."

"What happened to the girl? Do you remember her name?"

"Yolanda Gordon, and she went into care."

"Where was she at the time of the murders?"

"The boyfriend, Duane Miller, claimed she was at his place. He returned to his apartment, picked her up, and took her home where they discovered the bodies. He tried to say he stepped out to buy food for them and came back, but we found no proof he drove anywhere other than the family bungalow. Witnesses observed his truck, already familiar to the neighbours. There were no receipts and no recent grocery purchases."

"Stella here." The hard pound of her heart makes her breath come in gasps. "Any way we can obtain the foster records for Yolanda Gordon?"

"I'm happy to send you whatever I can find. Care to enlighten me?"

Aiden tells him the story. Stella contributes the information focused on Owen's reading and adds, "Greta Walmsley might be Yolanda Gordon. She found herself with opportunity. A motive makes sense if she felt Owen discovered her identity and threatened to reveal her past."

"You two may have connected a few dots. Greta Walmsley is popular. My wife bought her books and has often watched her on television. I remember she said the writer reminded her of Yolanda Gordon. I'll send you the file and the pictures. They aren't pretty. What's the fax number? You'll keep me posted, right?"

"Sure, Detective. We appreciate the cooperation."

"Before we sign off, let me describe Yolanda. For a thirteen-year-old whose family was murdered, she expressed minimal emotional response—

flat and unfeeling. I waited with her until the social worker arrived, and then she walked away without a care in the world." He pauses for a moment. "The boyfriend was no concern to her, either. Didn't even ask to talk to him."

"Thanks, Detective Bishop. I'll keep an eye out for your fax."

They sit in Aiden's office and stare at one another. Stella breaks their silence. "If Greta Walmsley and Yolanda Gordon are the same person, and Owen discovered the truth, we have our motive."

"Owen's reading implicated the daughter. Greta, or Yolanda, was never involved. Detective Bishop reported they bundled her off to foster care right away."

"She was thirteen, Aiden."

"Owen's story embellished the murders. What difference did his interpretation make to Greta?"

****

"Victoria Barlow, please. Detective Aiden North, RCMP Port Ephron and Shale Harbour. Thank you. I'll hold." He places the call on speaker and raises both eyebrows at Stella.

"Barlow here. How may I help you?"

"Good afternoon, Miss Barlow. Please be aware I have you on speaker, and my colleague, Stella Kirk, is with me."

"We spoke last week, correct?"

Stella leans toward the telephone. "Good afternoon."

Aiden clears his throat. "Miss Barlow, we are conducting an investigation which involves one of your authors, Greta Walmsley."

"Yes."

"We want to discuss the details of your relationship with her, her abilities with regard to her skills as a writer, and any history you might possess as to how she came to her craft and when she began her career."

"Detective, would information not have more value if you spoke with Greta, herself? I can't imagine what you will gain through my observations."

"May we meet with you in Halifax, Miss Barlow?"

She's hesitant. The phone line remains quiet. "I guess I'm unable to stop official police business."

"Perfect. Your office around ten tomorrow morning?" Aiden peers at Stella. She nods.

174

"Thank you, Miss Barlow. Goodbye."

They arrange to meet at the detachment the next day.

****

For whatever the reason, the trudge to her Jeep and the return trip to the park takes less time than she expected. Once on the back veranda, she's not sure she's fully prepared to confront or discuss the issue of Wilson Shobbrook. He fills the darkened doorway. Her watch indicates three in the afternoon. She assumed him to be at work on a trailer, or in the shop repairing a mower or another cranky piece of equipment. "Oh. You're here."

"I am indeed. I quit early." He's jumpy. "How did your meeting with Aiden go?"

"We learned new information. There's the distinct possibility Owen discovered how Greta Walmsley's family was murdered by her boyfriend thirteen years ago, and she has changed her name from Yolanda Gordon."

"What? How?"

"A newspaper report in Owen's box told the story, although the young girl in the true version didn't participate in the murders. They were her boyfriend's idea. We called the Winnipeg police and talked to one of the detectives involved. We are ninety per cent sure Yolanda Gordon is Greta Walmsley." She stops to take a breath. "I hope you don't mind if I drive into Halifax with Aiden tomorrow. We have an appointment scheduled with Greta's publisher at ten. We are both convinced she knows more."

"Not at all. Can you stop at Murphy's Auto Supply and buy oil and a filter for the park truck?"

"Certainly. Write a list for me and call them to have the stuff ready. I don't want to inconvenience Aiden. Rosemary comes home on Monday night or Tuesday and he's pushing to move the investigation to a conclusion, one way or another." She nods. "But, yes, I will purchase truck crap at Murphy's, if there's time." She giggles. Nick does the tasks she hates to do. He keeps the old yellow Ford between the ditches when the vehicle should have been scrapped years ago.

"Want to guess what's for supper?"

"You said pot roast."

"Right! I told you already." He frowns. "No surprises, then," he exclaims with a nervous flourish. "We'll lock the doors, turn off the phone, and I will remind you why I love you."

"With pot roast?"

"Sort of." He dances from one foot to the other. "Never mind. Tea on the veranda? There's no wind on that side of the house. I'll explain Wilson and her mission."

Stella struggles with unbearable curiosity but contains her emotions, nods, and plugs in the kettle, dying to hear Nick's story but knowing not to rush him.

They curl together on the rattan settee, cups in hand, and feet stretched out on the coffee table. She waits.

"Wilson Shobbrook, I came to understand, was acting as an emissary for my father."

"Tobias? He sent her to Shale Harbour?"

"Oh, yes," he nods with enthusiasm. "Six weeks before we finalize our business deal. I guess Wilson represented Dad's last-ditch attempt to convince me to return to the States and invest with him."

Stella frowns. "Why Wilson? I've never even heard you mention her before. Was she ever an important part of your life?"

"Not in any special sense. We entered the service at the same time. We were aware of one another in high school but were never close friends. We sort of developed a friendship in the military before I left. She became a nurse and rose in the ranks. From what she says, she called my folks when she visited the area and asked where I finally located."

"Do you believe her?"

"No, but I needed two days to find the truth. She had no idea I was granted a full pardon. I wondered if she contacted Mom and Dad to locate me for the service."

"My God, Nick. That's mean."

He shrugs. "She's a company girl, army through and through. The force has given her a good life. She swears by the hoopla. She claimed Dad asked her to come here to convince me to go back." Nick turns to meet Stella's gaze. "He paid her way, Stella."

Disappointment fills her chest—for Nick and the lost kinship he believed was re-kindled with his parents; and for her, in the vaporization of an acceptance she assumed she'd found. "I thought he endorsed our plans for the future here at the park."

"Me, too, but we were sucked into the Tobias Cochran vortex when I believed he supported me for once in his life. Dad asked her to come round me up without any mention of my pardon because he suspected Wilson wanted to score points with the army if she turned me in." He wraps an arm around Stella's shoulder and exhales. "He conned her, too. No need to worry. A trip to Florida won't happen any time soon."

She sips her tea for a moment while she revels in the warmth of him beside her. "I guess we've been enlightened. Will you call them?"

"Nope."

✿

CHAPTER 19

The Concept Held Value

A twitchy and sweaty young woman Stella expects attends university and works part-time shows them into an office carved from an upstairs bedroom in a neglected heritage home in downtown Halifax. Vague and clumsy, she seems impatient to return to the foyer which doubles as reception. The scarred hardwood floor is strewn with extension cords. The awkward space is anchored by an oversized, laminate-topped, grey metal desk. If Sailboat Publishing is successful, neither their location nor the calibre of their hired help reflects affluence.

They perch on mismatched chairs—one upholstered in a dirty-brown canvas-like fabric and the other a standard-issue stacking variety.

The demeanour of Greta Walmsley's editor and publisher proves to be miles from expectation, too. They stand when she bursts through the door and dashes for the protective barrier of her desk, while she motions for them to return to their seats. As often happens when Stella imagines a person from the sound of their voice, Victoria Barlow bears no resemblance. Stella expected a tall, formidable woman. Instead, they are confronted by a bird-like creature, frail and skittish. She's sixty, if a day, and attired in a yellow and brown argyle vest over a white blouse paired with a shapeless skirt. Stella suspects the waistband has been rolled to keep the hemline from dusting the old floorboards. Her fingers are twigs, her nails chewed beyond repair.

She studies her guests through wire-rimmed glasses, which refuse to stay in position. She nudges them up the bridge of her nose every few seconds. She rests her elbows on her desk and clasps her hands.

Aiden breaks the silence. "Good morning, Miss Barlow. I'm Aiden North and let me introduce my colleague, Stella Kirk. Thank you for meeting with us."

"Ask your questions. I will try to be forthright, but I am uncomfortable with your presence in my office."

"Suspicious deaths are uncomfortable, Miss Barlow." Aiden pursues the interview with a calmness that appears to rub off on their interviewee. Her twitches settle. "Let's start with your history and role here at Sailboat Publishing, after which please explain how you met Greta Walmsley."

"To be sure." She adjusts her glasses and squints. "I am one of four editors on staff. Two of us act as publishers." She raises a finger. "I am not an owner. Sailboat Publishing is owned by a much bigger company. Our branch has a limited focus. I do non-fiction, but no cookbooks. The others handle short story collections and poetry."

A person might assume, with inspection of the surroundings, this organization runs on a minimal budget, but Greta's books have been successful. "Both of Greta's self-help volumes were published through Sailboat, correct?"

Victoria grimaces in response to Stella's unspoken observations. "The company moves money around. Our little branch does not benefit from the profits in an obvious cause-and-effect fashion."

"I see." Aiden delves further. "How did you become involved with Greta?"

The editor sits straighter in her chair. "Authors forward query letters." She makes eye contact with them. "We receive many, many query letters. Most are trashed. We answer ideas with merit. Greta Walmsley sent a sub-standard letter, although she illustrated a solid premise. She revealed bits of her life history and said she wanted to explore how a person can carve out a new and better future."

"She wasn't much of a writer, but the premise held value," Stella contributes. A picture has started to build.

Miss Barlow claws at her glasses in obvious discomfort. "I imagined a lousy query with an exciting idea could magically morph into an actual book. My mistake."

"What happened?"

"Sailboat advanced her a significant sum. She produced two chapters." The woman squirms in her seat. "A fifth-grader effort." She glances away from her tormented fingers. "Don't be fooled—the fundamentals, focused on the re-creation of yourself after a difficult childhood, were solid. The girl couldn't write to save her soul, though."

"But the idea proved too good to toss." Stella has figured out the answer.

"I rewrote every word of her ramblings and scribblings, as if I were her ghost writer—in the sense of celebrities who employ a writer to craft their memoirs. As one of the publishers, I'm responsible for the advance. We needed to earn back the money paid out earlier."

Stella determines Victoria is ready to level with them and asks, "When did you discover Greta's real identity?"

"There was an incident when she turned into another person in seconds. She threatened me." She stops for a sip of water.

"Tell us the details of what happened, Miss Barlow." Aiden sits on the edge of his chair.

"Her concepts were good, but when I told her I did not have either the time or the inclination to write a second volume and attach her name, she asked me if I was aware of who she was. When I said no, she became incensed. She screamed how her parents and brother were murdered; she lived in foster care for six years; and her ideas for *Creating a New Self* and *Improving on Self* are based on her experiences. I couldn't comprehend what her rants meant. The story sounded fabricated."

"Was her information enough for you to decide to write her next installment, which I assume you did?" Stella suspects more details yet unsaid.

"No. I didn't want to do another book for her."

"What happened?" Aiden asks.

"She threatened to accuse me of sexual abuse and said she could rattle off every detail to police because of frequent assaults in foster care. As a result, she could fabricate the experience except to change the name of her abuser. She insisted I write the book and help make Greta Walmsley famous." Victoria's hands vibrate as she clutches them on her desk.

"Do you want to press charges, Miss Barlow?" Aiden murmurs.

"No, but I hope you discover if Greta, as a party in your investigation, is involved. Maybe I'll be rid of her."

"Will you tell us what she revealed to you about our current inquiries and the death of Owen Ellis-Thomas?"

Victoria still has more to say, and Stella listens intently.

The woman twists her fingers. "She called me, at home, late on the Friday night of the retreat. She said a kid wrote a story which implicated her in her family's murder. She was distraught. I convinced her the work was a macabre coincidence; how anyone could access a newspaper article and exaggerate the facts." She nudges her glasses for the hundredth time. "I failed to see the relevance. In any event, my response calmed her."

"Are you able to share more with us?"

"No, Detective. Are we finished?"

On the return trip to Shale Harbour, Stella remains troubled. "You asked if she could assist with other information, and she said no. She lied, Aiden."

****

Often, Stella feels she spends more time in Shale Harbour at the RCMP detachment than she does at home. Nick doesn't object. Today, they slept in and ate a late breakfast. His mind is focused on the preparation for septic installation. Although raked with guilt at her lack of involvement, discovering what really happened to Owen has become her priority. The organizational flow of poop will wait until later.

Aiden stands propped in front of the reception desk with a sheaf of papers in his fist.

"I'm not late," is her standard phrase. She was tardy once, and the circumstance embarrassed her. No one had any idea why, but the details didn't matter. Her momentary mortification stays with her.

"Perfect timing. I received the file from Winnipeg not two minutes ago. Detective Bishop must have been up all night. What's the time in Winnipeg? Seven o'clock?"

Stella nods. She wants to see Yolanda Gordon's juvenile record, convinced Greta and Yolanda are the same person.

They sift through the faxed documents for an hour. The information is heartbreaking if one separates the current personality of Greta Walmsley from the child whose parents and brother were brutally murdered by Duane Miller when she was thirteen years old. Additional facts come to light. In the first place, Yolanda Gordon acted out and social workers intervened from the time she turned ten. She ran away from home, refused to attend school, stole from friends, family, and local businesses, took her parent's car on a joy ride, and became involved with boys much older. Her last social worker was a woman named Janelle Daly. The proof of their suspicions jumps off the page. Ms. Daly assisted Yolanda in her transition out of foster care, set her up in an apartment on social assistance, and found a legal aid lawyer who paved the way for her to change her name to Greta Walmsley. The unabridged story emerges in black and white.

"Here's my question, Stella." Aiden leans back into his office chair. "What justifies Greta's degree of upset? An invented tale, which may have taken the details of her personal tragedy, implicated her. Her boyfriend committed the crimes. He's in jail. Thirteen years have passed. No one knows her identity. Her response, as told by Victoria Barlow, was an over-reaction. Why not ignore the kid?"

"Besides threatening her publisher into writing a second, and now third book, Greta over-reacted to Owen's story. What have we missed? I wonder if Detective Bishop can interview Duane Miller for us."

Aiden reaches for the phone. "He sent the fax. He must be around. Let's give him a shout."

"Good morning, Detective. Yes, we received the information. I've put you on speaker."

"Hi, Detective Bishop."

"Please call me Bish. Everyone does. Are the documents useful?"

"Absolutely. I was surprised you could access juvenile records, though."

"They were unsealed when she changed her name. Not convinced personnel followed protocols, but our good fortune."

"Well, we have lots of questions for Greta Walmsley a.k.a Yolanda Gordon, if I can convince her to come in for an interview without the need to charge her first. We have a favour to request."

"Sure."

"Are you able to visit Duane Miller?"

"He's a half-hour away. No problem. What's your line of inquiry?"

"Room for doubt. Did he cover for Yolanda? Could she have been involved in her family's murder?"

"Man, your theory's a long shot. I read his file after we talked. Duane's a model prisoner. There has never been a report to suggest a story different from what happened at the trial. He has two years before he's even eligible for a parole application, but I'll call and see if I can talk to him today."

"Perfect. Second issue. Does Janelle Daly still work in the area?"

"Yeah. I found her contact information, expecting you'd ask."

"Bish, Stella, here. We appreciate what you've done. Thanks for your help to connect the dots."

"The Gordon Family murder was a big case here in Winnipeg. No one had seen a similar crime before. The pictures of the scene were too much for some seasoned cops to sift through. Forensics were on the property for days."

Stella recalls Owen's story, the violence, and the gory details. After they sign off with Detective Bishop, Aiden calls Owen's parents and asks if they can visit later in the day.

"To be sure, Detective North. Have you made a break in the case?"

"No, Ms. Ellis. Stella and I want to explore Owen's creative process, and the research he put into various scenes. I hope the topic won't be too unpleasant for you."

"He read his best work at Stella's party. I was delighted to edit for him and proud of his efforts." Her voice wobbles. "Others were unsettled by the subject matter, and I understood."

As Aiden replaces the receiver, Stella suggests, "Let's talk to Janelle Daly, if we can reach her. I want to hear her impressions of Yolanda."

Detective Bishop's contact information proves accurate, and after Aiden identifies himself, a receptionist transfers his call.

"Janelle Daly. How may I help you?"

"Good morning, Ms. Daly. I'm Detective Aiden North of the RCMP in Nova Scotia. I am with Stella Kirk, my community liaison. We hope you can assist us with details related to Greta Walmsley, or Yolanda Gordon. She is involved in a mysterious death case here in Shale Harbour."

"Good morning. Nice to meet you. Most of my interactions with clients are confidential. I often testify in court, but file content is revealed with a warrant."

"Paperwork won't be needed for our questions. We are in possession of her juvenile record, released after her legal name change."

"I didn't agree at the time, afraid for her privacy."

"Yolanda wanted to make a new life for herself. We understand and appreciate her concerns."

"She has done remarkably well, Detective, if one considers her past. I gather you're aware she identifies herself as the Greta Walmsley of the self-help books now?"

"We are indeed. Were you surprised at her writing skills?"

"Pleasantly. When she told me how she planned to write a book, I assumed, at first, her goal was to stay on social welfare and avoid furthering her education or learning a trade. She proved me wrong and has made a successful life."

Stella attempts to knock the social worker off guard. "How often did she bully you, Ms. Daly?"

"Odd question. She was adamant she wanted to change her name. I rendered assistance not strictly in my mandate, but she could be persuasive."

"And her lack of work after her transition out of the system?"

Janelle hesitates before she assumes control once more. "Many nineteen-year-olds want to scam the government. They expect to be provided for. They try to avoid the responsibilities which come with aging out. Yolanda was different. She didn't want to follow the rules either, but she concocted a plan of her own."

"What were her problems in care?" Stella pushes. "I noticed five homes in six years."

"Issues overwhelmed the girl. No surprise. Everyone in her family was killed. She was troubled, even paranoid. Counselling never worked. I've revealed too much. Are we finished?"

"Thank you for your time, Ms. Daly. We appreciate the help." Aiden stabs the button to end the call.

"Social workers never change." Stella props her cheek on her fist. "She didn't reveal what we couldn't read in the file."

****

The calendar proclaims the date as October 15. Stella harnesses her embarrassment at the lack of obvious progress in the investigation. She swallows an apology when Edward answers the door.

"Come in, come in. When you called, we expected a break in Owen's case."

Aiden frowns. Stella jumps in. "We need to chase additional leads, Edward." She glances at Aiden. "We hope to have a report for you soon."

"Any sort of report sounds nice," Frances mumbles, as she rounds the corner from the little kitchen with mugs of tea.

Both Aiden and Stella choose the low sofa again, although both are aware of the consequences when they're ready to leave.

"We aren't on a quest to determine *who* murdered your son, Frances. We must decide *if* he was murdered, or if Owen was the subject of tragic accidental circumstances. Thoroughness is critical, and we appreciate both your patience and your cooperation."

His recitation resembles a paragraph from the police handbook on how to support victims' families. Stella jumps in before Owen's parents have too much time to react to Aiden's response. "Frances, Edward. You were both supportive of your son's writing, correct?"

"In every way, Stella. He was a talented young man. He needed our understanding and blessing."

"When I reviewed the box of research gathered from his basement room, the number of newspaper articles, and the age of particular examples, stuck out."

Frances peeks above her teacup. Her nod toward Edward is barely detectable. "My brother, Rex, is your culprit. He lives outside town and has a barn full of newspapers. He bought a collection at an auction, and he's kept, collected, and stored the dirty rags ever since." She sips her tea. "If you walk into the barn, he has a path shoulder high with papers on either side. He loved Owen. To be honest, and I don't need to confer with Edward, Owen took after his Uncle Rex in many ways."

"Rex allowed Owen to cut pieces from his collection? Sounds odd for a hoarder of sorts."

Edward enters the conversation. He's sat, mute, in his recliner until now. "Rex did whatever Owen wanted. He doesn't have a family of his own and delighted in Owen."

"We're not sure if Owen favoured Rex because of heredity or their similarities were because they spent hours together," Frances interrupts. "We realize Owen found an article. He used the basic facts and elaborated." She turns to Edward with puddled eyes. "As our Owen could often do."

"Could Owen have gotten in touch with anyone connected to a family slain out west thirteen years ago?"

"Mercy, no! To be honest, Detective, Owen wasn't remotely interested in the real people or their circumstances. He saw the story as the foundation of a piece, while he visualized potential for much worse than the facts represented." Her brows furrow. "His attitude bothered me, but I can't explain the reason. Simply put, he cared not one whit for the original victims. They were merely vehicles for his own creation."

Owen's perspective, as portrayed by his parents, doesn't surprise Stella.

"Did he express concern he might meet someone from a news story he 'elaborated' on?"

"I don't imagine the idea crossed his mind." Frances' lip quivers. "He was twenty, Stella—not the mastermind you describe."

Stella silently checks with Aiden before she continues. "Two quick additional questions. Are either of you acquainted with the details of Mayko Doan's history?"

Frances sputters. "I've read her memoir. She's a nice young woman, but skittish."

"Did Owen ever express an interest in her story?"

"Never," Edward added. "Not the least bit curious. We discussed this before."

"Your patience is appreciated. And Bryce?" Stella needs to understand what Owen knew.

"Everybody in our circle knows Bryce is a big fraud." Frances interrupts. "To be frank, no one cares. Whatever sells books."

"You've been a huge help today, Ms. Ellis, Mr. Thomas. We're grateful for your time. If your son's death was not an accident, the person who killed him needed a motive. He wrote a story which incorporated someone's life circumstances, terrible as they were, and proceeded to create a fictional narrative far worse."

"Owen wrote stories based on real events. He never talked to relevant parties or the police. He fabricated detail. The end." Edward rises from his chair.

Stella clambers to her feet. "Thanks for the tea, Frances, and thanks again for your patience. Aiden and I want to find the truth." She extends her hand to Owen's mother and then his father.

Aiden copies her actions.

Back in the car, Aiden sputters his relief. "We've disturbed them once too often. I don't blame them for their defensiveness."

"We found one important detail, at least. Owen didn't research any cases he discovered in Uncle Rex's barn. He created his stories around articles which served as inspiration. Owen never contacted Duane Miller." Their work makes more sense if her assessment is wrong, but it isn't. "Nonetheless, I'll be curious to hear what Detective Bishop has to say after he interviews the guy. Thirteen years in jail. He might be ready to tell a new story." Stella settles in for the ride back to Shale Harbour.

"Let's complete the phone calls tomorrow. If you come into the office mid-morning and no other inconveniences—death or a major crime—confuse our Friday, we can review the Fredericton and Québec City police reports due by then." He scowls while he drives. "I don't anticipate any further issues, but we must eliminate both Bryce and Mayko."

"I agree."

"Next, Detective Bishop will no doubt contact us early in his day, after coffee here. Finally, let's try to wrangle an interview with Greta Walmsley. I want to see her on Tuesday, in Port Ephron, because I need to be nearby."

"Are you worried about Rosemary?" She knows the answer.

"Concerned." He turns his face away from the windshield for a split-second. "I'm scared to death, Stella. I have no idea what to expect. Toni says she's worse than ever, whereas Mary Jo wants to believe they'll have smooth sailing. Mary Jo has rented her house to a college instructor for the winter. I'm supposed to manage on my own and visit my wife on occasion. Smooth sailing...." He studies the road ahead.

She attempts comfort. "If we have an opportunity to interview Greta, since we now understand the story Owen wrote was based on an exaggeration of her real-life experience, we can complete the investigation before the 'Stang has been in Toni's yard for twenty-four hours."

❦

CHAPTER 20

A Simple Case of Misadventure

"I'm back to the detachment today."

Nick squints over his coffee cup. "Oh, yeah. What else is new?"

"Are you cross?"

He rises and approaches her. "Never. You and Aiden need to find out what happened to Owen, and the tick of Aiden's domestic clock bangs louder by the day."

Stella leans into his hip while he stands. "Rosemary arrives Monday unless there's a problem. We'll try to arrange an interview with Greta for Tuesday. If you have a work list for me, Monday might be okay." She tilts her face upward and beams.

"I've managed to keep us under control. The surveyors will be back any time and the big shovels are scheduled for two weeks from Monday. And I have Duke, remember? He's my secret weapon." He chortles while he returns to his chair. "Any theories yet? I expect you have one by now."

"Yes, but Aiden won't appreciate my idea."

"Why not? Can you share?" He plasters more jam on brown bread toast—a personal favourite.

"Owen might have stumbled on Greta's identity. His parents claim he embellished a news story from years ago, but the concept is too simple. Owen was secretive and searched for the weaknesses in people. Even if Owen threatened to expose her, what's Greta's issue? She lived through a tragedy and made a success of herself after horrific circumstances. Worse case scenario, she has a personal history to be proud of." She pouts.

"Possibly the kid's death was a simple matter of misadventure. The little thief toppled."

After a hug which almost convinces her to stay home, she trots to the Jeep and makes the drive into town. She discovers Aiden parked with an elbow on the elevated front desk, deep in conversation with Sergeant Moyer. "Hi. The faxes from Fredericton and Québec City arrived. We can take them to my office to review."

"Good morning." Stella nods toward Moyer before she follows Aiden along the hall.

"Here. You read Mayko Doan's interview and I'll tackle Bryce Blanken's."

Stella reaches for the curled, waxy papers and studies them in silence. She chews her lip as she scans familiar data. The real Mayko Doan died before Mai Phan—her legal name—left Vietnam in 1975. Domestic abuse by the soldier who brought her to the United States in the same year forced her to hide. After Mai immigrated to Canada in 1978, she adopted her dead friend's name and wrote a memoir based on Mayko's life. She continues to live under the assumed name. Aiden gave strict instructions. She's cooperative and is to suffer no ramifications. Her admission to Canada was legal. Her theft of Mayko Doan's identity is not. The report reiterates known information. On Saturday, September 26, once the afternoon workshops ended, Mayko accompanied Hester as far as the café, and continued to Mrs. Carlyle's. She changed and took her dog, Tanchau, for a walk. When she travelled west on Birch, she saw Bryce Blanken enter the community hall. She trudged north on Maple, and east on Elm. Greta Walmsley strolled ahead of her. She remained behind Greta at a respectful distance until the self-help author entered the hotel at ten past five. Mayko wandered Shale Harbour and the beaches near the wharf with Tanchau until six o'clock, when she returned and ate supper with Hope Carlyle.

"I see not one shred of new information here, Aiden." The papers roll in Stella's hands. "Mayko Doan didn't hurt Owen. He wasn't aware of her identity. If his parents were correct, he cared less. Did you discover a fresh scrap regarding Bryce?"

"Nope. He was straightforward with the local cops. Provided them the same history he gave us. I don't see a motive. He opened the door of the hall and hollered for Greta. After no response, he left and shopped at Parlour Antiques before he parked nearer the hotel." Aiden's shoulders heave and he expels a huff of frustration. "I expect Owen was dead at the foot of the stairs."

"Okay. If you're correct, the timings suggest Greta was inside when he fell, or she might have pushed him to his death."

"Do you have a theory?"

"Yes. Somehow, and with his parents unaware, Owen discovered Greta's identity. He waited until everyone left and yelled downstairs to the classroom, 'Hey, Yolanda', at which point Greta panicked."

Aiden squirms to get comfortable. "Say you're right. Why did she panic? Let's imagine he knows she's Yolanda and exaggerated the murder of her family to implicate her. She would suffer no ramifications. Owen's writing is fabrication."

Stella frowns. "Correct. Without a motive for Greta, we're left with the idea he fell accidentally. Or she surprised him, and he stumbled."

"Hopefully, your scenarios are the end of the story, Stella. We'll conduct an interview with Greta the first of the week and wait for Detective Bishop to call back today after he's seen Duane Miller, but I need to wrap the case sooner rather than later."

"Rosemary?"

"What else? Home in three days and, although she'll be with Mary Jo and Toni, their expectations of me are high." He winces. "Perhaps you've noticed." Then, he mutters to himself, "She should be in hospital."

"Your wife has made spectacular recoveries in the past."

"Not this time, my friend. Toni told me they have her on a dozen medications—turned her into a veritable zombie. Mary Jo wants to take her off the pills to see what happens."

"And what do you want?"

With stealthy avoidance, he replies, "Coffee, but let's call Greta Walmsley first."

****

Before they adjourn to the café, Aiden telephones Greta Walmsley at home. No answer. She has a machine which directs her calls to her publisher. "Good morning, Miss Walmsley. Detective Aiden North of the Port Ephron and Shale Harbour RCMP. I wish to schedule an appointment with you. I have a few further questions related to our investigation into the unfortunate death of Owen Ellis-Thomas." He glances across to Stella and lifts his brows. "Please contact me at your earliest convenience." After he rattles off the detachment number and returns the handset to the base, he checks his watch. "Let's go find an early lunch. I expect Bish will call near noon, our time."

"Okay. I need to tell Nick. May I use your phone?"

"Sure. Come out to the front afterward." He grabs his topcoat before he leaves.

Nick answers on the second ring. "Shale Cliffs RV Park. How can I—?"

"Hi."

"Hi, you. I bet you're standing me up." His tone holds enough humour for Stella's confidence to emerge.

"Yes, as a matter of fact. Aiden and I plan to scrounge lunch at the café, because he expects the detective from Winnipeg to call soon."

"No problem. Duke and I won't starve. When are you coming home?"

"Teatime." An idea pops into her head. "Nick, let's invite Aiden to supper tomorrow night. His life will be chaotic once his sisters-in-law return with Rosemary."

"Sure. Don't forget, we're to meet Trixie and her new flame on Sunday at the Purple Tulip."

She blushes. "I hope we can find time for 'us', too."

"If you stop standing me up," he jokingly admonishes.

Once settled at the café, Aiden and Stella sip their coffee and wait for corn chowder and biscuits to make their way from the kitchen under Tiffany's supervision. The little restaurant isn't busy. They've chosen their favourite bistro table in the back. "Come to supper tomorrow night."

Aiden's eyes narrow while he peers over the rim of his cup.

"An evening at the park might be the last time you have a chance to relax before Rosemary returns."

"What did Nick say?"

"Nick doesn't need an excuse to roast a chicken. We have a date with Trixie and Valentin Reguly at the Purple Tulip Sunday night. Tomorrow is perfect.

"Okay, although I'm convinced you've issued me a pity invitation."

She can't tell if he's joking. "Aiden, Nick and I are acutely aware of your challenges with Rosemary. We want to help—call it our attempt to be supportive."

Sounding both grateful and sad, he adds, "I expect she's off the rails. Toni said to be prepared." He stops as Tiffany approaches.

Stella meets the owner's eyes. "Thanks. Lunch smells scrumptious."

"You two are my guinea pigs. If the chowder needs any more spices, wave."

"The normalcy in my marriage is gone for good," he mutters, once they're alone.

"Oh, Aiden." Stella frowns. "Come for dinner. We can talk."

After a delicious meal, they return to the detachment to discover Detective Bishop has called and left a message for them to answer as soon as possible. They rush to Aiden's office and close the door.

"Detective Bishop."

"Good morning, Bish. Aiden North and Stella Kirk here. Sorry we missed your call."

"Hi. No problem. I interviewed Duane Miller yesterday, after we talked. He was cooperative, but I didn't uncover much."

"Did he have his lawyer with him?"

"Nope. Met with me on his own, with a guard in the room. I'll send you a transcript of our discussion. You might notice an indicator I overlooked."

"Describe Duane Miller."

"Nice enough fella. Polite. Soft spoken. After thirteen years inside, I found his demeanour tough in the beginning, but he relaxed when he found out I wanted the truth. He told me he struggled for the first twenty-four months, but now he works on the prison farm, with the animals and in the gardens."

"What about Yolanda?"

"He loved her, but her family refused to allow him near. She was thirteen, and he was of age. Her parents threatened to go to the police and claim statutory rape. He said he lost his mind and went after the whole family, although he admitted he regrets killing the younger brother. He said he can't find a way past the murder of a child." Bishop pauses.

"Did you ask if Yolanda was involved?"

"Yes. I questioned him about his original statement. Told him I understood if he took the fall for the girl. He was adamant she stayed at his place and clueless until he drove her home."

"I'm surprised."

"Yeah. Me, too. I asked him to explain his clothes because he must have returned to his apartment covered in blood. He said the washer and dryer were in the bathroom, right at the front entrance. He had hidden fresh clothes in there, changed, and Yolanda never saw him until after he made the switch. He told her he needed a piss."

"Plausible." Stella grimaces. "The report says they found items of her clothes in the dryer."

"Correct, but she stayed with him often. Forensics discovered her items mixed with his, but by then any blood residue on her clothes was considered cross contamination. He also mentioned he has two years before he applies for parole, and he's landed a job at a market garden farm when release is granted. He doesn't want to ruin his chances."

"Is he afraid if he implicates Yolanda, he'll be denied?"

"I asked. He gritted his teeth and muttered his time will be done and he wants to move on."

"Okay. Thanks, Bish. We appreciate your hard work in such quick order."

"Most welcome. If Yolanda Gordon played a part in the slaughter of her parents and younger brother, you'll only find out from her. As for this Owen kid—Yolanda was one tough cookie as a teen. Easy to imagine, as an adult, she gave the guy a shove."

****

After the discussion with Bishop, Aiden calls Greta one more time. "No need to contact Sailboat Publishing. They're in no position to make an appointment for her. I want to schedule an interview for Tuesday in Port Ephron."

"Okay by me." She understands the pressure he's under because of Rosemary's return.

As Aiden holds the receiver to dial, Moyer appears in the doorway and waves a slip of paper. "Greta Walmsley left a message"

"Great—we were on the phone for half an hour," he mutters in frustration. "I'll call right away."

"Not necessary, Sir," Moyer interrupts. "Talk to her lawyer...a person named Aloysius Fitzgerald." He guffaws. "What mother gazes down on her new baby and says, 'I'm gonna name my kid Aloysius'?"

Aiden reaches for the note and ignores his sergeant. "Guess the next step is Mr. Fitzgerald."

Stella settles in a straight-backed chair as Aiden picks up the phone. "Good afternoon. Yes, I want to speak to Aloysius Fitzgerald, please. Detective North of the RCMP in Port Ephron and Shale Harbour. The matter relates to Greta Walmsley. Thank you." He widens his eyes at Stella.

She twists the straps of her shoulder bag, curious why Greta has a lawyer on standby.

"Mr. Fitzgerald. Hello. My name is Detective Aiden North. I've put you on speaker to enable my colleague, Stella Kirk, to join our conversation."

"Good afternoon, Mr. Fitzgerald."

"What can I do for our fine members of the police today?"

"We were directed to contact you by Greta Walmsley. We wish to re-interview her in relation to the Owen Ellis-Thomas death which occurred here in Shale Harbour at the time of a writers retreat on September twenty-sixth, or into the wee hours of September twenty-seventh. Are you able to accompany her to Port Ephron on Tuesday, at one o'clock?"

"Listen Detective North, correct? Miss Walmsley is resistant to the idea of additional interviews. She asked me to convince you to postpone or cancel such a request. She is deep into edits of her third book and no longer wants to partake in your investigation."

Aiden leans back in his office chair to the point where Stella fears he might fall over. "I hope she pays you pots of money to make such comments, Fitzgerald. I want to talk to her, and I've asked you nicely if you will come with her to my detachment in Port Ephron. Miss Kirk and I are happy to travel to Halifax if we must."

The lawyer's smoky chuckle conjures pinstripe suits with vests, and fat cigars.

"You realize an arrest could be necessary to gain her compliance. If you don't have enough evidence, you have no reason to insist. Charge her."

"Greta Walmsley may well be the last person to see our victim alive. She has a colourful past. The kid who died collected other people's secrets. We need to have a discussion with her to determine Owen's understanding of her life as Yolanda Gordon."

"I have been involved with Greta for many years. She holds no secrets from me. I'll convince her to travel to Port Ephron on Tuesday, October twentieth. My office will confirm."

"Thanks, Mr. Fitzgerald. Why the change of heart?"

"Let's say a good lawyer likes to keep the players in mind."

After Aiden replaces the receiver, Stella frowns. "He no doubt knows Greta Walmsley's background better than us, and the details are to his advantage. Does he suspect her involvement in the murders?" She stands, not expecting an answer, and gathers her purse and scarf. "Off I go. Tomorrow night any time after five, okay?"

Elbows on his desk and chin in his hands, he nods. "I'll bring a case of the local brew Nick likes."

She waves before she treks along the hall and out into the brisk sunshine toward her Jeep.

****

"I said I'd be home for tea." She finds him on the top step of the veranda, tears up the stairs, and wraps both arms around him, while she inhales the smell of wood and motor oil. "Glad to be back."

"Long day?"

"We didn't make much progress, to be honest."

"Duke's gone. Site jobs are done. Septic company is scheduled. Let's take a break. You invited Aiden for supper tomorrow night?"

She blinks at him. "He's a wreck. An evening in the park might be a distraction." She giggles. "If he expresses any interest in septic systems, you can keep him busy for hours."

"Good idea! I'll take him on a tour to show off the field and the tank locations. Good idea," he repeats.

His remark is a tease, but the concept has merit. The aroma of blackcurrant tea wraps around her as the comfort blanket it has come to represent over the years. They sit side by side at the kitchen table, not end-for-end as they do for meals. "We had a conversation with a detective from Winnipeg who interviewed Duane Miller for us yesterday." She answers the question in his eyes. "He's the guy who murdered Yolanda Gordon's family. Greta Walmsley is Yolanda Gordon. Duane Miller was her adult boyfriend when she was thirteen." She stops for a sip of tea. "The Winnipeg detective remains certain she wasn't involved. Miller repeated what he said in court and didn't budge from his story. We contacted Greta's lawyer, Aloysius Fitzgerald. He has agreed to accompany her to an interview in Port Ephron on Tuesday. Aiden wants Monday at home for when Rosemary arrives. I'm not sure what difference the day will make. She sounds over-medicated. He needs time off."

"Do you and Aiden conclude Greta Walmsley killed Owen because he found out who she was? Lots of people change their name and start a new life. She has no reason to be ashamed. She's famous now, right?"

"Indeed. What motivated Greta to hurt the kid? He wrote a story which exaggerated the actual circumstances. The details were gory and put her in a bad light, but it's not factual and no one would be the wiser. Why bother with him?" She studies his eyes, as if an answer might be hidden away. "Love the tea. I needed the break...and your company, too."

Chapter 21

Reality Invades Her Brain

She alluded to a chicken dinner for Aiden, but Nick has thawed steaks. The last barbecue of the season, she expects. When his Citation crunches in the driveway, she stops chopping vegetables for the salad, and makes her way to the door. Fall is her favourite time of year. The mornings are crisp, the afternoons warm, and dusk rolls in by early evening. They planned a tour before dark. Potatoes are in the oven to bake, the greens will chill for an hour, and they can wander the park before Nick starts the grill.

Aiden clutches a box of beer as he alights from the car. She considers the passage of time as she watches the only two men she has ever loved shake hands and climb the veranda stairs together. "Welcome, my friend."

He peers at her through a shock of white hair which has fallen over one eye. He pushes a strand out of the way. "No chance for a haircut," he adds as a means of justification. "I'm happy you invited me, otherwise I'd be back at the detachment with pizza and a few files." He hands the beer to Nick.

"Even though the invitation was out of pity?" She notices Nick's surprise. "He accused me of issuing a pity invitation when we spoke yesterday." She grins at both men.

"Beer after the tour, Aiden. I want to show you around and explain the septic. We scheduled your trailer for hook-up in the spring once you arrive." Nick can't contain his excitement and hops from one foot to the other.

"I'll put the beer in the fridge and check on the potatoes." Stella reaches for the carton.

****

"Each flag represents a spot where a holding tank gets dropped, Aiden. You should see them—huge cement cisterns. Every site with septic services will be connected to lines dug throughout the park. They'll converge on one of ten tanks." The wind off the water whips at their hair. Nick shouts to be heard.

"Then what happens?"

As Stella walks along beside them, she wonders if Aiden is feigning interest.

"Once a week, a staff member—or me," he giggles, "has to pull a septic collector around the park with the loader and siphon each tank. The septic collector contents are dumped into the big tank near the field. The septic field will be constructed in the manner of a traditional contour system where the solids sink, and the liquid is pumped into the field. Filtration occurs over time and via the slope. The house, cottage, and public washrooms can be integrated later, as needed. They're fine for a few years yet. We'll install a large capacity pump, to push the liquids away from the shore. Can't have human waste run into the ocean. You should see the permits."

"Big bucks."

"Oh, yeah. No question." He wraps one arm around Stella as they make their way toward the area designated to be the field. "The investment is huge, but lots of rigs won't come to a park without full-service facilities. The bonus becomes more seasonal sites on offer, too." He points out where the pump house will be situated, explaining filtration and biological enzymes for the third time.

"I must admit, the idea of no honey wagon every week is positive. Do you expect your rates to increase?"

Nick glances at Stella.

"Not for now, Aiden." She brushes wisps of hair away from her face. The wind has begun to blow harder. "If the project stays on budget, we can manage the payments without higher costs to our customers." She hopes. "We expect to finish much of the work before the weather turns. Let's go back to the house." She checks her watch. "Time to put those steaks on."

The air has developed a chill, but they gather on the veranda for beers while Nick barbecues. The potatoes have a few more minutes, and the salad is ready. She scrounged in the freezer for an apple crisp she made a few weeks ago. She'll tuck the deep dish into the oven before they sit for supper.

Since the discussion on septic systems and their variations has been exhausted before they begin to eat, thankfully, she changes the subject to the case at hand. "Do you think we can interview Greta in one afternoon, or will we need two?"

Aiden settles into his meal and studies her from across the kitchen table. He takes a deep breath. "I hope the former, but if we're the least bit suspicious she pushed the lad, we'll have to take advantage of the second date and see her Wednesday as well." He reaches for the butter. "God, I wish they'd kept Rosemary."

He sips his beer and continues. "Let's start with verification of her identity and a determination of who else knows she's Yolanda Gordon of the Winnipeg Gordon murders. We might discover a link between Owen and another person besides Duane Miller."

"There's the possibility the entire set of circumstances was random. Maybe she believed he knew her, but he didn't. She could have over-reacted to an innocuous remark he made. He was mean to folks for sport."

"I wonder if her lawyer, Fitzgerald, could tell us the whole story if he were able. From our phone call, I think he tried to imply a message, but we heard a riddle."

"Fancy apple crisp for dessert? Who's ready for tea?"

The conversation reverts to Rosemary. Aiden's apparent confusion and lack of clarity on the exact parameters of her condition makes Stella nervous. He has depended on Toni and Mary Jo to keep him informed from the start, and Stella's afraid he's in for a few surprises when she returns on Monday.

****

Before her eyes have an opportunity to open, reality invades her brain. Money management and the murder investigation wrestle to take control. She prepares to toss the blankets aside and face the bedroom's icy Sunday morning air when his arm stretches across her bare breasts. His calloused hand cups her shoulder.

"Are you awake?" The muffled voice is buried in her neck.

"I am now." Her lack of response to his touch doesn't last for long.

When they emerge into a sunny, although damp and cool, kitchen Nick departs for the living room to make a fire while she rummages for breakfast ingredients.

She boils eggs and turns on the oven to heat buns, which she wraps in foil, and places on the lower rack. Nick has braved the frosty temperature to load in more wood from the veranda. He'll want the fireplace to be ready to light when they return from supper tonight, too. After twenty minutes and hot coffee, the house offers a pittance of warmth. Sunshine will improve the conditions, but the thermometer has struggled to maintain a civilized level for almost a week.

The combination of boiled eggs and cinnamon buns is one of her favourite Sunday breakfasts, harder to realize in the summer, because staff dig in the freezer to find treats for lunch. Sweet butter, brown sugar, and spiced filling drips around her fingers. Nick watches her lick them off.

"Need help?" he teases.

"Sure. And how do you propose we finish our work?"

His manner is playful while he munches.

"On a more serious note," he continues, "I talked to the lawyer on Friday, as we agreed now that you've cashed the company GIC. The paperwork is ready for Trixie to sign at year end. We've completed the offer to purchase her shares by both you and me. Our partnership agreement is ready with the roulette clause, and the pre-approval papers from the bank arrived." He slurps coffee. "I'll confirm the dig for October 26."

"I'm pleased we found a property lawyer in Port Ephron. Cavelle helped," she adds. "I didn't want to deal with Stephens and Stephens."

"Me, either. But not because Carter and Brigitte are a couple."

"No. His firm has a hand in every legal transaction on this side of the isthmus. I wanted separation. Better to be out of town. Andrea Picard specializes in property and business law. She's a perfect fit."

Nick has handled most of the legalities as the primary purchaser. She expects to have more involvement as they move forward. "Agreed. She took my call, answered my questions, and has managed the sale, to this point from her office. She said she could write our wills, as well. I appreciate her professional approach. She's business-like."

"Shale Harbour Savings and Loan said the payment for the septic system loan will be one thousand dollars a month, the same as what I've paid Trixie for the last three years. If interest rates ever drop, we might pay the note off before the term concludes."

"Don't count on a windfall, my love."

"I should be so lucky." She wrinkles her nose at her own sarcasm. "I can hope. Now," she claps her hands together, "we have today and tomorrow before I'm due to meet Aiden in Port Ephron. What do we need to accomplish?"

He lifts his eyebrows and leers.

She giggles.

"Oh, you meant chores. Well, let me see. Around the house wants the services of a rake and the flower beds are a mess. I'll water in the new trees we planted. The loader needs to be serviced in case they want me to help with the septic. Your Jeep should be washed. A loaf of fresh brown bread sounds nice." His soft laugh overrides any attempt to add to his list.

"Enough. I'm tired of listening to you," she responds to his teases. "Since we don't have to prepare supper tonight, let's tackle the work outside. You rake, I'll clean flower beds, soup for lunch, perhaps a short nap." She lifts her brows in much the same way he did. "Then off to the Purple Tulip." She scrapes her chair when she pushes out to take her dishes to the sink.

Companionable servitude to the yard areas near the old house occupy the remainder of the morning and through until after one o'clock. Eve manages the gardens most of the summer but the tasks of cutting back the Hosta, tending to the bulbs, and trimming the myriad of ornamental bushes fall to her each autumn. Nick rakes leaves, not for the last time. He carts the piles in wheelbarrows to the field behind the parking lot. The soil will become richer for his efforts.

While she works, Stella reviews their looming interview with Greta Walmsley. She prays Aloysius Fitzgerald is not the type of lawyer who refuses to permit his client to answer a question, regardless of the context. The truth hidden beneath Greta's story, and what she perceived Owen knew, will be her focus. She expects Aiden to be preoccupied with Rosemary and her return. Her expectations of his involvement are low, and she chastises herself when her thoughts place him in a negative light.

"Hey. No work, no lunch, Missy." He has caught her crouched in the weeds, fixated on her trowel.

"Busted. I wonder if Aiden will find time to prepare for our big interview on Tuesday."

He reaches out an arm and hauls her to her feet but doesn't respond.

"Thanks." She prattles on. "I expect his mind to be at home, so I want to review what we have to clarify before we decide if Owen was murdered or if his death was by misadventure."

"He's still responsible for case-management, Stella. You're his consultant, not another detective assigned. Don't under-estimate him—or Rosemary, either. Her arrival will go fine, and he'll call you on Monday, fully prepared."

"No." She pushes a wisp of hair off her cheek with a soiled glove. "Rosemary is in a bad way. I think her condition has worsened more than he realizes, although Toni has tried to tell him. His emotions are all over the place." She shrugs. "One day he wants her home with him and life back to normal. The next, he's convinced she should be in an institution. I sympathize, but he has to find his own path."

****

"I've decided to wear linen pants and a turtleneck sweater," Stella muses, not necessarily to Nick, inside his closet in search of a shirt. "I love the Purple Tulip, but cement and metal make me feel chilly, even with those little gas fireplaces stuck in the walls."

"Do we have much time?"

"Trixie told me the reservations are for six. We need to hurry." She drags a faux stone necklace over her head. "Finished. Passable?"

He fakes serious consideration—his response obvious. "Beautiful, my love." He reaches across the space between them to run a finger along her arm. "Now, help me find a shirt."

"Big job to find a shirt to match jeans." Her sarcasm goes unnoticed. "Wear this plaid one. The fabric's soft and cozy. You'll appreciate my choice at the restaurant."

Twilight has settled on the landscape as they cross the isthmus and point the old Jeep in the direction of Port Ephron and the Purple Tulip. The evening promises to hold an element of interest.

"How long have Trixie and Valentin Reguly dated?"

"Not sure. She didn't say much at first. They met at the Gorman's. Mallory is Valentin's sister and a friend of Trixie's."

"She's sick, right?"

"Mallory's family doesn't expect her to see Christmas, from what I've heard."

The Purple Tulip is impossible to locate if you're unaware of the hidden side street. The building served as the doctor's office and surgery over a century ago. The veranda-style deck, across the front, sports a trellis trim and becomes a popular place to gather in the summer. As they enter the gloomy interior, Mitchell greets them. "Hello, Stella. Your sister and Mr. Reguly are already seated. Let me show you through."

Dark and polished cement floors echo the sound of chairs as they move and heels as they click. Soft guitar music wafts in the background. Mitchell whisks them across the expanse and deep into the dining room. Stella takes a moment to admire the light fixtures which pepper the ceiling—each unit constructed with twenty metal cheese graters. The lights shine with an eerie, disco-ball effect.

Valentin rises as Nick drags red basket chairs against the unforgiving floor. Stella leans over to pat her sister's hand.

"I can't forget my manners." Trixie bubbles and her curls bounce. "Val, meet the love of Stella's life, Nick Cochran—soon to be a fifty percent shareholder in Shale Cliffs RV Park. Nick, Valentin Reguly, but we call him Val." She sips a green frothy drink in a stemmed Margarita glass.

Nick and Val shake hands. Each of them sits, save for Trixie, who didn't stand in the first place. Her sister has, with relish, returned to her old self. Her attire consists of a frilled denim skirt, a strapless halter-top, and a white leather jacket. White heeled ankle boots with fringe trim on the backs are visible to Stella as Trixie leans sideways and crosses her legs. Uncontrolled glamour meets country and western groupie crosses Stella's mind. From her point of view, Russ Harrison has been shoved into her sister's past with swift firmness.

"First, Valentin." She catches Trixie's glare. "Val. How's Mallory?"

"Not much better, Stella. Thanks for your concern. My brother-in-law, you know him—Ted—is goin' to pieces right in front of her eyes. She told me yesterday she wanted to die and give him some peace."

"Poor Theodore. He would hate to think she's burdened with concerns for him."

Before she takes a breath, Marnie Webb, the manager of the business, approaches the table. "Hi, folks. Can I refresh your drinks? And Stella and Nick, what will you have?"

"White house wine for me, Marnie. Nice to see you again. Hope your summer was successful."

"We were busy every day. I imagine life wasn't great over your way. Two murders since May. Nick?"

Hollow silence follows her remark. Before Stella can respond, Nick replies.

"A local brew you have on tap, Marnie."

"We have a full-bodied amber. Finishes with a touch of blueberry."

"Perfect."

"And another whatever she's drinking." He points to Trixie's glass, "And a Molson's."

"Back in a jiffy."

Trixie's latest flame appears rather academic when not dressed in the garb of a caretaker. Stella's thoughts return to the day she and Aiden interviewed him in the basement of the community hall—not yet a month ago. "What? I'm sorry. I am fascinated by the décor in here." She attempts to cover her drift away from the conversation. "Funny how the place can feel warm and cold at the same time."

"Val asked an investigation question, Stella." Trixie sounds impatient. "He found the body, remember?"

"Here we go." Marnie approaches, and with the dexterity of a gymnast, she serves their drinks from a tray and removes the empties from the table. "When you have a chance to examine the menus, wave and I'll be back. The special is slow roasted pork ribs with root vegetables and garlic smashed potatoes. The house salad is included."

"Thank you, Marnie. Give us a few minutes," Trixie replies.

Stella turns to Valentin. "I can't discuss the investigation. I imagine the aftermath of the discovery of his body has been difficult, though."

"You can listen, right?"

"To be sure. What do you want to tell me? Do you have information to add to your statement, Val?"

"I watched the kid. He made me nervous. I found him in the janitor's cupboard, rootin' around. He didn't care I caught him and sent him on his way. He sneered at me. No respect for people's spaces."

"Thanks, Val. You may have to drop into the detachment and revise the comments on your original statement."

"Don't know if my idea matters." He glances at Trixie and nods.

Stella suspects Trixie insisted on the conversation.

"Shall we order dinner?" She attempts a subject change and waves to Marnie.

Nick orders the special, as does Val. Trixie chooses a mushroom risotto, while Stella decides on apple and apricot stuffed port tenderloin with the same vegetables as the special.

Their plates arrive and Trixie requests her third, or perhaps fourth, drink.

"I have a theory regarding Owen's unfortunate demise. His story might be the truth. Did the thought ever cross your mind? Say, somehow, he wrote what turned out to be non-fiction, and the murderer was at the retreat?" She leans forward and points a wobbly index finger at Stella. "My theory works if the killer came to the reading at your place. They listened, figured Owen uncovered their dirty little secret, and bumped the brat off the first chance they found." She relaxes back against the basket chair and winks. "See? Crime solved, and we haven't even ordered dessert yet."

On the drive home, Stella continues to mull over Trixie's theory born of drunkenness and devoid of any concept of Greta's history. "Nick, what if Trixie's right? What if Owen's piece was true, but he didn't realize? What if Duane Miller has covered for her and she thought Owen found out? His idea was to write a grizzly narrative—the embellishment of an actual murder. The trouble was, he stumbled on the truth."

"Too much of a coincidence, Stella. For Owen to exaggerate a Winnipeg massacre from thirteen years ago, and then read his words in front of the real murderer? Can't happen. And what's his genre—fictional truth?"

Reflected in the lights from the dashboard, his expression is difficult to interpret.

CHAPTER 22

She Knows She Has No Choice

"Stella! Can you grab the phone? I hear her. She's out of the shower."

"Who is it, Nick?" Stella hollers from the top of the stairs.

"Aiden. He sounds upset."

Dressed in underwear and a towel wrapped turban-style around her head, Stella stumbles to the extension beside their bed. "Hi. What's the matter?" He's supposed to be off, and they have an interview tomorrow. A call at seven-thirty in the morning indicates an issue.

"Toni and Mary Jo arrived home last night after supper. Moyer tried to contact me, but I was at Toni's. We've been played."

"What do you mean? Is Rosemary in bad shape?"

"Yes, but worse. Fitzgerald called yesterday afternoon and rescheduled our interview with Greta to today at one. I can't come. Rosemary must see her psychiatrist, and I'm required to be present."

She holds her breath and hopes her suspicions aren't true.

"Will you handle the initial meeting?"

"Me? Alone with Greta Walmsley and Aloysius Fitzgerald? Aiden, this is a joke, right?"

"No. He left a message where he offered to come to Port Ephron today and tomorrow afternoons, but no future times *prove* convenient." He snorts into the phone. "Oldest trick in the book—try to put us off guard."

"Well, his ploy worked. Are you not able to reschedule Rosemary's appointment?"

"Not a chance. Lucky we were given an emergency time in the first place. Listen. No need for you to be alone. I'll assign another detective to sit in and take notes. Do the interview. They'll record and compile the transcript afterward. We'll debrief Tuesday morning and prepare for the afternoon."

"We could postpone for a week. The lawyer can't stall forever."

"You heard him. He knows I have little leverage without concrete evidence. His call indicates a moment of cooperation, and we need to grab hold."

Her brain has turned to jelly, and her knees are numb. Convinced from the start Greta pushed Owen, she's been sure a confession will be their singular avenue to uncover the truth, but she never expected to fly solo.

"Okay, if you trust me enough to ask the right questions." Her shoulders shudder. "Do you have time to review what you want covered in the first interview?"

"Verify her identity by her admission she's Yolanda Gordon. Try to knock her off balance because we're aware she didn't write the books herself."

"Sure. I can knock her off balance. No problem with her lawyer in the room." Sarcasm makes an appearance.

Aiden doesn't respond to her attitude. "You handled the interviews with Meredith Tompkins and Opal Painter like a pro. I have faith in you. Gotta go. Greta and her lawyer will be in the Port Ephron detachment at one. Good luck."

After she drops the receiver into the cradle, the urge to vomit overtakes her. This interview could determine whether Greta Walmsley killed Owen Ellis-Thomas. Where's Nick? Duke arrived and the veranda door closed while she was on the phone. She hauls old corduroys and a bulky sweater over her still-damp skin, races outside, jumps on the golf cart, and speeds along the road to find the park pickup. Duke and Nick are hard at work loading fire pits into the box. Kiki stands in the driver's seat with both front feet on the wheel. Her sweater resembles Stella's—an unnerving comparison.

Duke pauses when he sees her approach. "What did Aiden want?" Nick grunts as he tosses another fire-scorched rim into the truck.

"The sisters arrived with Rosemary last night. They have a psychiatrist appointment. Rosemary's behaviour turns out to be more than the three of them can handle."

"Good he took the day off. Are you here to help?"

"No. The lawyer called over the weekend and rescheduled the interview for today at one." She waits a moment to allow the next rim to rattle against the assembled collection piled in the bed. "He asked me to conduct the first part by myself."

Nick stops. Duke stops. They both stare at her as if she's dropped in from outer space. "You aren't a detective, Stella. Sorry. You're good, but he can't expect you to do his job." A flush spreads across Nick's face.

His anger is counterproductive. She touches his sleeve. "A colleague will be assigned to be in the room, run the recorder, and take notes. He wants me to ask the questions based on the details of our investigation." In a sudden fit of shallowly buried insecurity, she asks, "Don't you think I can handle the interview?"

"You can handle whatever you put your mind to, Stella."

Duke moves toward the cab and pats Kiki. Stella appreciates his feeble attempt to wander out of earshot.

"Aiden has imposed on you. Now he won't be in a position where he needs to wrangle with a smart lawyer. He's the one with the family problem. Your job isn't to solve his issues, or the case, for him."

"I'll manage." She flips from insecurity to defence of her acquiescence with Aiden. "I'm to set the stage—let her realize we understand the trauma she experienced and how we're impatient to resolve the matter—to find out her impression of Owen."

Nick approaches her with rusty palms raised. "I'd doff my hat to you if I wore one. I admire your courage, but don't allow Aiden to take advantage of you, okay?" He leans over and kisses her on the cheek.

Duke makes his way to the back of the truck once more.

On her return to the house, she wonders if Nick could be right. Has Aiden found a path to shirk his responsibilities? She's committed to support him where Rosemary's concerned, but he may well have succeeded in transferring responsibility of their case squarely on to her shoulders.

****

"I made you lunch." Nick's voice drifts up from the kitchen.

"Thanks. No appetite." After three or four attempts, she dons a pair of dark-blue pleated trousers and a white long-sleeved cotton sweater. She peers at her hair in the mirror over the dresser and dispenses with any attempt at the use of a clip. Her wavy and wispy style must suffice. *Do I see more grey streaks? No wonder.* Despite the date, she settles on sandals.

A quick grasp of the banister proves necessary when her gallop threatens to topple her to the bottom of the stairs. *Such a potential circumstance is beyond ironic.* "No time for much." She spies the table. He has made her a ham and cheese sandwich, a cup of tea, and chopped a banana in a bowl for dessert. She lifts her lips to show appreciation while her stomach lurches.

After she consumes the forced nutrition of half the offerings, she leaves the rest and runs upstairs to finish getting ready before her race to Port Ephron. She wants to arrive thirty minutes early and review her questions. And she must meet the detective Aiden has assigned to sit in. Her imagination conjures an old-fashioned guy who expects her to keep her mouth shut. Hopefully, Aiden gave clear instructions related to her role.

When Nick wraps his arms around her shoulders and plants a warm kiss on her lips, the oasis of the moment transmits needed courage. "I will cook and be here when you return. You're good at what you do, Stella. Don't forget."

"Gotta go. Thanks, Nick. I love you, big guy."

"Yes, you do," he snickers, as he opens the door. "Call me before you leave for home."

The drive across the isthmus and into Port Ephron is a blur. Her thoughts race. Over the years, she has come to understand how her brain works for her, even when she isn't focused. It happened in university, too. Mountains of issues rolled around in her mind, but when crunch time came and performance was needed, the facts aligned and the information she was afraid was lost would emerge available, organized, and ready. She clenches the wheel and wills her poor noggin not to disappoint.

When she enters the Port Ephron detachment, a familiar awkwardness overtakes her. In Shale Harbour, she's recognized, and dare she say, respected, for the role she plays with Aiden. Here, she knows few people, and has felt herself an oddity at best. She approaches the desk and addresses an officer she has, again, never met. "Hi. I'm Stella Kirk, scheduled to meet with Greta Walmsley and her lawyer at one. A detective has been assigned to attend the interview because of Detective North's unavailability."

The person on duty lifts bored eyes. "Yes. The paperwork is in order. Have a seat and I'll call Detective Matkowski."

Stella does as she's told, uncomfortable with the lack of familiarity.

Heavy heels clunk along the hall and the glass door opens. A broad right hand, with nails manicured to a short and square finish, extends toward her. "Detective Estelle Matkowski assigned to assist you. You may call me Essie when we're alone."

"Hi. Stella Kirk. Nice to meet you" The proffered hand feels warm, and the shake heavy. "Any sign of our guests?" In an attempt not to assess, Stella observes the slim-cut black suit with the white T-shirt, and the badge barely visible where the single button of the blazer covers the waistband of the pants. Her dyed red locks are cropped short and combed straight back from her forehead and temples, obviously fixed in place with extra-hold hair spray. *No judgment.* They walk in silence to the interview room.

"They're tucked away inside. We can call when we're ready." She takes a seat beside Stella, in the middle of one long side of the conference table.

Stella prefers she sit on the corner and suggests the same.

"Direct contact with interviewees is vital. I pretend I'm able to read their minds. We'll start with the fact we've uncovered her real identity. The file says she didn't write those books. We should confront the sham," she huffs.

Maybe Essie is the primary interviewer, and she missed the point when she and Aiden discussed strategies. "Those are the topics, Essie, but I want to create a path for Ms. Walmsley to find her way to admit the truth, if you can be on board with my approach."

"Aiden instructed me to be your wing man. Flap away. Shall we have them brought in?"

She nods. *Did Detective Matkowski give in too quickly?* Essie reaches for the telephone.

Greta Walmsley glides into the conference room, followed by Aloysius Fitzgerald, who is far from the figure Stella expected. From the sound of his voice, she assumed a tall, barrel-chested man with chiselled features, great hair, and a pinstriped three-piece. Instead, she finds herself confronted by a slightly better-spoken version of Duke Powell. Greta's legal representative shuffles behind her, dressed in a pale grey and coffee-stained suit. Short, almost bald, and with an inadequate comb-over, he carries a briefcase the size of a car door.

The author nods. She's come to the Port Ephron police station in a low-cut lace dress with a crocheted shawl.

"Please have a seat." Essie points to the chairs opposite. "Water, coffee, or tea?"

They refuse in unison.

Stella meets Essie's gaze, assumes she sees agreement, and begins.

"Detective North will not be with us today. We decided against inconveniencing you further and have honoured the revised schedule with the help of Detective Matkowski. Shall we begin?"

"I have no additions to my original statements, Stella." Greta pouts with a practised purse of her lips and slump of her shoulders. "I am busy."

"We have new information to review and want to address potential revelations immediately." Stella paces her response.

"Why are you babbling?"

The attempt to unnerve her with the insult fails. "Yolanda, when did you come to realize a change of your name and a re-invention of your childhood presented a possible path to a normal life?"

"What?" She turns to Fitzgerald. "Can they refer to my previous identity?"

He nods his acknowledgement.

"My mother read cheesy paperback romances and Yolanda, after *it* happened, made me too easy for people to remember. I needed a way for the public to see me and not Yolanda Gordon, whose parents and brother were slaughtered by Duane Miller. I was at the mercy of everyone until I found a cooperative social worker."

"Has the name change worked?"

She pouts. "Not if people like you dig around and find out." She points a finger at them. "Right? The two of you regard me in a different light now." She folds her arms. "And how does my old life relate to Owen Ellis-Thomas, anyway?"

"Owen collected personal information. He was known to use the secrets of others to manipulate them. I wonder if he found out who you are."

"I'm Greta Walmsley, and I often say, 'I have the paperwork as proof'."

"You intimidate Victoria Barlow to write your books." Stella allows the statement to settle in the air between them.

"Listen. Barlow works as an editor—she edits. I admit I didn't have much of an education and paragraphs and punctuation aren't my strong suit, but the ideas are mine. Dear old dried-up Vicky structures sentences and fiddles with the commas." She glances across the table at Essie. "Have you met Vicky? She couldn't have an original idea if a revelation thumped her on the chin. I've made piles of money for Sailboat Publishing. She knows she has no choice." She puffs with a satisfied smirk.

"Greta, I understand this will be repetition, but please outline your movements on Saturday, September 26, from the time classes were completed around three forty-five." She casts a quick glance at Essie. "Detective

Matkowski will benefit from hearing your account."

After she wiggles in her seat as if settling in for a long train ride or a lecture, she proceeds to deliver a well-rehearsed version of her afternoon. She leaves no detail to chance, referencing her departure from the Shale Harbour Community Hall and Playhouse, and her walk on Birch, north on Maple, and then east on Elm to the hotel. She gushes as she describes her dinner at the Purple Tulip with Bryce Blanken. She mentions what she wore and what she ordered from the menu in a perfect recitation.

"I'm sure your comments have helped Detective Matkowski arrange the facts in her mind. Yolanda—sorry—Greta, we're finished for now, but we need you and Mr. Fitzgerald to return tomorrow, as scheduled, to explore other avenues of our investigation."

"Is a second interview necessary, Miss Kirk? Miss Walmsley is busy, and her preference was today."

Stella senses Fitzgerald's eyes reveal information different from his words, giving her added confidence. "Yes. Back-to-back interviews were the agreement and I want to have Detective North involved. Shall we say same time tomorrow?"

"Agreed." The lawyer places a never-referenced folder back in his briefcase.

Greta whines but acquiesces after a stern glance from Fitzgerald.

Once the two women are alone in the conference room, Essie reveals her thoughts. "You should have pushed her more. Aiden said you're a great interviewer. I'm afraid, Stella, I don't agree."

"I followed Aiden's instructions. I ensured Greta understands we're familiar with her background and the game she's played with Sailboat Publishing." Exhausted, Stella struggles to remain calm. "The woman left today apprehensive. Dear old Aloysius of the tall-suits-on-a-short-man club proved far more supportive than what I presumed."

Essie doesn't argue. "I'll write the notes."

"Aiden said he'd call tonight, so we can review the interview. I expect you may attend part two if you're interested."

****

She leaves a message on the answering machine at home. "On my way." Nick wanted her to telephone, but he must be outside somewhere. With a mind-weariness she has come to find familiar, she reminds the front desk of the appointment tomorrow, and trudges to her Jeep. Drizzle settles on the windshield and a storm is predicted for overnight. Her bare feet are cold and clammy in leather sandals—an acceptable choice at noon but not now. Nick will no doubt be cruising around the park in search of items which need to be secured ahead of the weather.

What information might Owen have used? She reviews the options in her mind. Did he discover she's Yolanda? Did he suggest she participated in the murders? *Was* she part of the murders and Duane Miller covered for her? Did she believe Owen revealed her truth, whatever her truth happens to be—the change of name and identity or a cover-up? Stella blinks into the gloom and tries to focus, as abject weariness threatens to overtake her.

During the drive to the park, a healthy red fox runs across the road in front of the Jeep. She imagines him curled in his burrow this damp and rainy night, wrapped in tight with his nose buried in the warmth of his fluffy tail. She could be envious if she were destined to return to a drafty and dark house.

The backyard lights are ablaze. The inside door opens, and she sees his blurred form behind the screen. As she mounts the stairs, which seem steeper tonight, he approaches the top and extends his hand.

"Tired, my love? Supper will be ready in no time."

He's moved the dining table over in front of the fire. The smell of stew drifts to meet her. He found buns somewhere. He pours her a glass of wine, and they snuggle on the sofa while his concoction bubbles away in the kitchen.

"Thanks. I'm exhausted, Nick."

"Not surprised. Did she confess?"

She shakes her head. "Not quite. The detective Aiden assigned felt I should have begun with an accusation. In any event, we're back tomorrow. I'll muster my confidence with Aiden in the room. And I have a funny notion related to Greta's lawyer. I didn't give him much credit after the phone call, but I suspect he wants to discover the truth, too."

Stella continues, her head now rested on Nick's shoulder. "Aiden suggested Fitzgerald rescheduled the initial interview to knock us off balance, but I suspect Greta instigated the manoeuvre. When I said I wanted to meet as promised, he agreed. Greta pouted, but he ignored her." She stops to sip her wine. "What's happened here today? You were out when I left Port Ephron."

"Went to the machine shed for a few minutes prepping for morning. The site engineers will be back to do the final measurements for the holes and trenches. Expect hundreds of little flags everywhere—different colours for each task. Duke said he would come out to help."

While she tries to pay attention, her thoughts drift toward Trixie's drunken suggestion that Owen's story might have been true, and the reading set Greta off. Trixie has no awareness of Greta's history, but what if her cockamamie idea has merit? She'll discuss the concept with Aiden when he calls tonight.

❧

CHAPTER 23

A Thread of Anger

"Detective North is not in his office, and I thought I'd call you. I hope you don't mind."

"No, Victoria. I'm surprised you couldn't reach Aiden. Did the detachment give you my number?"

The publisher responds with subtle sarcasm. "I can be a detective, too. You left your contact information with the receptionist when you first called Sailboat Publishing."

"Right." *Aiden should be at work.* "How may I help you today?" The morning has begun in a quiet enough fashion despite her concerns. Aiden failed to ring her last night, and when she tried the house, no one answered. The machine didn't kick in. Reluctant to call Toni's number, she fretted instead. Yesterday's interview requires review. She felt uneasy and jumpy throughout the evening. Sleep proved elusive, and now here's Victoria Barlow on the phone.

"I fear I made light of Greta's remarks related to Owen and his reading at your party."

Stella closes her eyes to focus for a moment. "Tell me, Victoria. Don't make assumptions regarding importance. Every detail may have merit in the investigation."

"When you and Detective North came to my office, I told you how Greta called me after Owen read his piece. She said he implicated her, and she wanted him stopped. I calmed her."

"Yes." She suspects there's more.

"The way Greta framed her concerns suggested Owen discovered information unknown to the public. I tried to convince her the whole experience amounted to a macabre coincidence, but she rattled on and insisted Owen must have talked to Duane Miller, the man who killed her family."

"Did she say Owen's reading told more truth than fiction?"

"She managed to avoid blurting out such a conclusion, but every concern she voiced suggested Owen didn't fabricate his story. I reminded her how anyone can scan old newspaper articles, take a report, and expand on the facts to create significant differences."

"And she wasn't convinced?"

"She repeated she needed to discover how Duane and Owen met."

"Not *if*, but *how*?"

"Her emphasis."

"Thanks, Victoria. Your information will be helpful."

"My apologies because I didn't reveal the details sooner."

"Better late than never. Thanks again."

Before she has an opportunity to telephone the Port Ephron detachment and find Aiden, the phone jangles a second time. "Good morning. Shale Cliffs RV Park."

"Your father has started to wander and snap at staff. We need a modicum of family assistance, if possible. He hasn't had company for a month."

The statement is accusatory, but true, nonetheless. She's been involved with the writers retreat, the case, park end-of-season activities, and septic systems since Owen's death. "Three weeks, to be precise, but I appreciate your concern. I have been embroiled in a police matter and should have alerted my sister and her daughter to drop in to see Dad. I will now, but what appears to be the problem?"

"Mr. Kirk insists one of our female residents disappeared."

"Has she?" Stella appreciates her father's flair for the dramatic. The woman may be on vacation with family, and he doesn't understand.

"By no means. She moved into a smaller, private residence some months ago, and I'm told she settled well."

"Did you tell my father?"

"Without doubt, but he refuses to believe me. He says she's been abducted. Despite your busy life, you might find a moment to visit."

The bite of her criticism stings. "Today is bad for me, but I'll contact my sister. She'll come to Harbour Manor and speak with Dad."

"Please ask Trixie to schedule beforehand. We need to be informed of her arrival time." The Harbour Manor supervisor disconnects the call.

"Is Detective North around?"

"I'm afraid he isn't available. May I take a message?"

"When do you expect him?"

"I can't say. May I take a message?"

"No, thanks."

"Hi, Toni. Stella here. Is Aiden with you? He's not at work and there's no answer at his house. Sorry to bother you and Mary Jo, but it's critical I touch base with him."

Toni whispers, "He's here. Give me a sec."

"Stella." His breath comes in gasps. "I imagine you've figured out you're on your own for the interview."

"Aiden, I'm a civilian. The circumstances are inappropriate. Our wings will be clipped, for sure."

"Can't help," he pants. "Rosemary's fallen completely off the rails. She punched Mary Jo, Stella. Her psychiatrist is searching for a bed in the psychiatric hospital in Halifax, but the wait could be days, or a week. Says she's a danger to herself and others. Essie can sit in again."

He sounds disinterested and distracted. She doesn't bother to provide feedback from yesterday or share Victoria Barlow's revelation and decides to forge ahead with her gut as her guide. Stella's opinion hasn't altered. Greta pushed the kid although, possibly, didn't expect him to fall. She will conduct the interview her way and work hard to discover the truth. An element of her confidence stems from her sense that Fitzgerald, the lawyer, wants her to be the catalyst to reveal buried secrets. "I'll do my best, Aiden."

She touches the receiver to the cradle long enough to engage a dial tone and calls Yellow House.

"Yellow House Book Store."

"Hi, Trixie." No time for preamble. "We have a problem with Dad. Can you go over to the manor today and have a talk with him?"

"Why?" Her whine annoys Stella, who has less patience than required at present.

"I have an interview—the Owen Ellis-Thomas case."

"What's the issue with the old geezer now? Did he pee in a corner?" She giggles at her joke.

"No. The supervisor tells me he's convinced a female resident vanished.

The manor says she moved out. Who knows? If you discover where she's moved, take Dad for a visit."

"More your department, Stella."

She closes her eyes for a second. "You're right, and I promise to pull my weight once we wrap this case. Aiden is up to his ears with Rosemary, and I'm left holding the bag, Trixie. Can you help?"

She acquiesces, no doubt due to the anxiety she senses on Stella's end of the conversation. "Sure. I'll include Mia to give Brigitte a break and call later tonight to tell you what happened."

****

"Did you say Aiden bailed on you again today?" Nick's tone holds a thread of anger.

"I guess. They are waiting for an emergency bed in Halifax. Rosemary is violent, and he doesn't dare leave her with Toni and Mary Jo. She slugged Mary Jo once already."

"Good God, Stella. The interview needs to be cancelled. Aiden mustn't believe you have much of a case if he can't find a way to postpone or attend."

"We need a confession, or she walks away."

"Refusal to meet until he has Rosemary under wraps isn't an option?" His eyes search hers.

"I'm sure I have an ally in the lawyer. The right question asked in the right manner is the key." She studies her slippers. "I may regret my actions, but I'll do my best." She meets his gaze once more. "Aiden expected Owen's death was a case of misadventure from the start, but we interviewed many potential suspects, and the investigation developed a life of its own."

Shuffling toward him, she's close enough to wrap her arms around his neck. "I understand your concerns. Allow me to manage today, which should put an end to the matter. Afterward, we can spend whatever time you want discussing the finer points of septic systems." She gives him a smooch on the chin. "Gotta change now."

Detective Matkowski is waiting in reception when Stella scrambles in the door of the detachment thirty minutes before Greta Walmsley and her lawyer are due to arrive.

"I gather you and I are the interviewers again today, Essie."

"Not necessarily. I spoke to Halifax branch, and we can assign a second detective to take North's place. The interview isn't your responsibility."

Don't blame her because she wants to put the run to me. "Well, let's carry on as planned. If I make too much of a mess, I'll back off and leave the case to the experts. Aiden told me you are assigned to sit in again."

"Lucky you. You managed to speak to the great North. He notified the overnight sergeant the rest of us were to stick to phone messages."

"Make no mistake. Aiden didn't call me. I called him. He's in the middle of a family crisis. He needs everyone's support these days."

They enter the interview room and Essie closes the door. The click of the latch has an ominous sound and Stella's senses go on alert.

"You and North have been in a partnership of sorts for a while now, right?"

"A year or more. The work wasn't contracted until our last case. I helped out on an informal basis at first, because I own a business on the isthmus and have local connections." She widens her eyes for effect.

Essie leans toward Stella and places her elbows on her knees.

Stella sits back in her chair.

"I might as well tell you myself," the detective continues. "I've applied to be North's partner in the future. The brass think he needs professional support when he has 'family crisis' issues. You'll be free to spend more time at your trailer park. Your place is a trailer park, right?"

Detective Matkowski's expression hovers between taunt and challenge, but Stella finds her voice. "I guess the folks 'higher up' will make those decisions, Essie. For today, I want to concentrate on steering Greta into an admission of culpability in Owen's death." She squares her shoulders. "My methods may appear unorthodox to you, but please wait until we break, and are alone, before you question me. I imagine they've arrived."

******

Greta's tendencies toward the flamboyant have increased. Today, she has paired a floor-length gauzy top with skin-tight jeans, visible as the slits in the sides of the gown-like blouse flutter when she walks. She has wound a narrow, sequined scarf around her thin and ropy neck. She wobbles on platform heels, which threaten to sprain even the most robust ankles. Aloysius Fitzgerald follows behind, ever the obedient dog focused on his master, and sits once Greta has partially removed her red off-the-shoulder crocheted wrap.

Essie fiddles with and rearranges files while Stella focuses on her breathing. If Greta doesn't confess today, to an altercation with Owen on Saturday afternoon after the workshops concluded, she expects no further actions in the case. Owen's death will be declared misadventure and she will be forced to abandon her instincts.

"Are we settled? Anybody need water?"

Yesterday's null response to Essie's attempt at hospitality is repeated.

"Thank you for your attendance. Let's begin, shall we?" Stella avoids the mention of Aiden's name on purpose.

"Where's Detective North, Ms. Kirk? I thought he'd be here for the second portion of our interview." Fitzgerald sounds curious; not annoyed or upset.

"Detective North remains unavailable." Stella gathers as much authority as she can muster. "We will," she glances at Essie, "endeavour to carry on."

"I guess we are to enjoy amateur hour once again." Greta's forced bravado doesn't escape Stella's notice.

"May we begin today with an exploration of your attitude toward Owen Ellis-Thomas?" Without pause for a response, she continues. "Did you befriend him?"

"Absolutely not! No one *befriended* Owen. Authors tolerated him because he was the son of Frances and Edward. Most of his contemporaries avoided the little creep."

"Examples?"

"Well, he rifled through others' belongings if they were unattended. He harassed, leered, hid in corners, made snide remarks under his breath, and wandered around in a suspicious manner."

"Describe suspicious."

"Stella, you people interviewed everyone at the retreat. He spent an average of ten minutes in a class and then roamed the halls where he watched who left with whom and who went to the bathroom. He was a creep—common knowledge."

"Were Frances and Edward aware of his behaviour?"

Greta sucks in her breath—an overt attempt to curb her hostility. "They aren't idiots. People complained from the time Owen was a toddler. I heard about the story of one book festival in Montréal—Bryce was an organizer— where Owen became such a distraction the promoters hired babysitters so Frances and Edward could read and sign books. He was four, and a handful. I can't imagine the concept of motherhood. I'm terrified after hearing about

Frances and Edward's experiences."

In a soft tone she contrives to focus Greta's attention, Stella mutters, "I wonder if your mother felt the same way."

"My mother was a control freak." Greta rolls and unrolls the edge of her crocheted shawl, still draped over one shoulder.

Fitzgerald sits straighter in his chair, and Stella senses Essie's gaze on her ear.

"Owen's story bothered you, and he deserved to be confronted." Oftentimes overt statements, with questionable accuracy, push a witness to clarify and elaborate.

"Idiot Owen did not, and I repeat, did not bother me."

"He troubled you."

"Don't be obtuse. He took a newspaper report and turned the whole nightmare into reality. If people were aware of my identity, they would believe he wrote the truth."

"You found an opportunity to confront him after class on Saturday." Stella states what she expects are the facts. "He tried to make a fool of you."

Fitzgerald lays his hand on Greta's arm. "Those are statements, not questions. No need to respond."

She ignores his support. "I left him at the door on the lookout for a girl. I told you what happened." The corner of the red shawl unwinds in a sudden jerk.

"We should take a five-minute break, eh, Stella?" Essie stands.

"What? Sure, I guess."

Once removed to Aiden's office, Stella finds her temper in tatters. "What the hell, Essie? She pushed him and she needs to tell us the truth. What is your problem?"

"You're on the hunt for a nonexistent confession. I think we should go back inside and put an end to the interview. You could make matters worse if she feels forced."

Stella takes a moment to grit her teeth. "Essie, I am the interviewer in Aiden's absence and the woman has her lawyer with her. My understanding is you are to follow my lead. Greta Walmsley pushed Owen, and she will tell us what happened before we're done. Please take notes and manage the recorder as you were asked." Her heart thumps. Damn Aiden.

As they re-enter the conference room, she meets Fitzgerald's gaze. She wants to interpret the softening of his facial expression as encouragement, but her observations may be a vague and faint hope on her part.

"Let's start with the murder of your family." Stella pats the papers in front of her. "Owen described your mother's brutal death in his writing."

"You aren't obliged to discuss the murder of your family," Fitzgerald once again intervenes, albeit unenthusiastically, in Stella's opinion.

"I don't know what happened."

"Did Duane Miller reveal your involvement directly to Owen, or did Duane tell a third party who gave sordid details to the kid?"

"Duane killed them. He's in jail."

Fitzgerald and Essie remain fixed on Greta. Stella continues.

"You're certain Owen uncovered your identity? Did you confront him at the hall?"

"No." Greta rolls and unrolls the corner of her shawl. The yarn threatens to become unravelled.

Stella presses. "Owen described one scene incorrectly."

Greta lifts hooded and angry slits toward Stella.

"He wrote your mother screamed for her life. She didn't, did she? She stared into your eyes when you killed her."

Now, Greta faces Stella with unnerving directness, devoid of emotion.

"You're wrong. She screamed. Rattled the windows." A crazed smirk envelopes her face. "Duane let me do her, but he did my father first, and then my brother. I asked him not to kill the kid, but I was too late. After thirteen years, Duane ratted me out, didn't he?"

"Tell us what happened the night your family died, Greta—in your own words, please." The young woman glances toward her lawyer, who nods.

"Duane's confession was true, except I talked him into letting me tag along."

Stella smothers a gasp. Greta spoke as if she *tagged along* to a party or a football game.

"When we drove to my house, he told me to wait in the car, but I followed him in and watched him kill Dad—over in two seconds, max. My mother screamed her head off. He tied her to a chair. I wanted him to leave my little brother alone, but he went upstairs and finished the job. Before he came back, I stuck a wad of napkins from the kitchen counter in her mouth." She stops to grace Stella with a satisfied smile. "You were right. Mom shut up. Duane handed me the knife and let me do the honours." She turns to face her lawyer. "You suspected from the start, but you worked for me, anyway." Her body relaxes in the chair, emptied of the secret she's carried for thirteen years. "How did idiot Owen find out?"

"What happened in the community hall on the afternoon in question, Greta?" Stella packs away her horror for the time being, not ready to stop.

"The little worm stood at the top of the stairs. On my way up, he asked me if a slut named Hester was in the bathroom and I said no, we were the last two in the building. I took the opportunity to quiz him as to who described the murders in Winnipeg. He claimed his Uncle Rex let him cut articles out of papers and he turned them into stories."

"I demanded again who told him, and he lied. He insisted he added the extra bits to make the story sound worse. When I grabbed him to shake the truth out of the little snot, he lost his balance and fell. I'm sure Duane talked."

"Any more to say, Greta?" Stella fights to control her gag reflex.

Essie stifles a cough and squirms in her chair.

"He fell. I didn't kill him. I didn't slit *his* throat, right Al?"

Aloysius Fitzgerald meets Stella's eyes. She's certain she sees relief.

****

"What am I doing? Stretched out on the couch with my feet on a cushion, ready to consume a bucket of wine. How's Dad?"

"Paranoid as hell. He thinks one of the old ladies, someone named Wilhelmina Saunders—they call her Willy—has vaporized, even though the supervisor says she moved out months ago."

"Can we take Dad to see her? Do they have her address?"

"Management reports a volunteer helped her move. I stopped in to check with Del Trembly for a minute, and she verified Dad's story, but staff say the old lady has simply gone. No one knows why Dad has this bee in his bonnet now." Trixie, as usual, sounds frustrated.

"And the volunteer?"

"The supervisor claims the person no longer visits. Talk to Dad and pretend to be an amateur sleuth," she teases. "You're pretty good at the role."

"Okay. I'll go see Dad," Stella replies, while ignoring her sister's dig for the moment. "The home should have records, at least." She raises her eyebrows at Nick, who nods agreement. "As for my role as a sleuth, Aiden has been off and assigned a detective named Essie Matkowski to sit in with me throughout the Greta Walmsley stuff. She claims she's applied to be Aiden's partner. My consultation days are over, I expect."

"Have you talked to Aiden? What does he say?"

"No. I'll call tomorrow if I don't hear from him. We're finished. I imagine the whole sorry mess will be in the papers sooner rather than later."

"Were you right?"

"In fact, *you* were right."

CHAPTER 24

Allies and Associates

When the phone rings while she and Nick are washing dishes, Stella expects the caller to be Aiden. "I hear you enjoyed a banner day," he blurts, the moment she says hello. He sounds proud of her.

"Did Essie call you?"

"No. I contacted the station and found her still in the office. She's finished the report. I gather you were pretty unorthodox with your series of questions, but you reached the finish line."

She groans. He no doubt heard. "Greta, or Yolanda, participated in the murder of her family and she grabbed Owen by the throat. She claims he lost his balance and fell."

"Essie said Yolanda was a juvenile when her folks died, and the current evidence goes to the Crown as manslaughter at best, but you did a good job. I didn't see a confession happening without you."

He's made a frail attempt to pacify me because Essie will soon be his partner. Tired and not interested in becoming ensnared in a long discussion, she cuts the call short. "Any chance we can meet tomorrow in the Port Ephron office, Aiden? I'll review the interviews with you then, and I want to take a few minutes to visit with Frances and Edward while I'm in town. I hope you'll go with me—and share Rosemary's latest news, too, if you find time," she adds, as an afterthought.

"I'll be at the detachment for the morning. We think they've found a bed for Rosemary, which means I won't be around later than noon, but we can meet with Frances and Edward. Let's say nine? Hi to Nick. See you tomorrow." He hangs up before she constructs a response.

****

Wednesday promises to be a bright and typical fall day. She knows. She's been awake for most of the night. Under normal circumstances, the soft rumble of Nick beside her soothes, but not last night. She couldn't sleep. She rambled around the house, peeked out the windows, and sat on cool leather before the darkened fireplace. The damp of the wee hours forced her back to a warm bed, but comfort didn't help. Today, she suspects Aiden will tell her that her services are no longer required. She wants to spend more time in the park and decides to be home for lunch, regardless of what happens.

Both Aiden and Essie are positioned in front of the reception desk when she breezes into the Port Ephron detachment.

She inhales. "Good morning, you two." She eyes the sheaf of papers clutched in Essie's fist. "The report?"

"Done and dusted." She cradles the pages to her chest. "Let's go talk in Aiden's office." At the exact moment she tries to make eye contact, he turns away. Once inside, Essie shuts the door and makes her way to a chair near Aiden and the side of his desk—the spot often reserved for Stella when they meet with witnesses. Relegated to one of those chairs which faces them both, her location feels vulnerable. She can't put her finger on why. She isn't their equal. She understands, but the seating arrangement gives her external position with the department an unpleasant emphasis.

Aiden clears his throat, a habit more obvious when he's uncomfortable or nervous. "I've read Essie's report, Stella." He coughs again. "As usual, your tactics aren't necessarily police service condoned, but from where we stand, we believe Greta's lawyer will negotiate a plea." He stops to study a fingernail. "Thanks for your help."

For a second, she contemplates confrontation of the obvious; to ask if he and Essie Matkowski are now partners and her services as a consultant are no longer required. Instead, she decides to tolerate the thorny and awkward atmosphere in favour of delicate manipulation—to force one of them to play their hand. "I'd appreciate a read, if the report isn't confidential."

"No problem, Stella. Here." Essie hands the papers across the desk. "They can't leave the office."

"Thank you. After I scan through the document, I still believe Frances and Edward must be debriefed today." She meets the eyes of each of them in turn. "I assume one of you wants to accompany me."

"I have time to go with you right away."

She watches him frown the instant he realizes she understands the current unspoken circumstances.

"I said yes when we spoke yesterday," he adds with unnecessary emphasis.

"Great. Let's take two cars. I know you want to shorten your day, and I'm impatient to return to my *trailer park.*" She focuses on Essie when she accentuates the phrase. Aiden acts none the wiser.

****

Frances and Edward greet them at the door, nervous for information. Their visit is no surprise. Aiden called before they departed the station.

"Come in. Come in. I've made coffee."

"Thanks, Frances. Shall we sit at your kitchen table?" Stella can't face another excruciating perch on their living room couch.

"What a practical idea." She glances at Edward for a moment. "We consider the two of you family, now. You have been kind over the last...why, almost a month!"

They struggle around the heavy maple dining set, too big for the cozy nook. Stella finds herself wedged against the wall in the fourth chair, the one no doubt pushed out of the way and never used. She ducks to avoid the bottom of the glass-doored cupboard which hangs above. Room for three suited their requirements before the death of their only child.

Aiden begins, elbows on the table, and coffee cup in his hands. "We want you to know Owen's story of the triple murder in Winnipeg is, in fact, true. Greta Walmsley was known as Yolanda Gordon. Her family was the one killed on the night Owen described."

Owen's parents sit frozen in anticipation of Aiden's words. After Frances reaches for a napkin and dabs her eyes, Edward holds her chapped hand.

Frances finds her voice first. "Oh, how horrible for Greta, to hear her tragic story told with such violence and detail—and he included the poor child as if she participated in the homicide. Owen exaggerated. She must be devastated." She turns to her husband. "I should contact her."

Stella steps into the conversation. "Are the two of you certain Owen didn't talk to anyone involved in the Winnipeg case?"

"Positive." Edward's soft but emphatic voice catches her unawares. "Owen never bothered to research a story. He was lazy if the truth be told. He wanted to use his imagination after he found a hook to provide inspiration. I hope Greta was not unduly hurt by his scribblings."

Afraid Aiden wants to leave the conversation before more can be revealed, she plunges forward. "Did you know Greta Walmsley was born Yolanda Gordon?"

"No idea, Stella." Frances turns to Edward, and he shakes his head. "No idea," he repeats.

Aiden reveals additional details. After fifteen minutes, Owen's parents understand their son died because he wrote a fictional account of an incident; whereas in truth, the murders happened the way he imagined. Yolanda Gordon assisted in the brutalization of her family and pushed Owen to his death late Saturday afternoon, September 26, after a heated discussion and an altercation. Accident or not, the Crown, or the courts, will make the decision.

Before they leave, Frances asks Stella if she plans to be a sponsor for next year's retreat. "We've spoken to Farley, and he wants to strike another committee."

As they depart the house, the couple stand behind the dented aluminum storm door and Stella ponders the process of grief. Perhaps they've found their path.

"We need to talk, Stella."

"Understood, but I have a few issues right now. Call me on the weekend." She refuses to hear her fate today.

****

When she arrives at the park, muffins and cheese are on the table. Local apples are displayed in a rectangular antique dough bowl, and the kettle is ready to boil. He's curious. He makes no secret of his emotions.

"Aiden and I never discussed my consultancy role, Nick. He said he'll call on the weekend. He was worried and wanted to return to Toni's. To be frank, I appreciated the break." She sighs. "He included Essie in our debrief. Awkward doesn't begin to describe the situation. For the moment, Aiden can address his wife's issues and I'll find out what's wrong with Dad."

"Works for me. Sit. Let's change the subject. I think we're right on schedule for septic. I hope you're ready." He munches on a muffin.

"Great table conversation." She smacks him on the arm. "I plan to take the afternoon to organize and invite people to lunch here in the park on Friday. I want everyone who helped me with Owen's case to spend time with us. Are you game?"

"You bet. Let's scratch out a menu." He taps the wooden surface. "I'll make buns, okay? Who do you expect to come?"

"Trixie, Hester, Mildred, Cloris, and Duke. Brigitte and Cavelle are more than welcome but they'll be working."

****

The next day, Stella decides to call Harbour Manor and confirm a time to visit. She can shop afterward for the groceries she'll need for Friday lunch.

"Good morning, Ms. Martin." Stella remains unable to muster enough courage to address Maura Martin, RN by her given name. "I want to stop by later today to see my father and Mrs. Trembly. Will one o'clock be convenient for you and your staff?" She's cognizant of how formal she sounds.

"To be sure, Stella. You may come to Harbour Manor any time you desire. Although he won't recall, I'll let both Norbert and Del know you'll be here." She pauses. "Does he remember you? I thought he didn't."

Stella's heart twists. "No, not anymore. He sees me as Nick Cochran's wife. No matter, but to be honest, Trixie was the right person to send in the first place."

"Your sister did little to assuage your father's concerns." The phone clicks in her ear.

"May I come with you?"

"Your presence is a big help, my dear. Dad will listen to you. We can visit with Dad and Del together." In a sudden burst, she develops enthusiasm for the task thanks to Nick's support.

****

Maura Martin scuttles out from an office tucked away behind the nurses' station.

"Do you have an updated address for Wilhelmina Saunders? I want to take Del and Dad to see her."

"Her personal information is confidential. Frankly, I'm not sure of the location, but tell your father she's moved into a guest house, and I'm told is happy." Supervisor Martin turns her back on the reception desk.

They arrive at Norbert's door, shoulder to shoulder. He's snuggled in his chair, swivelled to face the window and the grounds. "The colours of the leaves are real nice, eh Norbert?"

"Nick, my man. Great to see you. They told me someone was comin' to talk to me today, but they didn't say who." He makes a valiant attempt to hop to his feet. Nick reaches a hand to steady him. "And you brought your darlin' wife." He glances from Stella back to Nick.

"Stella, Norbert. Her name is Stella."

"Right. I know her name." He gives Nick an affectionate nudge.

"Norbert," Stella weighs in. "Maura Martin asked us to talk with you because you've been worried. A resident moved away?"

"Willy didn't move anywheres. She vanished. They took her." His agitation emerges with a force. "Go ask Del."

As is often the case when Stella visits the manor and pops in to say hi to Del Trembly, they discover her flaked out in her lounger, smothered in a red velour track suit, and focused on the television, the sound notches too high.

"Well, the gang's all here. Come on in," she motions with her arms while her body rolls. "Turn off the squawk box and find a scrap of bed to sit on." She waves her arms again. "Bring another chair from out in the hall. Norbert needs one."

Once settled to her satisfaction, she asks, "To what do I owe the pleasure?"

"Dad is worried about a former resident named Willy, Del."

"Yeah. We both are—Willy Saunders. Been months since we've seen her. I'm sure you noticed her on your visits. She wears a man's grey topcoat and carries a string bag purse—the kind where you can see your stuff inside."

"Supervisor Martin says she moved out," Stella reminds Del. "She reports Mrs. Saunders now resides at a guest house.

"Not true," pipes in Norbert. "Willy yells goodbye when she goes somewheres."

"Nick and I will discuss Willy's whereabouts with Maura Martin again to determine where we can find her. We'll take both of you to visit soon. Okay?"

"Maura won't tell you much. I asked for the umpteenth time last week. Confidentiality," Del parrots although she sounds both resigned and disgusted. "She won't tell me anything about my buddy Jasper, either."

"And who is Jasper?"

"One of the bridge club. The fellas haven't played bridge since he took off."

During their short visit, they exchange news related to the writers retreat. Del asks of Hester, her niece, and Stella mentions how much help Hester provided to the investigation. Eve will soon be home from university for her break. Since she's Del's granddaughter and a summer park employee of Stella's, they always find a moment to chat about her.

Afterward, they walk Norbert to his room. His final remark serves to settle her concerns. "Willy wanted a cat. They won't let us have pets here. I bet they gave her a cat at her new place. Who knows why Jasper left? He liked livin' here."

****

Duke and his lady-friend, Cloris, are the first to arrive for lunch on Friday. Stella smothers a laugh when she sees them. They're dressed in coordinated turquoise silk cowboy shirts with white fringes and piping. Cloris attempts to pat down her black skirt mounted on piles of crinoline. Duke's black trousers are pressed with knife-like precision. "Where's Kiki?"

"Home alone, Stella. Don't happen often, but Cloris and I are off to our square-dancin' club for three o'clock. I left her at my motel room because the weather's too cold for her in my girlfriend's truck." He snuggles into the mounds of netting.

Cloris' guise speaks to her absolute pleasure because the dog is among the missing today.

"Come on in. Trixie's on her way. Nick has run off to pick up Mildred and Hester. What's your preference—wine, beer, iced tea, or warm cider? Take your choice." Both settle for cider and cuddle together on a leather sofa as Trixie navigates the veranda stairs with a potato salad in one hand and her purse in the other. "Brigitte's contribution, because she couldn't leave Yellow House." She motions to the salad with her nose and giggles in a conspiratorial tone. "Mia is thrilled to be able to 'work' with her mom. I didn't sense as much enthusiasm from her mother." She hobbles on heeled boots into the kitchen. "I have shrimp in the truck." She waves her hand. "I know you said not to bring food, but the plant was selling a load of shrimp." She sets the potato salad on the table and hugs Stella. "I still have contacts."

"We're here," Nick shouts from the living room. He's on the mat at the veranda door, flanked by Hester Painter and Mildred Fox.

What a picture. Nick balances a crate which overflows with root vegetables, no doubt from Hester's garden. Outfitted in her standard wool skirt and knitted sweater, Stella trusts Jewel double-checked Hester's clothes to make sure they were clean before Nick arrived to fetch her.

"Mildred, my dear. Aren't you the fashion plate?" She rushes across the space and grips the old woman's shoulders.

"I'm not given invitations to luncheon often and wanted to wear my best outfit for the occasion." She cackles and pats the calf-length skirt of her two-piece dark grey suit, paired with a bright red blouse that ties at the neck. "It ain't a funeral, but do I pass inspection? Your man's bin givin' me the eye." She turns to wink at Nick, before she sees Trixie on her way out of the kitchen. "I can't manage the high heels, Trixie, but I thought I'd provide some competition today."

"Hot stuff, Mildred." Trixie responds, more toward Stella than Mildred.

"The vegetables are from Jewel and me, but I gathered them."

"Thank you, Hester. No better gift in the world." She brushes her hand against the woman's arm. Hester isn't given to hugs.

Stella silently assesses the room. When dropped into the middle of a community, you become friends with personalities you could never imagine as allies and associates. When she came home to help her father, the people now around her table embraced her...and she's blessed.

She reveals to her guests the basic information related to Yolanda Gordon, and the circumstances behind her name change to Greta Walmsley. She emphasizes how they helped, more than they might realize, in their recollections of the newspaper article upon which Owen based his story. Although there's detail she can't share, each of them played a role and she is grateful.

"Despite his frequent questionable behaviour, Owen didn't expose Greta, did he, Stella?"

"No, Hester. In the end, Owen was the innocent party. If Greta had controlled her paranoia, I expect Owen would still be alive."

****

"Trixie has changed." Stella and Nick sit side by side on a sofa, while they ponder supper. Her watch says five and they've opted for soup later.

"Correct," Nick replies. "She'll soon be independent. She won't be obliged to arrive hat in hand each month to accept a cheque from you to survive.

"I admit, you're no doubt right, but I'm surprised, nonetheless. She has an unfamiliar air."

"Take a gander in the mirror." He leans over and kisses the tip of her nose. "You are a confident woman and Trixie will soon be the same. Speaking of confident women, I took a call from Andrea Picard while you were on the veranda as people left. She wants to see us sometime in early November to review the loan agreements and the paperwork for the share transfer. We can pick a day over the weekend, and I'll contact her Monday." He adds as an afterthought, "Please God—nobody else die between now and the end of December."

"No matter. I expect Aiden will break his news before Monday and tell me the RCMP no longer require my services. He hinted, when we left Owen's parents yesterday, how we need to talk, and Essie made her point when she told me she's applied to be Aiden's partner." Bravado props her confidence.

"Never gonna happen."

****

"Shale Cliffs—"

"Hi, it's me," he interrupts. "Have you time?"

"Sure. Want to come out to the park for coffee? I expect the weekend to stay quiet."

His hesitation percolates along the phone line. "No. To be frank, I prefer not to see the emotion on your face."

"You're a coward, but okay. Rosemary is sick, and I'm not without sympathy. I'll make the conversation easy for you." She presents her most professional and impersonal voice. "Essie Matkowski has applied to be your partner and your boss thinks the idea has merit, because you asked a civilian to interview a potential murder suspect. Although this civilian managed to obtain the necessary information needed in the local case and, in addition, shed light on a thirteen-year-old Winnipeg homicide, said civilian's methods are unorthodox and her services are no longer required. Because your wife has health problems which are unpredictable, an argument can be made for you to work beside a police colleague, able to step in if the need arises." She stops for breath. "Did I adequately sum the circumstances?"

"You received a call."

"No."

"Essie talked to you." His remark makes another statement and doesn't ask a question.

"She told me she applied to partner with you."

"I'm sorry."

"Me, too, Aiden. I hope Rosemary receives the care she needs."

"Yes. Placement has turned out to be one of the worst experiences of my life. We called for assistance, and I managed to get help from two female constables. Toni and I sat in the back seat of the cruiser to take her to the city. Mary Jo tagged along behind."

"A psychiatric long-term care facility?"

"Rosemary will remain in the institution until stable." His voice wobbles. "I don't know, Stella. She's a shell. There's no light in her eyes. The volume of medications over the years has taken away any personality—Annette Funicello or otherwise."

****

Is Nick's wet nose pressed against hers? Her mind cranks toward wakefulness. *Today's Monday. The septic system is scheduled to be installed today.* She peeks through her lashes to meet the whiskers of Kiki, on her bed and intent on the study of her face. From this angle, the little dog looms large. The minute their gazes connect, Kiki jumps and nuzzles. Fur flies.

"Why are you here with me, wee one? Duke must be outside with Nick, and I've overslept." She can hear the faint sound of machinery.

About the Author

L. P. Suzanne Atkinson was born in New Brunswick, Canada and lived in both Alberta and Québec before settling in Nova Scotia in 1991. She has degrees from Mount Allison, Acadia, and McGill universities. Suzanne spent her professional career in the fields of mental health and home care. She also owned and operated, with her husband, both an antique business and a construction business for more than twenty-five years.

Suzanne writes about the unavoidable consequences of relationships. She uses her life and work experiences to weave stories that cross many boundaries.

She and her husband, David Weintraub, make Bedford, Nova Scotia their home.

Email – lpsa.books@eastlink.ca
Website – http://lpsabooks.wix.com/lpsabooks#
Face Book – L. P. Suzanne Atkinson – Author
Face Book – lpsabooks Private Stash

Titles:
Emily's Will Be Done (2012)
Ties That Bind (2014)
Station Secrets: Regarding Hayworth Book I (2015)
Hexagon Dilemma: Regarding Hayworth Book II (2016)
Segue House Connection: Regarding Hayworth Book III (2017)
Diner Revelations: Regarding Hayworth Book IV (2018)
No Visible Means: A Stella Kirk Mystery #1 (2019)
Didn't Stand a Chance: A Stella Kirk Mystery #2 (2020)
Sand In My Suitcase: A Stella Kirk Mystery #3 (2021)
Fictional Truth: A Stella Kirk Mystery #4 (2022)

If you liked any one of the author's books, please consider leaving a review on Goodreads, Amazon, or your favourite social platform. Thank you.

Watch for:

Mallory Gorman Won't Be Buried Today: A Stella Kirk Mystery #5

The fifth in a series of cozy mysteries, set in Shale Cliffs RV Park
Coming in the spring / summer of 2023